MADDY MADRIGAL MYSTERIES BOOK 4

MORTAL MAGIC

DEBRA CASTANEDA

SHADOW CANYON press

ISBN: 979-8-9994829-2-1
Edited by: Lyndsey Smith, Horrorsmith Editing
Cover design by: Jacqueline Sweet

To the original Ripper.

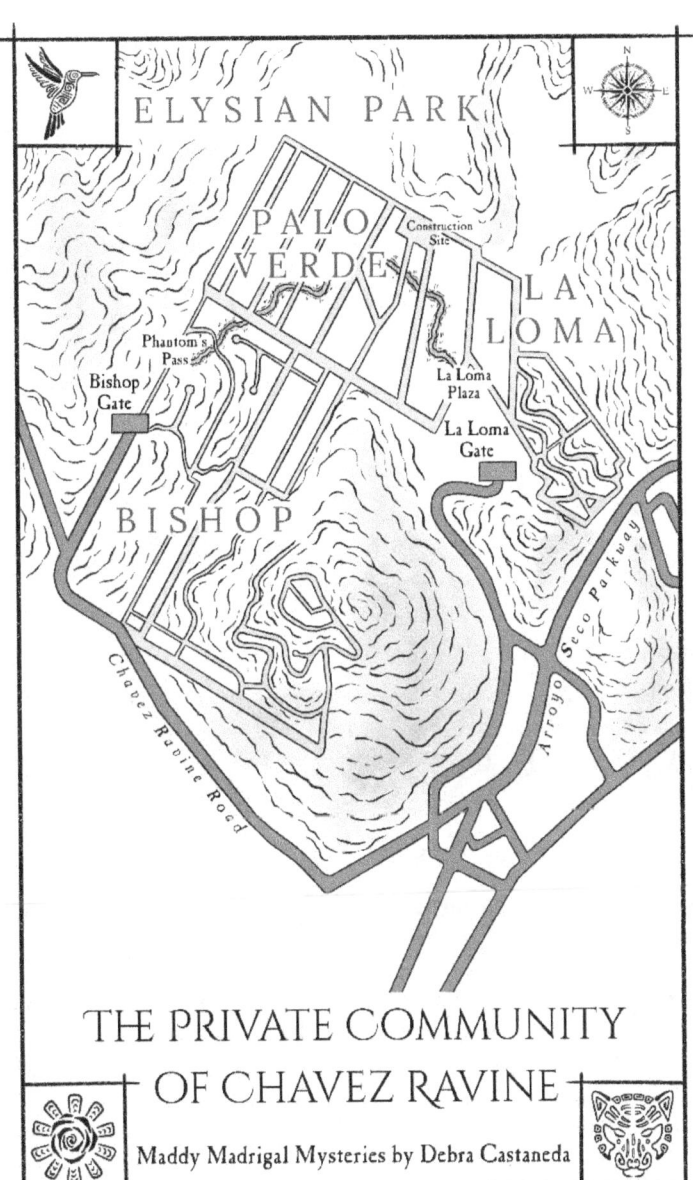

ELYSIAN PARK

PALO VERDE

Construction Site

LA LOMA

Phantom's Pass

Bishop Gate

La Loma Plaza

La Loma Gate

BISHOP

Chavez Ravine Road

Arroyo Seco Parkway

THE PRIVATE COMMUNITY
OF CHAVEZ RAVINE

Maddy Madrigal Mysteries by Debra Castaneda

Chapter 1

It was just a feeling, a sensation twanging along my spine like an out-of-tune guitar. My cat, Sam, appeared to sense it too. He leapt off the couch and dashed toward the French doors in the sunroom, where he began chattering.

Something was in the backyard.

Heart thumping, I hurried into the room. A gray form was moving around on the hill behind my house.

Oh, please no. Not another chupacabra.

Chupacabras were bad—mean and hard to subdue—but they had never broken through my protection spell over Chavez Ravine. If a chupacabra showed up, it would have meant my magic had failed and my team was in for a tough fight.

Sam stood on his hind legs, teeth clacking. The noise was so god-awful it made my toes curl.

Outside, the creature nuzzled the dry grass.

I laughed.

It was a goat.

I had completely forgotten about Ben Tomas's plan. Correction: Ben Tomas, Master Landscaper. He had brought in goats to gnaw on the hard-to-reach vegetation on the steep slopes and deep gullies of the gated community. The HOA board loved the idea: Eileen Simpson and Dan Berman because it was cheap and didn't involve pesticides; Cora Bernal, Charlie Perez, and Hernan Frias because it was a throwback to the first residents of Chavez Ravine, who had kept goats. They had been a familiar sight back in the day and had occasionally found their way into a burrito.

"Calm down," I told Sam. "It's just a goat. Nothing to worry about. For once."

The words were as much for my own reassurance as they were for his. A few weeks earlier, I had spotted something enormous in a tree late one night, and I had lived in a state of hypervigilance ever since. Whatever it was had flown away and hadn't reappeared.

The only thing I knew for sure was that it wasn't an entity. The heatmap in the command center hadn't detected a thing.

I flopped back down on the couch in the living room. My first few months as head of security for Chavez Ravine had been quite a roller coaster, and I hadn't realized how much tension I had been holding, waiting for the next awful thing to happen.

But while I watched the lone goat nibbling the hillside weeds, I began to relax. It was, after all, Saturday, a day off. My boyfriend, Stu, was running security for some high-profile celebrity event, and I planned to spend the day cleaning, shopping, and cooking ahead for the week.

Boring stuff for most people, but to me, it sounded like heaven.

I glanced at Sam, who had lost interest in the goat and was lazily grooming himself in a patch of sunlight. Typical cat behavior, but my big red Bengal was no typical cat. He was a supernatural guard kitty and personal assistant. As I worked to enhance my Mexican witchcraft skills, Sam had my back.

I had inherited my magic from my great-aunt, Lencha Bantacorte, a famous bruja who had once lived in La Loma, but I still had to work hard to focus my powers. It was comforting to know Sam was at my side in case things went awry. Which, of course, they sometimes did.

My cleaning routine always started the same way: I tied back my hair, put on some Tito Puente music, and carefully dusted the clay figurine of Lencha, made by my sculptor friend Julia Suarez. Lencha didn't blink, glow, or come to life anymore, but that was fine by me. She had helped me get started and had given me the inspiration I needed to improve my skills on my own. Thanks to her and Sam, I had survived my first few months as head of security for Chavez Ravine, even though they had been chaotic, intense, and even deadly.

Sam stayed in the sunroom, watching the goat, while I swept and mopped the floors, scoured the bathroom, and changed the sheets.

"It's not a shapeshifter, if that's what you're worried about, weirdo." I wiped down the windowpanes with glass cleaner.

Sam glanced up at me with huge green eyes. His expression said it all.

Stupid, trusting human.

I paused, studying the goat. He had reached the bottom of the hill and was eyeing my herb beds.

But like any good master landscaper, Ben Tomas had known this might happen.

When the HOA had told the community about the goat project, some residents expressed concerns that the goats would destroy their gardens. But Ben Tomas had explained that motion-activated sprinklers would take care of the problem.

And sure enough, just when the goat sauntered toward my herbs, the sprinklers switched on. The goat turned and raced up the hill.

I tapped out a message to let Ben know what had happened.

Glad to know it worked!

When I finished cleaning and doing the laundry, I decided I deserved a treat. A nice lunch at Muertos Café was just what I needed.

I showered, got dressed, grabbed a book—my latest thriller obsession—and headed to La Loma Plaza in my Jeep.

After settling in at a table with an umbrella on the café's back patio, I ordered one of their specials: a grilled shrimp salad with a side of poblano pepper soup. It didn't matter what time of year it was; Muertos served freshly made caldo all year round.

I had just finished my soup when a woman's voice cut through the chatter filling the patio. "Aren't you Maddy Madrigal?"

When I looked up, a woman around my own age, with dark hair and serious brown eyes, stood in front of my table. I recognized her immediately—as one does when one meets someone they've spent time stalking.

"Yes, I'm Maddy. And you're Hernan Frias's granddaughter."

She nodded but didn't smile. "Right, Valeria Torres. It's nice to see you again."

"Are you picking up some pan dulce for Hernan?" The man was addicted to the sweet Mexican pastries.

Valeria smiled wearily. "No. I was grabbing something to go when I spotted you through the window and thought I'd come say hello. My abuelo is always talking about the place, and I've never been." She glanced down at my plate. "I'm sorry to interrupt. Your food is getting cold."

"No worries. It's just a salad. Would you like to join me?" I really wanted to read my book, but it seemed like the polite thing to say.

Valeria shook her head. "Thank you, but I better get going. Did you hear about the goats they brought in to control the weeds and stuff? My grandpa left town, and he was really worried about them getting into his garden and eating all the roses, so I said I would come and check."

"All the way from Pomona?" I asked in surprise.

"He was *really* freaking." Valeria widened her eyes for emphasis. "And he gave his caretaker a few days off, so it was down to me."

When I had first met Valeria at the hospital, where her grandfather was recovering from a heart attack, she mentioned she was his only living relative, besides some far-flung cousins. Hernan wanted her to train as a bruja, even offering to send her to Mexico to learn the craft, but she had refused. Instead, Valeria was pursuing her dream of opening a bookstore. I figured she stood to inherit her grandfather's home and any money he left behind.

Back then, she had called him difficult and an egomaniac, but she still seemed fond of the man. Fond enough to drive some thirty miles to do his bidding.

"I didn't know Hernan was out of town. Does he still go to academic brujo conferences?" I sounded more sarcastic than I intended.

Valeria smiled, her teeth very white against her smooth brown skin. "No. I'm not sure where he is, to tell you the truth. He just said he had some urgent business out of town. He was a bit mysterious about the whole thing."

My relationship with Hernan had evolved. We had started out as mortal enemies, but a couple of months later, we found ourselves in the you're-dating-my-mother-and-there's-nothing-I-can-do-about-it stage. We were far from besties, but since he and my mother were so close, we had developed a semi-friendly truce. If I cared enough, I could call my mother and find out where he had gone. But that would mean talking to my mother—a sure-fire way to ruin my nice, relaxing, low-key weekend.

"So, were the roses okay?" I asked.

Valeria chuckled. "Fine. But I did see a few goats coming out of the parking lot at Phantom's Pass, so who knows how long the roses will be safe."

I sat up straighter in my chair. "You know, we have surveillance cameras all over Chavez Ravine. I could ask my team to keep an eye out, make sure the goats aren't getting into stuff they shouldn't."

Valeria's eyebrows shot up. "Oh. I didn't know you had cameras. Though I should have guessed, what with the HOA and all the security and everything."

I gave a distracted nod, surprised it hadn't occurred to me to use the cameras for goat monitoring. As soon as I was done with lunch, I would call the command center to set it up. All that equipment had cost a fortune, and I needed any extra rationale I could find to help the HOA board justify it.

"So, there are cameras everywhere?" Valeria shuddered. "If I lived here, I would hate that. Feeling like I was being watched all the time. So much for the right to privacy. Then again, that's typical of this place. All that micromanagement and arbitrary rules."

Here we go.

I took a deep breath. "I understand what you mean," I said in a neutral tone. "But people like feeling safe, and the cameras can be quite useful."

The door to the kitchen opened, and a server stuck his head out. "Order for Valeria?"

Valeria raised her hand and gave a little wave. "That's me! I'll be right there." She turned back to me, clearing her throat. "Well, time to get back to my shop. It was nice seeing you again, Maddy."

I watched her go, wondering about Hernan's sudden departure. In the time I had known him, he had only left Chavez Ravine to go to the hospital. I finished my meal and walked back to the Jeep.

Halfway through the parking lot, my phone rang. It was Ben Tomas. When I picked up, he was breathing heavily.

"Something bad happened," he said without preamble.

Ben wasn't prone to exaggeration, and the panic in his voice filled me with dread. My thoughts skittered in a dozen different directions, all of them alarming.

"What's going on?"

"Two of the goats." His voice sounded strained. "They're dead. Something's killed them."

Chapter 2

Ben Tomas met me outside the gate of the equipment yard on the border of Palo Verde, next to Elysian Park. Behind a tall hedge, the yard was filled with vehicles, an enormous nursery, a greenhouse, and all the other stuff needed to keep the grounds of Chavez Ravine beautiful.

"Where are the goats?" I asked.

Ben looked down at my sandals and frowned. "Did you bring any other shoes?"

That wasn't a good sign.

I kept a pair of socks and old hiking boots in the back of my Jeep, so I tugged those on.

Ben gave a grim nod. "They're in the back."

The master landscaper wasn't in the mood for chitchat while he pushed open the gate. I shuddered, remembering the last time I had been there, when an enormous bat-like creature had sunk its claws into Bailey Nixon's copper hair and tried to carry her away.

The air was heavy with sweet, floral scents mixed with just a hint of bitterness. We passed rows of marigolds, pansies, and snapdragons still growing in neatly tended beds. Ben's crew had put a lot of care and attention into the flowers, and their healthy growth was a testament to their skills.

"Marigolds for fall," Ben said. He was a man of few words, but he was kind and thoughtful.

We continued to the back of the yard, squeezing behind a potting shed, where Ben unlatched a wooden gate.

He pushed it open and pointed to the hill rising to Elysian Park. "They're up there."

I would have never made it up the slope in sandals, at least not with my dignity intact. The hillside was covered in rocks, dry brush, and weeds.

"I let two goats out here yesterday," Ben said. "This hill is a fire hazard, so it's a top priority. The fire department said it's nearly impossible to get permits for a controlled burn this close to homes, so they suggested we try the goats." He sounded mildly guilty, like he was responsible for whatever bad thing had happened to the animals.

I was busy staring at the ground, trying to avoid twisting an ankle on the rough terrain, so when Ben stopped, I ran into him and nearly fell. He shot out a hand and steadied my arm.

"Thanks, I…" The words caught in my throat.

Brown, furry legs ending in black hooves poked out from behind a large boulder. I stepped aside for a better look and immediately wished I hadn't.

Ben cursed under his breath, his usually stoic demeanor cracking at the disturbing sight before us.

I stepped closer, blood whooshing in my ears. The bodies were shrunken, like they had been drained of blood.

"We've got coyotes out here, but I don't think they did that," Ben said.

"No. Of course not." It was sad, but it wasn't a crime scene or an entity attack. At least, I didn't think so. But just in case, I added, "Can you take some pictures?"

"Already did."

"I'll ask Occult Affairs to pick them up and examine them. See if they've seen anything like this before."

"You think it could be an entity?"

"Not really," I replied. "The heatmap would have caught it. But the nerds in Occult Affairs are always worried about a new super-charged entity that can evade detection. Better to let them take a look. Can't be too careful."

"What should we do?" Ben asked.

I turned away from the goats and stared down at the big, tall trees around the equipment yard, thinking about the shadowy, winged creature Stu and I had seen not long before.

"You ever see anything hanging around in the trees? Something that shouldn't be there?"

Ben scowled. "If I had, you would have been the first to know. Have *you* seen something like that?"

"Yeah, but just once, and just for a moment. If Stu hadn't seen it too, I might have thought I'd imagined it." I scraped a hand through my hair. "Okay. Does anyone else know about this? Did you tell any of your crew?"

Ben shook his head. "No. Just you."

"Good. Since we don't know what really happened—and for all we know, it was a coyote—I don't see any reason to panic anyone. Where can we put these poor creatures until Occult Affairs arrives?"

"I can move them to one of the potting sheds. It's nice and cool, and I can put a lock on it. But I'm going to need help from some of my guys. I won't be able to get them off this hill on my own."

I thought for a moment. "That's fine. But say a coyote did it."

Ben snorted. "A vampire coyote?"

"Good point. Maybe wrap them up in a tarp first? Before your guys see them?"

"I can do that." Ben rubbed a thick, dark eyebrow. "What are you going to tell the board?"

"Nothing. It's too early for that. I don't want everyone freaking out."

I knew I ought to call Coral Bernal, the HOA president, but considering I didn't know what had killed the goats, even that seemed premature.

Ben gave a curt nod. After all the trouble he had gone through to get approval for the goat program, he was probably worried the board might overreact and cancel it.

I turned and stared at the top of the hill, trying to remember if we had cameras up there. No, we did not. We had installed them in areas closer to homes. Still, I would have my team check all the feeds for signs of a goat killer.

"I need to know how many goats are wandering around and, if possible, their locations. I'm going to ask the command center to keep an eye on them through the camera feeds. If they see something, they'll dispatch a security crew."

Ben brightened. "Really? That would be great."

Yeah, in theory. Since I was so close to the command center, that was my next stop. The new guy, Rafi, was there, so I gave him the instructions. Of everyone on the security team, Rafi dressed the most professionally. He wore a pressed blue Oxford shirt, and his hair was neatly combed, not a sleek black strand out of place.

"And what is it we are supposed to be looking for, ma'am?" he asked in his usual polite and precise way.

A blood-sucking fiend.

"Not sure," I said. "Could be anything, really. Honestly, anything that shows an unhealthy interest in goats."

Rafi swiveled in his chair and pulled up a feed on the large screen attached to the wall. A goat grazed on a hill above the new housing development just up the street from my house.

"I would say a chupacabra, ma'am, but the heatmap would pick them up."

Smart guy. He had done his homework. We'd had chupacabra incidents, but those had been before his time.

I thanked him and crossed the lawn to my office, where I made myself a latte and then composed a message to my team. After letting them know about the dead goats and the plan to monitor them, I emailed the photos of the goats to Occult Affairs researcher Steve Zhou to see what he could make of the wounds. He was one of the few OA nerds I trusted.

When I got home, the weight of the strange events settled into my bones. The day had started out so well. Despite the caffeine jolt from my latte, all the energy drained out of my body. The Saturday that was supposed to have been filled with happy domestic duties had taken an ugly turn.

I poured myself a glass of cold water and drank it down. A glance at the clock showed it was nearly four. Not too late for a quick nap.

In my bedroom, I closed the shutters and collapsed on the bed. Sam meowed loudly.

"Oh, for crying out loud. What do you want, an invitation?"

Apparently, that was exactly what he had been waiting for. He jumped up on the bed and pressed his big furry head into my side. While my eyes fluttered closed, I was haunted by the feeling that something sinister lurked in Chavez Ravine. Again.

I pushed the thought away and fell into a restless sleep.

Chapter 3

"When was the last time you had a weekend off?"

The question almost caused me to drop the phone. I thought Stu was calling about dinner plans, not a romantic getaway.

But he had asked a good question. I couldn't remember the last time I'd had two whole days to myself.

My thoughts leapt ahead. It was Wednesday. Did that leave me enough time for a bikini wax? I had never had one, but it sounded like the kind of thing one did before a sexy weekend trip.

That *was* what it would be, wasn't it?

Speaking of bikinis, I didn't own one, and my boring black one-piece was better suited to laps at the gym. Time to go shopping.

And then there was the cat. He had spent long stretches at home alone, but never an entire weekend. The mere thought of leaving him filled me with panic. And guilt. He wasn't just any cat. Our relationship was complicated.

I called my friend Julia Suarez in a panic. Sam tolerated me, but he loved Julia.

"Of course, I can cat-sit!" she squealed. "I can house-sit too. That will make it easier, yeah?"

It would. With Julia around, Sam probably wouldn't even notice I was away.

One problem solved. I turned my attention to the next one. Stu wanted me to decide where we would go. After the massive earthquakes that had unleashed entities on Los Angeles, finding a hotel had become complicated.

Most Angelenos opted to vacation out of town to get away from the daily nightmare of entities. The airlines had caught on quickly and jacked up fares on flights from all the LA airports. So had hotels in destinations like Palm Springs, San Diego, and San Francisco.

Stu owned a successful security company, but he had a mortgage and a daughter with hefty private school bills, so spending thousands to get out of town seemed irresponsible.

Staying local made the most sense, but even that presented issues. Los Angeles hotels had quickly adjusted to the new reality and had developed strict policies prohibiting last-minute cancellations in case there were entity eruptions on their property.

We decided the safest thing to do was wait until Friday morning to check the heatmap and pick a place that appeared safe.

It was an uneventful week. No monsters, neither supernatural nor human. No board problems or squabbles among my staff. Not even a nastygram from Eileen Simpson, which was unusual.

In the absence of drama, I made steady progress on my projects while tranquility reigned in the neighborhoods. I let Cora know I would be leaving a little early on Friday, and she immediately suspected something was up.

"I presume Stu Wells will be unavailable Friday as well?" The smile in her voice was audible.

The new guy, Rafi, seemed a little surprised when Stu and I strolled into the command center early Friday. "Is something wrong, ma'am?"

"Not a thing," I said, feeling lighthearted. I had already dealt with a long and scary string of "something wrongs," including a dark, shadowy creature in the trees of La Loma, spotted by a tipsy yours truly. Stu had seen it too.

It was like Rafi could read my mind because he said, "I checked the camera feeds first thing, ma'am. Nothing unusual. No sign of our Winged Thing." That was the cute nickname someone had come up with for our mysterious visitor." Rafi nodded politely at Stu.

Stu smiled in return, but from the way he was pacing behind the massive control console, he was impatient to start our weekend before something work-related clawed it back.

"I need to check a few things," I said hurriedly. "How about taking a quick break and be back in, say, fifteen minutes?"

Rafi's eyebrows shot up. It was an unusual request. I normally didn't need first-hand access to the heatmap, but he dipped his head and got up. He paused at the door. "If you need me back sooner, ma'am, just give me a call."

When he was gone, my fingers flew over the keyboard, expanding the view beyond Chavez Ravine to include all of Los Angeles. Stu stood behind me and massaged my shoulders. A slight tremor swept through my body, and a wave of heat rippled down my spine.

Focus on the screen, or you'll never get out of here.

"The Hollywood Hills, Mid-Wilshire, and Exposition Park are the usual shitshow." I pointed at the red dots on the huge wall screen.

"We wouldn't want to go there anyway," Stu replied. "How does Zuma Beach look?"

Zuma was in Malibu. I expanded the map, zeroed in, and sighed.

"Uh. Not good." I tapped at the keyboard and read the brief description on the screen. "Undetermined aquatic entity or entities. They've closed the beach."

Stu's fingers spasmed on my shoulders. "Shit. How about Santa Monica?"

"Checking." I had fallen into work mode. A moment later, a series of pulsing red dots appeared on the map. "Oh no. What are the chances of that? Two beaches? Come on."

"Forget the beach," Stu said. "How does Pasadena look? There's a new place I'd love to try."

We were in luck. Pasadena was in the clear, and it was a short drive away.

Stu pulled out his phone. A minute later, he announced, "I got us a cottage suite." He pulled me to my feet. "They've got an awesome spa. We can get a couple's massage if you're into it."

I laughed. "Oh? You're planning to leave the room?"

Stu was about to reply—something naughty, by his expression—when Rafi walked back in, holding a large to-go cup.

I knew Rafi would probably check the logs as soon as we left and try to figure out what I had been up to, but that was fine. It had taken me a while to settle into my new role as a boss. I didn't owe everyone an explanation about everything.

We climbed into Stu's new SUV and drove to Pasadena. The hotel was a sprawling, stately monument to Spanish architecture and old-school railroad money. It was a former estate, with stucco walls, red-tiled roofs, and arched windows, set on several dozen acres of perfectly manicured lawns and lush landscaping. The lobby floor was so shiny it resembled glass, and the whole place smelled amazing—warm and woody with a hint of citrus.

Through floor-to-ceiling windows, a glorious pool sparkled in the sun, surrounded by chaise lounges, day beds, and umbrella tables. Honestly, it was all a little overwhelming. Stu must have been more accustomed to five-star luxury because he seemed unfazed.

I was glad I had taken Julia's fashion advice and had worn a stylish, flowing boho dress in turquoise and green. With my strappy gold sandals, I fit in just fine, though I still felt awkward. The other guests were dressed casually, but in that calculated, perfect sort of way. It was late summer, and Stu wore pin-striped, black shorts and a light blue polo shirt that brought out his eyes.

The clerk at the front desk flirted with him shamelessly and hardly seemed to notice me standing at his elbow. When Stu stepped away to answer a call from his daughter, Clare, the clerk fanned himself and grinned. "He's so hot."

I couldn't help but laugh. The clerk was a burly guy with a shaved head, stuffed into a too-tight navy suit. The remark might have been unprofessional, but I think he sensed it would make me feel more comfortable, and he was right.

I winked. "He totally is."

We didn't have much luggage—just two small bags—but Stu handed them over to a porter to deliver to our rooms. Stu and I held hands while we made our way through the maze of perfectly tended gardens. Our cottage was at the far end of the grounds, nestled among the trees.

Inside the room, a chilled bottle of champagne awaited, along with fresh flowers. "Someone thought of everything," I said.

Stu winked. "Someone ordered the romance package."

"Hmm." I headed toward the bedroom. "If there aren't rose petals on the bed, I think you should ask for your money back."

There were only two fluffy robes on the bed, but rose petals had been sprinkled around a large hot tub on an elevated platform in a corner of the room. More rose petals decorated a gold box of chocolates sitting on a beautiful wooden table. The whole setup looked like an advertisement for one of those fancy stores that sold luxury linens with unimaginable thread counts.

17

I stepped into the bathroom—more understated elegance with lots of marble and warm wood. The towels were thick and sumptuous. I quickly washed my hands with the lemon verbena soap and dried them with a hand towel so soft it felt like velvet. Then I gazed at myself in the mirror, amazed by how much my life had changed for the better in a few short but action-packed months. My bones softened while I contemplated my choices: champagne first and then sex? Or sex and then champagne and maybe that couple's massage?

I hadn't heard a peep out of Stu for several minutes, so I walked into the living room.

He stood on the patio just beyond the open French doors, looking out onto the lawn. His posture was all wrong. His shoulders tight and stiff.

"Stu? You okay?" My voice was quiet. Barely above a whisper.

When he turned around, the answer was written all over his face. I looked past him.

Shit. All that grass between us and the other cottages…all that dirt underneath it…

It was moving.

"You're kidding me," I mumbled.

"I wish. It looks big." He cleared his throat. "Did you bring any…supplies?"

I swallowed hard and shook my head. Cute two-piece bathing suit? Check. Small, expensive bottle of sandalwood-scented massage oil? Check. Black satin nightie? Check. Smoke Bomb to sedate entities? Nope. Magic-infused pouches? Also no.

Stu closed the gap between us and pulled me in for a hug. Tears welled up in my eyes. No matter what I did or where I went, entities seemed to rule my life.

Stu patted my back. "It's okay. Take a deep breath. We just got here. Everything is going to be fine. This is not your responsibility. Occult Affairs will deal with it, and we'll be back on track in no time."

I sniffed. "Yeah. For sure. Okay. I'll call the command center." Which I did, but not before closing and locking the French doors.

Entities never ventured indoors, but one could never be too careful. Occult Affairs had long suspected a new kind of entity would eventually emerge, and when it did, it might not behave like the others.

With a wobbly sigh, I pulled out my cell phone from the pocket of my dress and called the direct number of the OA command center. The guy who answered the phone was new and too preoccupied with whatever emergency he was dealing with to do anything but take down the address.

"I'll send a crew as soon as I can. We've got a bit of a situation over in the Hollywood Hills. Have you alerted hotel management? If not, please do that as soon as we hang up. Please stay inside and don't forget to lock the doors."

Blah Blah Blah.

I felt like screaming. Stomping my feet. Throwing my phone. Falling to the carpeted floor and rolling around. My sexy weekend getaway was on the verge of being ruined by a fucking entity right outside our cottage.

Technically, I didn't *have* to do anything. We could have climbed into bed and pretended it wasn't happening. But it was just a matter of time before an unwary guest wandered into the area and started screaming. And there was no telling what was under that perfect grass. It could have been something rare and scary, like a ghoul or a vicious troll. Maybe a nasty chupacabra.

I kicked a trash can and sent it flying. Stu jumped, startled. I stomped toward the door.

"Maddy? What are you doing?"

"Duty calls," I said through gritted teeth.

Stu lunged toward me and grabbed my elbow. With his free hand, he cupped it against his ear. "Uh, I'm not hearing anything."

Outside, someone shrieked.

Stu coughed. "Okay…well, except for the screaming. But I certainly don't hear anyone calling your name. Let's just stay inside and let others handle things for a change. This is a good opportunity to practice emotional detachment. Or at least try a different kind of attachment." Stu wiggled his eyebrows.

I tried not to laugh. He was adorable, and he had delightfully naughty intentions, but Stu had no idea how OA operated. It could be hours—*many* hours—before a crew showed up. Until then, there would be more yelling and mayhem. I might not have had a Smoke Bomb or magic pouches, but I did have something I had been reluctant to use. A new, weird psychic connection to entities, and it seemed like the right time to put it to the test.

I kissed Stu on the neck.

"I'll be right back. You won't even know I was gone." I pulled away, slipped through the door, and ran toward the screams.

Chapter 4

I didn't know if the resort had a master landscaper like Ben Tomas, but whoever was in charge of the landscaping was going to be furious. The emerging entity was making a mess of the resort's perfect lawn. The flawless green field had been reduced to clumps of sod and grass churning in a massive, slow-moving circle.

Eyes watched me while I approached the swirling earth, and voices shouted through open windows, asking what the hell I thought I was doing. Now that I was standing just a few feet away from the entity entry point, I was beginning to wonder that myself. I was defenseless, except for my magic, which I still hadn't completely figured out yet.

My heart thumped in my chest while I focused on the roiling dirt. My toes curled. Damn it. I was outside in my bare feet. In fact, I had none of the basic protections against entities, like sturdy boots, an outfit made of durable material, and hair tied back so desperate entity claws couldn't grab it.

But there was no turning back.

Seconds later, a head emerged, followed by broad, meaty shoulders. Humanoid. And big, maybe twelve feet tall. Too small for a troll or ogre, but too large for a ghoul. It was a giant.

The thing hauled itself out of the far end of the hole, which wasn't easy because dirt kept falling back in. When it stood, I was graced with the view of its naked ass.

I cleared my throat. "Hello. Over here! My name is Maddy. I'm just here to greet you into our world."

The giant swiveled around. Dirt fell off him.

I blinked. It had a beard of black bristles and tusks like a wild boar. While I didn't know what it was, I was grateful it was exhibiting the classic signs of entity disorientation. It stared at me, swaying back and forth, and for a moment, I thought it would fall back into the hole. Instead, it collapsed onto the lawn, staring up at the blue sky.

I took a few cautious steps forward, hoping he would stay down until Occult Affairs could get there. Newly arrived entities often were too disoriented to move fast, especially the large ones, but there were always exceptions.

I began talking to it, keeping my distance and explaining about the earthquake that had introduced entities to Los Angeles. That he wasn't the only one and life would be very confusing for a long time, but there was a nice refuge in the desert where he could hang until someone figured out how to get them all back to wherever they had come from. He swiveled his head toward me, pointy ears twitching. The giant seemed to be listening but in a zoned-out kind of way. The emergence was hitting him especially hard, the poor sucker.

The chatter from onlookers in the background continued, but I was so focused on the giant that it all seemed far away.

I was getting no mental images like the ones I had received from the gnome at my mother's house and the horned worm at Griffith's Park. My mother had made it sound like entities just started yakking away in her head and she was able to communicate with them without words.

She had a gift, and she thought, as her daughter, I might have inherited it too.

And maybe I had. Maybe my connections with the worm and the troll were the beginning. And maybe I could do it again. I hoped so. Without my Smoke Bombs or magic pouches, it was the only hope I had.

I kept a safe distance of several yards, crouched, and held out a hand. To my surprise, the giant lifted his enormous arm and reached toward me.

"That's nice," I said soothingly. "There we go. Why don't you tell me a little about your home world? Let me see what it looks like?"

His tusks twitched, and I crab-walked back a few paces, just in case.

My brain began vibrating. It didn't hurt exactly, but it wasn't a pleasant sensation either. A moment later, I was crashing through a lush forest, chasing a shirtless, tattooed, brown-skinned man. I was seeing through the eyes of the giant and could feel the sharp pains of hunger in his stomach.

Damn it. A flesh-eater.

I shook my head to rid myself of the image, but not fast enough. The man's screams and the noise of crunching bones assaulted my mind before my vision returned to the ruined lawn.

"We don't do that sort of thing here," I said quietly.

An OA crew could not arrive fast enough, with a few Smoke Bombs to knock out the giant. I needed to buy more time.

The giant turned on his side and regarded me with dull eyes. His nose twitched.

"Okay, big guy. I get it. You're probably wondering what's going on and why you're here. Let's try communicating again. Maybe tell me about your friends and family?"

The giant's mouth opened slowly, revealing lots of big yellow teeth. Some razor sharp. Others like washboards. Yuck. I probably looked delicious.

The giant stirred.

"Maddy!" Hands grabbed my shoulders and pulled me to my feet.

It was Stu. I spun around. His mouth was straight and angry, eyes wide with alarm. He began dragging me toward the cottage.

The giant was trying to get to its feet. Someone was taking his snack away.

Shit.

Our conversation had been interrupted, so there was nothing to do but run. Try to get to the cottage. I had made a mental connection with the entity, but it hadn't resulted in anything beyond discovering he was a predator.

We had almost made it to the patio, the giant in lurching pursuit, when a group of men appeared, shouting war cries and brandishing patio umbrellas.

"What the hell are you doing?" I yelled. "Get back inside!"

The men, dressed like they had just finished a round of golf, ignored me. Apparently, they had seen one too many action movies.

Stu pulled me through the French doors, slamming them behind us. The men rushed forward, their makeshift weapons raised to charge into battle.

"Do *not* go back out there." Stu was breathing heavily, hands on his hips.

"That thing will kill them!"

For the most part, newly emerged entities were too confused to be dangerous, but there had been the occasional deadly encounter.

Stu's face was all hard angles. I was furious he thought I needed saving and pleased he had wanted to save me, all at the same time. It was confusing.

Outside, the giant roared. The windows rattled, and he swung a massive arm, sending one of the golfers flying across the lawn. The others scattered.

He lumbered toward the man lying on the ground.

"I can't just stay here," I said. "I've got to do something!"

Stu's face crumpled. He seemed to register that by trying to protect me, he had provoked the giant and set in motion the disaster unfolding on the lawn.

"Can you try your magic?" He sounded hopeful.

With a flesh-eating giant on the loose, it was time for *doing*, not *trying*, but I nodded. "Yeah. But no matter what happens, don't follow me this time." I glared at him. "Promise?"

Stu raked a hand through his hair. "No! I can't promise that."

I shot him a look. He tipped his head back and groaned.

"Okay. Okay. But if it looks like you're in trouble—"

"Then you'll call the Occult Affairs emergency number again."

I took a deep breath, trying to calm my racing heart before stepping outside, away from the safety of the cottage. The giant was looming over the fallen man.

I glanced back. Stu was staring at me. He gave a wobbly smile and a thumbs-up.

My stomach dropped, and a tingle raced up my neck.

Magic was hard enough under the best of circumstances. Doing it in front of an audience made it really awkward. Did Stu plan to stand there and watch the entire time?

Apparently, he did.

Lucky for all of us, the giant was hit by a second wave of disorientation. It swayed back and forth, nearly falling to the ground.

I didn't dare close my eyes, but my mind went inward, trying to find a thread of magic somewhere, anywhere.

But there was nothing. No heat. My hands felt cold and heavy. They might as well have been bags filled with damp sand attached to the ends of my wrists. Was there such a thing as magic performance anxiety?

It wasn't going to work. Not when I really needed it to put that monstrosity of a creature down.

Something whizzed by the side of my head, smacked the giant's right tusk, and exploded into a cloud of purple smoke.

I spun around. Malik, Occult Affairs recruit and former barista at Muertos Café, was standing there, getting another Smoke Bomb ready. A swath of dark hair fell over one eye. Despite the dorky uniform, he still managed to appear cool.

He lobbed a second Smoke Bomb, which left the giant twitching on the ground. Malik grinned. "Got here just in time."

I exhaled, then went to help the unfortunate golfer to his feet.

Malik took charge of the scene with swaggering confidence. He seemed to be having the time of his life. Occult Affairs suited him well.

I turned and walked toward the French doors of our cottage, my eyes cast down, annoyed I had needed saving, that I hadn't been able to handle things on my own. That my magic had failed.

At least Stu had stayed put. Sort of. When I looked up, he was standing on the patio, wearing swim trunks and holding up the bottle of champagne.

I had *so* earned that. And more.

Chapter 5

By lunchtime Sunday, I had managed to mostly forget about the nasty giant and my epic magic failure. After a very sexy morning involving the indoor hot tub, we were looking over the room service menu when my cell phone rang.

Stu picked it up from the nightstand and held it in the air so I could read the screen.

I sighed. "It's Jo." Jo was my friend who ran the command center at Occult Affairs. Half the time, she just wanted to chat. But sometimes, she was calling about something important.

"Go ahead." Stu squeezed my leg, rolled off the bed, and sauntered, naked, into the bathroom. "I'll jump in the shower."

That was the thing about Stu. He never tried to make me feel guilty for taking my job as seriously as I did. I couldn't say the same for the other guys I had dated, which was why they had never lasted long.

"We've got a situation, Mads," Jo said. "Make that *two* situations."

I snorted. "Hello to you too. And maybe you missed the memo, but I don't work for Occult Affairs anymore."

I sat up.

"Wait. Is something happening at Chavez Ravine?"

It was Jo's turn to snort. "You would have heard from your team if that was the case. Nope, it's about your mother. You know how she's on contract with us to provide her entity-charming services?"

"Yes…" I replied warily.

"Well, she's out of town, and we need her help."

"What do you mean, she's out of town? Where?"

"Mexico. Playa del Carmen, to be precise. At a fancy schmancy all-inclusive resort, from what I hear." Jo cleared her throat. "With a gentleman friend."

Hernan Frias. Retired professor of mystical studies, Chavez Ravine HOA board member, part-time brujo, and, apparently, irresistible to my mother.

The two had been spending a lot of time together, but I had no idea they had reached the lets-take-a-vacation phase. And I tried *not* to think about it. I really didn't want those pictures in my head.

So, my mother, the famous psychic, had decided to take a break from her entity whispering to enjoy some sun and sand with Hernan. I had never known her to do something so impulsive.

"Okay, well…I'm, uh, sorry she's not available." I probably sounded a little suspicious, but I had only heard one shoe drop so far.

"So am I. Aren't you going to ask why I'm calling?"

And there was shoe number two.

A warm breeze blew in through the French doors, and I began to regret taking Jo's call. "To vent about my mom?"

"No. I'm calling to ask for your help. Remember the last time we got together and had too much wine and you told me you had some kind of psychic breakthrough with a gnome? We're having some trouble with a new batch of gnomes, and I'd really like you to see if you can calm them the hell down. We'll pay, of course. Emergency weekend rates."

"Jo, I'm in Pasadena with Stu," I said, trying not to sound annoyed. "It's the first time we've gone anywhere together. We're supposed to have a spa day."

"You haven't checked the news lately, have you?" Jo sounded tired.

I eyed the half-empty bottle of massage oil on the nightstand. "No. We've been busy."

Jo sniffed. "I can imagine. Look, normally, I wouldn't even ask, but I'm desperate. Beverly Hills is in an uproar. The gnomes are squabbling over territory, and it's getting ugly. I've sent a crew, but you know how gnomes are. First sign of a squad car and they hide God knows where. And the Smoke Bombs don't work on them like they used to. I just need you to go over and see if you can settle things down. If it doesn't work, it doesn't work, but I'm out of options."

I cursed my mother, even though none of this was her fault. She could just blink her eyes at the pesky things, and they would fall all over themselves doing whatever she asked. I had managed a brief, weird connection with *one* gnome *one* time. That was not the same as communicating with them.

"I honestly don't think they'll listen to me." I could hear the resignation in my voice, and so could Jo.

"Thanks, Mads. I really owe you."

I glanced toward the bathroom. Stu was listening to the news on his phone, something he often did while shaving.

My weekend getaway was about to be interrupted. Stu had been so excited about this trip, and I didn't want to ruin it for him. For me. For us.

But I couldn't ignore Jo. "Fine. Give me the address."

Jo rattled off the location in Beverly Hills, then followed up with a text.

I'm really sorry about screwing up your weekend.

She sounded as sincere as a text could.

The whole thing felt like a fool's errand, with me playing the starring role.

Stu stepped out of the bathroom, his sandy hair still damp from the shower, a towel wrapped around his waist.

I opened my mouth to explain what had just happened, but Stu held up a hand and smiled. Crinkles formed around his blue eyes. "I heard the news about Beverly Hills. Plus, Jo calling you on a weekend…I put two and two together. So, let's go. Sooner we leave, the sooner we get back."

Stu's reaction caught me off guard. I expected him to protest. Remind me I deserved time off. Insist we stay and enjoy the rest of our weekend. But there he stood, the towel slung low on his hips, a look of sympathy in his eyes.

I felt warm all over. "Really? Are you sure?"

"Of course, I'm sure. Do you need to grab anything from home on the way?"

Good question. I thought for a moment. Not long ago, I had whipped up magic-infused pouches that subdued some wayward gnomes in Chavez Ravine, but they only paralyzed the gnomes temporarily and only with body contact. Basically, it was good for capturing them but wouldn't solve the problem in Beverly Hills. It wasn't worth the delay.

I shook my head. "No," I said, swinging my legs to the floor.

I showered quickly and pulled my hair into a bun. When I walked out of the bathroom, Stu handed me a to-go cup of freshly made coffee.

I took a sip. The dark roast was delicious, but it did nothing to calm my growing case of jitters.

When I needed my magic to subdue the giant, it hadn't worked. Did I have any magic left at all? Could I focus my new psychic powers enough to calm a bunch of angry gnomes?

I had no idea. I just hoped I wasn't trading my couple's massage for a massive solo disaster.

Chapter 6

It began at the famous Beverly Hills Hotel. Gnomes started popping up on the lush grounds, but the staff had run them off with rakes. The pesky things had scattered throughout the nearby properties, an area known as The Flats. Unfortunately, the new gnomes smacked right into some established gnome colonies, and a turf war ensued.

Gnomes seemed harmless, with their cute little pointy hats and bushy beards, but they were single-minded and stubborn. And when they didn't get their way, they could be downright nasty.

They also didn't behave like normal entities. They emerged without the classic signs of entity confusion, and they were escape artists. Occult Affairs had created a special refuge for them in the Santa Monica Mountains, but they refused to stay put. They even adapted to their new environment; over time, our Smoke Bombs began to lose effectiveness on them.

The impeccable properties of Beverly Hills had been irresistible to the gnomes, and there they remained. My mother had swept in and, with her psychic abilities, had convinced the gnomes to work together and beautify the area, but even that didn't stop the exodus of frustrated homeowners.

And now, with my mother doing God knows what with Hernan Frias in Mexico, it was up to me to solve the latest gnome problem. Stu drove slowly through the empty residential streets while I tried to come up with a plan.

"Let's go to my mom's house. I'll start with the gnome I connected with there. Maybe he can help."

Stu reached across the console and squeezed my knee. "They're a pain in the ass, but at least I don't have to worry about them gobbling you up."

My mother's house was just a few blocks away from where the trouble had started. Occult Affairs squad cars had blocked off the area, and about a dozen officers were talking to red-faced residents. Malik was there. He jogged over to the SUV, shaking his head and gesturing for Stu to turn around. I rolled down my window and stuck out my head.

Malik exhaled loudly when he recognized me. "Oh, it's you! Thank God. Jo said you were coming. It's a fucking disaster."

"I'm not sure what I can do," I said.

Stu squeezed my knee again but harder. "Think positive. You've got this."

A lump rose in my throat. His trust in me was touching but probably misplaced.

I slid out of the SUV and nodded at Malik. "What's the situation?"

Malik pushed aside the lock of dark hair that always seemed to fall over his right eye. "The new gnomes are causing chaos. They don't know the rules, apparently, so they're running around, yanking up flowers and stuff from yards and transplanting them in public spaces. But as soon as we approach, they vanish. Who knows where they go." He paused. "What's the plan? What should we do?"

"Just stand by until I do a little reconnaissance," I said. "I need to get to my mother's house on the other side of that barricade."

"I'll drive you in."

I shook my head. "I need to go alone. On foot."

Malik pressed his lips together. "Okay. I'll tell the others."

Stu leaned out the window. "Want some company?"

Yes, I did. Gnomes might have been cute, but I found them creepy. Especially the one I was about to try and "talk" to. But the gnomes who camped out at my mother's house at least seemed to recognize and accept me, and I didn't want to spook them.

"Thanks, but I think it's best if you wait here."

The streets were empty. People watched me from the front windows of their grand houses. Jo had messaged, saying she sent out an alert to residents, advising them to remain indoors until an expert arrived. Apparently, I was the expert. Talk about impostor syndrome.

It was eerily quiet. No cars, no lawn mowers. Just some distant birdsong.

I caught a fleeting glimpse of small bodies darting between houses.

My mother's place was easy to spot. The grounds were perfectly tended, and the Spanish-style house was immaculate.

I walked up the path toward the arched front door, and a hail of pebbles pelted my back. That was a hell of a welcome. I sprinted for the shallow porch. The assault stopped as quickly as it had started.

Heart racing, my hands clenched into balls, I turned toward the street. "All right. That's enough of that."

Deep, throaty laughter sounded from somewhere above my head. The little shits were in the trees.

I needed to stay calm. Yelling would only have risked antagonizing them. But I was pissed.

I counted to ten. "Everything's all right. My mother is away, so you've got me instead. I just want to talk, okay?"

They whispered to each other in their grumbly voices.

I kept my voice steady and called out again. "That was really rude, and you could have hurt me. My mother would be very disappointed. The last time I was here, I met one of you. Please, come out so we can talk again." I held out my hands. "I'm unarmed. I come in peace."

Which made me feel ridiculous. The gnomes giggled uproariously, mocking my attempts at diplomacy.

I stepped off the porch and stood under the tree. Six gnomes crouched in the branches, staring back at me.

I caught something in my peripheral—movement around the corner of the house. A blast of water hit me in the face.

I sputtered, wiping water from my eyes, and lunged forward. After grabbing the hose, I gave a mighty pull. The motion sent a gnome sprawling to the ground. I quickly knelt and pinned him in place.

Familiar beady eyes stared up at me.

"How about that," I said. "Just the gnome I happened to be looking for. I'm going to do my very best to pretend that didn't happen. And if you don't behave yourself, I'm going to tell my mother, and *she's* not going to be very happy with you. Do you understand?"

He grunted, his eyes never leaving my face.

"Good. I understand we have a bunch of new gnomes in the neighborhood. Do you know them?"

Mental images invaded my mind. They looked an awful lot like the ones he had sent before: a green rolling valley, a stampede of gnomes fleeing a terrifying dark shadow in the sky, and a tumble down a hole to escape it. Then, *boom*, the gnomes had appeared in our world.

"You told me that already." I sighed and loosened my grip on his arms, but just a little.

Beady Eyes shook his head and pressed his lips tightly together in frustration. The images came again, but I noticed a difference. The first waves of gnomes, including my captive, wore moss green tunics, thick leather belts, and sturdy boots. Their beards were iron gray. The gnomes I had just seen in my head appeared much younger. No beards. Blue overalls. They were thinner too.

Both groups of gnomes wore silly conical hats, which seemed to stay on no matter what.

"Okay. So, you are all from the same home world? Right?"

Beady Eyes nodded.

"Good. Thank you. Have you talked to them? Do the new guys know the rules that my mother set in place?"

Beady Eyes muttered something in a foreign language. To my surprise, I understood him.

They won't listen. They haven't been able to garden in a long, long time. Because of the monster in the sky.

So, the new gnomes had a pent-up need to get their grubby little hands into the dirt.

They won't listen, he repeated.

I gave Beady Eyes a sympathetic look. "Thank you for trying. It must be disorienting for the new arrivals. But we've got to get this figured out. They're causing chaos."

My knees, pressed into the hard stone of the entry path, ached. It was probably a mistake, but I sat back on my haunches. The gnome sat up and crossed his legs, frowning. His gaze shifted beyond me, and his mouth twitched.

When I turned, I noticed several of the beardless gnomes watching us.

"Hello," I said, quietly, so as not to scare them off.

The tallest one stepped forward cautiously, his eyes darting between me and my gnome friend, but just when he opened his mouth to say something, a cat burst out of the bushes and meowed loudly. It was a large ginger. Not anywhere near as big as Sam, but still, it was an impressive animal.

The young gnomes jumped, their eyes wide. They darted behind me to hide from the cat, muttering frantically to each other in their gravelly voices, clearly spooked.

The ginger cat seemed to enjoy the reaction he was getting. He sauntered over, tail flicking back and forth. I could sense the gnomes' agitation and thought they would make a break for it or at least hide in the bushes, but they appeared to be frozen.

Gnomes terrorized dogs, so I had assumed they would treat cats the same way. But seeing the effect the ginger had on the rogue gnomes gave me an idea.

Chapter 7

If, as my new gnome friend had said, the new arrivals were impossible to control, then I probably didn't have much chance of getting them to behave. But after watching them hide from the ginger cat, I realized I had a secret weapon.

Sam.

He was impressively large, and he was far from shy. Sam even made *humans* nervous. I could imagine how the unruly gnomes would react to him.

But could he really do it? Sam had been full of surprises since he first sauntered into my kitchen, but could he manage to corral a group of gnomes and help me coach them into good behavior?

My friend, the bearded gnome, was staring at me, waiting to see what I would do.

It was worth a try. I pointed at the gnomes. "Don't move. Any of you." I pulled out my phone and called Julia. "I have an enormous favor to ask. I'll explain when you get here, but can you bring Sam and meet me at my mother's house in Beverly Hills?"

"Oh no!" she said. "You got roped into dealing with that gnome craziness?" She paused. "Yeah, I think so. You don't have a crate or anything, do you? Never mind. He'd never get in anyway. Do you think he'll let me pick him up and put him in the car?"

That damn cat would have done anything for Julia. Or my next-door neighbor Leo. "For sure. But maybe just explain that I really need his help first."

Julia squealed. "That's so cute! For sure, for sure. Yeah. Send me your mom's address. I'll text you from the car."

We hung up. The gnomes were huddled together on the walkway while the cat circled them. Maybe Sam would convince the ginger to stick around.

Not daring to move until Julia arrived with Sam, I waited. I asked Beady Eyes to tell the others to sit tight too, and they did.

So far, the whole experience had been a win. I had been able to communicate with a gnome and had given him directions, I had learned about the new arrivals and witnessed how they reacted to the ginger cat, and I had a plan, sort of, for getting them under control.

It wasn't a couple's massage or champagne by the pool, but it was progress.

The ginger cat flopped on the ground near my knees and began grooming itself.

I called Malik and asked him to keep an eye out for Julia and Sam, and then I called Stu and told him to head back to the hotel. There was no telling how long I would be.

"No way," he said. "I'll go grab a coffee somewhere and wait for you. Good luck."

I would need it. My plan relied on a temperamental cat, and I didn't even have any treats to use as bribes.

Eventually, Malik's squad car pulled up, followed by Julia's ancient red Volvo. Julia got out wearing a yellow sundress, her auburn hair piled high on her head. She opened the passenger side door, and Sam jumped out. He paused on the sidewalk and looked around, as though assessing the situation with cool detachment.

The gnomes gasped and huddled together. The ginger cat stopped grooming, its tail flicking.

I beckoned Sam over, but he seemed more intent on making an entrance. He walked toward me, taking long, slow steps, like a model on a runway.

I was glad to see him but didn't know what to make of the attitude.

"Weirdo."

He sauntered up and sat, huge and Sphinx-like.

"Thank you for coming, Sam," I said, feeling like an idiot for talking to him like that. "Would you please watch these guys while I talk with my friend?" I jerked my head in the direction of Beady Eyes. "Make sure they don't go anywhere."

Sam blinked his green eyes and gave a low meow.

I took that as an agreement and gestured for my gnome friend to follow me inside. But when I entered the key code on the pad, he refused to budge.

He shook his head. *Outside.*

I had never seen the gnomes inside my mother's house, so maybe that was one of her rules. Fine. I walked into the backyard, and we sat on the deck under the shade of an awning. There, I fired off some questions. I learned there were twenty-five new arrivals. Not as many as I had feared. They were desperate to start working and had no concept of organizing their efforts or following a plan. And they were frenetic. They wouldn't sit still long enough to learn the rules the other gnomes followed.

I crouched down so my face was at eye level with the old gnome.

"Okay, my friend. Here's what we're going to do. Sam—he's the big cat—will keep the newcomers quiet and still while you explain my mother's rules. Then you'll split the new arrivals into groups of five and assign an older gnome to supervise each group as they work on a nearby yard. If the newcomers don't follow orders, they'll have to deal with Sam. And I'm putting *you* in charge. You'll keep everything running smoothly, or *you'll* have to face my mother when she gets back. Do we have an agreement?"

Beady Eyes pulled his shoulders back and puffed out his chest.

We had an agreement.

When we returned to the front of the house, Sam and the ginger cat were where I had left them, but now there were six cats instead of two.

Sam glanced over at me, looking smug.

"Nice crew you've assembled."

I could have sworn Sam nodded.

Julia had been chatting with Malik, but when she noticed me, she ran over and clutched my arm. "What about your weekend with Stu?"

My weekend had been ruined. By a bunch of short creepy guys in funny hats.

I tipped my head back and exhaled, thinking of the glistening pool back at the hotel and the massage oil on the nightstand. "I need to stay."

Julia stomped a sandaled foot. "No, you don't. Whatever you did, things seem to have calmed down. Not even Jo would expect you to stay around the clock. This isn't your full-time job. You already have one of those, and you deserve some time off."

I glanced over at Sam, who appeared to be in a stare-off contest with the tallest of the new gnomes. "I can't just leave Sam here," I said weakly. "What if something happens? Like, what if he starts chasing birds or the gnomes attack him?"

Julia snorted. "Sam? They wouldn't dare. But if you're worried, I'll stay." Her brown eyes flicked toward the house. "Your mother's home is gorgeous. I'd love to hang out here for a couple of nights! You don't think your mother would mind, do you?"

I didn't. Not if it meant putting an end to the gnome crisis and salvaging her reputation with Occult Affairs. It was bad form to run away with her boyfriend without telling her client, which my mother should have known.

"It's a lot to ask," I said.

Julia placed her hands on my shoulders, pulled me to her, and bumped her forehead against mine. "It's not, and you should never be afraid to ask for help. *Especially* after everything you've done for us in Chavez Ravine."

Julia made it sound so easy. She did have a point, though. I had promised to try and help, and I had. When I looked over at Sam, he was sitting regally, surrounded by his feline entourage. He seemed to be holding court with the gnomes, who still appeared nervous.

"Okay, you're right. Thank you." I pecked Julia on the cheek.

I went over to Sam to scratch his head, but he shot me the kind of look teenagers give their parents that said, "Don't you dare embarrass me."

I gave him a thumbs-up instead.

Malik was waiting at the curb. He opened the car door. "That's some cat you have there."

I looked at him, wondering if he thought I was nuts for leaving my cat to take care of such an important operation. But Malik had helped subdue a ghoul with sticky pouches of herbs, so he had seen it all.

"Yeah, he is something. I'm still trying to figure out what." I took out my phone to call Stu. "Malik, whatever you do, keep the media out. They'd have a field day. I'll call Jo and explain what's going on."

Malik sniffed. "She's going to love this."

Yes, she would. Mostly because the problem was being solved.

Stu arrived, and I climbed into the SUV. When we pulled away from the curb, more young gnomes emerged from the shrubbery. Beady Eyes and Sam stood closely together to greet them.

Chapter 8

Stu and I finally got that couple's massage, a leisurely swim in the glorious sparkling pool, and plenty of time lounging under the shade of an enormous umbrella while servers brought us food and drinks.

Plus, some other stuff back in the room.

But all that fun didn't completely chase away thoughts of work. Or Sam. I had left him alone to deal with the gnomes in Beverly Hills, and I felt like a bad mother. When I checked in with Malik and Julia, they said order had been restored, although Sam's cat army had doubled.

While Stu was swimming laps, I peeked at my phone for updates on the goats. Rafi had kept an eye on the camera feeds. The rest of the herd were alive and grazing away. Still no sign of blood-sucking entities, although he had spotted a pair of coyotes on the running trail bordering Elysian Park. Maybe it had been coyotes after all. It was a reassuring idea, but I still had a knot of unease in the pit of my stomach.

Stu emerged from the pool, droplets glistening on his bronzed skin. He strode toward me with a smile.

"Everything okay?" He stared pointedly at the phone in my hand and settled down beside me.

I forced a smile. "Fine. I just got an update from the command center. Some coyotes were seen near the goats."

Stu frowned while he toweled off. "Coyotes, huh? Could be, I guess. Nature can be brutal. But from what you told me, coyotes probably didn't attack those goats. And there's not been a single sighting of whatever it was that we saw flying away? The timing seems a little crazy to me."

I got to my feet, grabbed a tube of sun lotion, and rubbed some onto his shoulders. "Unless they're the next wave of entities. Bigger. Scarier. Capable of evading detection with the technology we have."

Stu shuddered. "I still haven't adapted to the new normal, which isn't so new anymore. I'm definitely not ready for whatever comes next. That's why I bought in Chavez Ravine, except, lately, things have been a little weird around there too. I will admit, it's got me worried. Just a bit."

My heart turned to a block of ice in my chest. I felt lightheaded, and my insecurity rose in my throat. Though I tried to choke it back down, I had no luck. I blurted out, "You mean, things have been weird since I moved in?"

Stu squeezed my hand and gave it a little shake. "No, of course not. Don't be silly. How could you have anything to do with everything that's been going on?"

He stared into my face. His blue eyes narrowed.

"Wait a minute. You're serious. You actually think you're somehow responsible for all the problems you've been solving? Come on. How does that even make sense?"

I bit my lip. Tears threatened to form in my eyes. "I don't know. Maybe my magic, as wobbly as it is, stirred things up? Chavez Ravine has a long history of supernatural activity, yet things seemed mostly fine until I moved in."

Stu's mouth opened, then closed. He drew me into a hug. His sun-warmed skin was hot and damp against mine.

"Maddy," he said into my hair, "stop it. You're just being paranoid. And remember what you told me? Strange things were happening before you *ever* stepped foot in Chavez Ravine, and that's exactly why Cora wanted to hire you in the first place. To use whatever magic you inherited, combined with your experience in Occult Affairs, to deal with it. And you did! So please, don't torture yourself like this."

He made it sound so simple.

"I guess."

Stu released me and studied my face with serious blue eyes. Sun lotion had settled into the crinkles of his tanned skin. "Is it possible you're feeling burned out? You've been working pretty much nonstop since you took the job. This weekend is the first time off you've had, right? And look what happened. You got called out on an emergency by an agency you don't even work for anymore, and you've been checking in with your team. You're not really getting a break."

I snorted. "The definition of the pot calling the kettle black."

Stu dipped his head. "Guilty as charged. I'm just saying it's possible you are having these guilty feelings because you have a big, important job that doesn't allow for much downtime. But maybe you can try a little emotional detachment?"

I barked out a laugh. How could I detach myself from a job that felt like it was consuming me whole? "Yeah, right."

Stu laughed too. "Okay, baby steps. How about we try not to think about the job for the next, say, two hours?"

"What are we going to do for two hours?" I probably sounded a little suspicious.

Stu rolled his eyes. He leaned in closer, his voice dropping to a husky whisper. "Do I really have to spell it out for you?"

That snapped me out of my funk. I gathered up my belongings and practically sprinted back to the cottage, my flip-flops slapping against the pavement, the sun beating down on my bare shoulders, and Stu laughing in the distance behind me.

By Monday morning, my weekend with Stu was a pleasant memory. I wound my way through the congested streets of Los Angeles, cursing up a storm, heading to Beverly Hills to collect my cat. Julia had left my mother's house for an artsy luncheon downtown, and I didn't want Sam to be alone longer than necessary.

I had just passed the La Brea Tar Pits when Stu called.

"Miss me already?" I asked.

"Of course." Stu sighed, but he was all business. "Hey. I hate to ask, but I'm wondering if you can do me a favor. A big one."

A couple of Occult Affairs vehicles were parked on the street near Museum Row. Not surprising; Miracle Mile was a popular entity emergence spot.

"Name it."

"Can you please pick up Clare? Something came up at work, and I had to leave her at her soccer game in West Hollywood. Her mother's out of town, and Clare is supposed to stay with me for the next few days."

"No problem. She can hang out at my place until you get home."

"I'm sorry about this," Stu said. "Are you sure you're okay with it?"

"Of course I am. I'm headed to Beverly Hills to get Sam, so it's a small detour. Maybe Clare can help me get Sam into the Jeep."

Stu laughed. "Good luck with that. Might be hard now that he's had a taste of freedom."

I pulled up to the soccer field just when the game was ending. Judging by all the jumping up and down and whooping, Clare's team had won. Although, there was something odd going on with their uniforms. I jogged toward the group of parents and waved my hands above my head so Clare would see me.

When she came running toward me, I noticed that her face had been painted in shades of blue and turquoise, with swirls of white on her forehead resembling a tiara. Pink butterfly wings decorated each cheek.

Over her soccer shorts, she wore a pink tutu. "What's all this?"

"Every season, we play a game of Silly Soccer. This year, we're The Poofy Princesses." She twirled around. "It's so much fun." She looked around, frowning. "Where's my dad? He said he would be right back."

I shook my head. "He's going to be longer than expected, so you're stuck with me."

Clare grinned. "I don't mind. I always have fun with you."

I took her elbow and steered her toward the parking lot. "Let's see what you say after we've finished trying to round up Sam. He's at my mom's house, playing gnome warden. I'll explain on the way."

Clare's eyes were as big as saucers when I finished telling her the story of the rogue gnomes.

"I always knew Sam was smart, but I had no idea he was *that* smart," she said.

At the roadblock, I stopped long enough for Malik to share a brief update. "Everything has settled down. We'll be staying another twenty-four hours, just in case, and then we plan to clear out. I don't know what you're paying your cat, but he deserves a raise."

Clare giggled. "Maddy can buy him a tuna steak."

"Like hell I will," I grumbled. "One taste of that and he'd never be satisfied with canned again."

"You're funny." Clare leaned over me to get a better look at Malik. Her warm breath brushed against my face. Half a block away, she said, "Oh my God, he's so cute."

"He's taken," I replied automatically. "And he's *way* too old for you."

Clare sniffed. "Well, now he is, but when I'm like nineteen or twenty, it won't be a big deal. Hypothetically speaking, that is."

At times like that, I was glad I wasn't Clare's mother. Teenage girls scared me. I tried to let it go, although I did wonder whether I should mention her interest in an older man to her father. Better to be forewarned and all that. I glanced over at Clare in her princess makeup. She was still just a child. I was overreacting.

And then I remembered what I had gotten up to at her age and shuddered.

Beverly Hills was quiet, almost eerily so. Some gnomes were visible, but they lingered in ones and twos, going about their gardening business in their assigned front yards. Cats patrolled the walkways and porches.

Clare was right. Sam *was* smart.

Clare pressed her face against the passenger-side window. "This is amazing! I've never seen gnomes in person before. They're so cute!"

I wondered what she would think if she saw them up close, with their grayish skin, wrinkled faces, and dark, beady eyes.

After pulling into my mother's driveway, I turned in my seat for a quick safety chat.

"Okay, Clare. I'm going to find Sam, but I need you to stay here. Inside. I won't be long, okay? But as cute as they are, gnomes can be a little unpredictable and—"

Clare threw open the door. "I see some!" Before I could grab the back of her jersey, she was running toward a palm tree.

49

Three gnomes in blue vests knelt on the ground, planting pansies around its trunk. They jumped to their feet, startled by the girl in the pink tutu racing toward them.

"Clare Wells!" I shouted after her. "You come back this second."

How the hell had I gotten a mom voice all of a sudden?

Less than a yard into the chase, I dodged a wheelbarrow full of dirt and stepped on a hand rake. My ankle wobbled, and down I went. When I lurched to my feet, Clare was surrounded by a half dozen gnomes. They inched toward her, hands outstretched.

Clare glanced over her shoulder at me, her dark eyes wide with fear. "Maddy!" she cried. "What are they doing?"

Crap.

"Sam!" I shouted into the air. "Where are you? I need you."

I stumbled toward Clare, but the gnomes swept her off her feet with surprising strength. She let out a startled cry before they whisked her away into the bushes, disappearing in a matter of seconds.

Chapter 9

Panic gripped me, and I frantically scanned the area. I was sweaty all over, and my heart was beating way too fast. The gnomes had abducted Clare right before my eyes, and I had no idea where they had taken her. My mind raced with horrifying possibilities. Had they disappeared into a hole in the ground? Taken her wherever it was they hid when Occult Affairs showed up?

Gnomes had never abducted a human before. Then again, these gnomes were young recent arrivals. Who knew what they were capable of?

Poor Clare had been with me for less than an hour, and I had managed to lose her. What the hell would I tell Stu?

Well, it appears your only child has been kidnapped by a band of gnomes. Oops. My bad.

I shouted again for Sam, but he was a no-show. Maybe he had developed a taste for freedom far from his boring life at home.

My hands were shaking when I called Malik. "I want everyone you have out looking for her."

"We'll find her." He didn't sound confident, and my heart sank lower in my chest.

Breathless, I sprinted around the side of the house and checked the backyard. Nothing. I ran down the middle of the street, scanning the front yards and in between the houses. Three old-school gnomes were erecting a trellis when I ran past. They glanced in my direction, startled.

"Have you seen a teenage girl wearing a tutu?" I shouted.

They didn't answer, but they bent their heads together and began chattering among themselves.

When I reached the end of the block, my vision became blurry. At first, I thought sweat had dripped into my eyes, but it wasn't sweat. I was crying.

Once when I was little, I had hidden inside one of those circular clothing racks in a department store. I didn't remember why—maybe to teach my mom a lesson because I hated shopping—but it was so warm and stuffy in there, I nodded off. The next thing I knew was my mother screaming my name.

When I crawled out, she scooped me up in her arms and cried. "Madre miá de Dios, I thought you'd been kidnapped!"

Her relief didn't last long. By the time we reached the parking lot, it was, as usual, all about her.

"You have no idea what you've put me through, Madeline."

Each second Clare remained missing brought me closer to understanding the panic that must have gripped my mother all those years ago in the fluorescent-lit aisles of May Company. The frantic worry shriveling my heart was so visceral it actually hurt. Clare wasn't even my own flesh and blood. I had no official role in her life, like "stepmother." I was just her dad's girlfriend. Yet here I was, caught in a riptide of emotions threatening to drag me under. It was absurd—almost illogical—how quickly she had wormed her way into my life.

My desperation wasn't caused by worry about Stu's potential wrath. It was something deeper. A more profound concern for Clare.

I needed to calm down.

They're gnomes. Not ghouls. They're harmless. She'll be fine.

I searched the next block, and then the next. Still no sign of Sam or of my friend Beady Eyes.

Dammit, Sam. Where are you?

When my phone rang in my pocket, I couldn't answer it fast enough. It was Malik.

"Did you find her?"

"Yeah. She's fine, for now. But you'd better check things out for yourself." Malik gave me directions to a small park nearby. I would get there faster on foot rather than going all the way back to my mother's house to pick up the Jeep.

By the time I got to the park, my back was drenched with sweat, and my leg muscles burned. I found Malik and a half dozen uniformed OA officers huddled together, staring at a gazebo built to resemble a castle. It was made of gray stone and wood, with a tower and thatched roof. A round stone base supported sturdy columns. The whole thing was straight out of a fairy tale.

Clare stood in the middle of the gazebo, hands pressed against her mouth. She saw me and gave a frantic wave.

"Maddy, please get me out of here!"

She's okay. She's okay.

I waved back while my legs went weak with relief.

Her small abductors—all of them newly arrived gnomes— were busily planting purple flowers at the base of the gazebo. A few others were standing guard, keeping Clare captive.

Malik walked over and folded his arms against his chest. "We've tried Smoke Bombs, but those don't work on these new gnomes. What do you want to do?"

I wanted to use my magic. If it worked, it would be the easiest and fastest solution.

"Give me a second."

I could sense Malik staring at me when I closed my eyes, willing myself to focus, thinking of vines coming out of the

53

ground and wrapping themselves around the small creatures, binding them in place. While my thoughts cooperated, my hands did not. They felt cold and stiff, like they had at the hotel when the giant appeared. No magical spark. Nothing.

My eyes flicked open. Clare appeared distressed and confused, her eyes pleading with me. Obviously, she wondered why no one was doing anything to save her.

There was nothing else to do but march over there and get our girl. Of course, I had left my slingshot and ammo in the Jeep.

I had no way of knowing what these new gnomes might do if we confronted them. If they got violent, it could be bad for Clare and the OA officers. And me. But I was out of options.

"We're going to have to do this the old-fashioned way," I said to Malik, pointing at his baton. "Use the batons, but only if you have to. Let's try to get Clare out without sending the gnomes into a panic."

Malik began talking quietly to the other officers, when something rustled in the bushes off to our left. I spun around, half expecting more gnomes, but a furry red head appeared, followed by a sturdy striped body. It was Sam.

"Took you long enough," I hissed.

Sam paused long enough to meow loudly.

I bent over and barked, "Don't you tell me to calm down!"

Sam strutted toward us, tail flicking. Behind him, a small army of cats emerged from the hedges and flanked him, their eyes gleaming.

"You going to let them handle this?" Malik said hopefully.

Sam swiveled his head and regarded the dark-haired officer. He let out a guttural meow as if to say, "We've got this."

With that, he guided his feline troops toward the gnomes, who froze when they noticed the approaching army. But before the gnomes could react, the cats pounced.

In a whirlwind of fur, barred teeth, and pointed hats, the two groups clashed in a chaotic battle. The gnomes shrieked when sharp claws came out. When the tallest gnome grabbed a spade and swung it at Sam's head, both Clare and I screamed, but Sam jumped away and bit the gnome on the rear.

With a chorus of cat screeches and gnomes' gravelly shouts, the battle was over in minutes.

Chapter 10

The gnomes were small and scrappy, but they were no match against Sam and the lightning-fast movements of his feline friends. The cats overpowered them one by one until a single gnome remained standing, clutching a pair of garden shears in his hand. He positioned himself at the top step of the gazebo, his jaw set firmly, clearly determined to keep Clare trapped.

I stepped forward and stopped beside Sam.

The gnome was panting heavily, a mixture of fear and defiance in his eyes.

"That's enough out of you today," I said loudly, but it wasn't my words he heard as much as my thoughts. "It's over. Time to let the young lady go."

The gnome's dark eyes darted between us while he weighed his options. He let out a high-pitched battle cry and charged. The gnome had just reached the second step when Sam head-butted his stomach, sending the gnome tumbling backward. Clare lunged and delivered a solid shove, propelling him off the steps and onto the ground. He ended up flat on his back, staring up at the sky.

Clare ran toward me. I opened my arms to embrace her, but she went straight past and knelt next to Sam, burying her face in his fur. Sam tolerated the attention for a second but obviously thought it undignified. He wriggled free and joined the other cats, who were surrounding the limp, defeated gnomes. The cats licked their paws, managing to look both triumphant and slightly bored.

"Wait until Jo hears about this," Malik said with a smirk. "She'll definitely want to put these guys on the payroll. I just hope they don't put us out of a job."

My friend Jo was practical, above all else. I could imagine her trying to put together a crew of police felines, but she would have to fly it by the chief first, and he would laugh her out of his office before she finished her pitch.

I reached out a hand to help Clare up, my heart still racing from all the adrenaline. "I'm glad you're okay, but your father is going to have a fit when he finds out."

That was enough to make Clare burst into tears. "We don't have to tell him. He'll be furious I wasn't more careful."

Malik had retreated to give us space, but he quickly stepped forward, holding out his phone. With a sniff, Clare peered at the screen, her eyes going wide.

"No! No! Crap!"

I looked at the display, then at the large group of people who had gathered behind us. Half of them had their phones out.

Malik tapped his screen and played a video that had captured the entire chaotic scene at the park. The headline read: "Cat Fight with Gnomes in Beverly Hills!"

Clare's shoulders slumped in defeat. She rested her head on my shoulder. "My dad is going to kill me."

I patted her back. "He'll kill me first. I was supposed to be the responsible adult."

"But I didn't listen." Clare sniffed. "You tried to warn me."

Malik put his phone in his pocket. "Clare…do you know why they took you? Why did they put you in the gazebo?"

Clare exhaled loudly. "This is going to sound crazy, but I think they thought I was a princess or a queen because after they carried me into the gazebo, they started chanting and bowing and stuff. Like I was some kind of royalty." She rolled her eyes. "I don't know where they got that idea. It's so stupid."

Malik and I exchanged glances. I tried to keep a straight face, but Malik couldn't manage it. He burst out laughing, tracing a circle around his face with his finger.

Clare's confused expression shifted to one of realization. "Oh my God, I completely forgot about the princess makeup!" She glanced down at her tutu and let out a groan. "Okay, okay, I get it now. But I still can't believe it happened."

I couldn't either, yet somehow, it oddly made sense. The gnomes had mistaken her for a figure from their realm whom they admired—maybe even worshipped—and had whisked her off to something that looked like a castle.

Occult Affairs officers came running up with crates and began stuffing gnomes inside them while Sam and the cats stood watch. Sam would have called it *supervising*, I'm sure.

If the new gnomes were like the others, they would escape the processing facility known as The Dump and head straight back to Beverly Hills. But hopefully by then, my mother would be back and could deal with them herself. Like she was supposed to do. Like she was paid to do.

I wanted nothing more than to go home with my cat, take a nice shower, and change into fresh, clean clothes. But first, I had to do the responsible thing and call Stu.

I was pulling out my phone when it rang. It was Stu's ex-wife, Vicki Wells. The only time we had ever spoken, she had told me to stay away from her daughter. Apparently, I had trouble following directions.

Clare noticed my expression. With one hand on my shoulder, she peered at the screen. "Oh shit, it's my mom. You think she saw the video?"

I inhaled deeply and answered the call. "Maddy Madrigal."

Vicki launched. "Did you *not* hear me the first time? What part of 'stay away from my daughter' did you not understand? And now look at what you've done. Clare is supposed to be playing soccer. All the other girls are off at a pizza party, having fun. But my daughter was kidnapped by some pervy little creeps who did who knows what."

Malik had just finished latching a crate. His head snapped up. The woman was yelling so loudly even he could hear her.

She droned on. I didn't even try to talk. Best to let her say her piece. Would she have even noticed if I hung up?

Clare's fingers dug into my arm. "I'm sorry, I'm sorry, I'm sorry," she murmured.

I took a deep breath. This was a whole new level of adulting. Getting screamed at by your new boyfriend's ex-wife and just letting it happen instead of yelling back and making things worse.

"If Clare was…touched by those things, I will sue you," Vicki continued. "Do you understand? Well, no. You don't, obviously, because I told you I didn't want you near my child, and now look what's happened. I told Stu. I did. But he didn't listen, and now he's going to be sorry because I'm going to court and ask them to amend our custody agreement. Either he keeps our daughter away from you, or that's it. I'll demand sole custody."

Vicki paused long enough to give me an opening.

"Vicki, I understand your concerns, but let me assure you that Clare is safe and everything is under control."

Malik gave me a thumbs-up.

Vicki scoffed. "Under control? You allowed my daughter to be *abducted*. She was a mess after the goblin incident. And now this! You are a walking disaster, and I will not allow my daughter to be collateral damage in your hot mess of a life."

Malik grimaced and hurried away, crate in hand.

Clare stared at me, stricken, silently pleading with me to fix things. But this was beyond my control. Stu had asked me for a favor. I had agreed. Things had gone badly wrong. I should have anticipated the danger but hadn't. Clare shouldn't have run out of the Jeep like that, but she did.

Vicki ended the call, so there was no more to say.

But I did have a question for Clare. "Did the gnomes…do anything…?"

The words drifted off. Vicki wasn't the only person who suspected entities of sexual misbehavior, although those concerns were greatly exaggerated. It had all started with the emergence of a giant who stirred the loins of the women who met him. The big hunk had even managed to sire the first and only entity-human child.

Clare made a yuck face. "No! Gross!" She tipped her head back. "My mom is so weird!" she wailed.

Yeah, so was mine. I still needed to call Stu. Our sexy weekend felt like it was a hundred years ago.

My phone rang. Speak of the devil. Clare and I exchanged nervous looks. I felt more like a teenager about to get in trouble than a grown-ass chief of security.

"Hey." Somehow, I sounded nonchalant.

"Can't leave you two alone, can I?" Stu said dryly. "I'm guessing things didn't go quite as planned at your mother's?"

I cleared my throat. "You can say that."

Clare's face was all scrunched up, and she bounced up and down. I squeezed her arm.

Stu gave a grim chuckle. "I'm sure I'll be hearing from Vicki."

"You can count on it."

Stu sighed. "Thank you for helping out with Clare, and I'm sorry things went sideways. From what I saw, it didn't look like fun. Well, except for the cats. They seemed to be having a blast. How about you both tell me all about it over dinner? Pizza? I can stop at Agostino's."

Stu wasn't mad. I couldn't believe it. If he had been standing in front of me, I would have thrown my arms around his neck and hugged him until it hurt.

Clare heard him, and her body sagged with relief. Her eyes lit up at the mention of pizza.

It was time to leave, but there was still the matter of Sam. He was sitting at my feet, staring up at me with his green eyes. I could swear he was expecting a tuna steak.

"Ready to go home?" I asked.

Sam peered over his shoulder at the other cats now lounging in the grass while the last gnome was carted off in a crate.

Without another glance, Sam trotted alongside us all the way to my mother's house. He leapt into the backseat of my Jeep, and by the time we were out of Beverly Hills, he was fast asleep.

Chapter 11

When we drove into Chavez Ravine, I almost immediately sensed a shift in energy. There was nothing obvious. It was more of a gut instinct that something was there that did not belong. I think Sam felt it too because he jumped into Clare's lap and looked out the window.

Sam clacked his teeth together when we entered Palo Verde.

"Look!" Clare cried. "There's a goat! They're *so* cute!"

The brown animal with black spots was munching some dry grass on the path running alongside the gully. I filled her in on Ben Tomas's goat project.

After dropping Clare off at Stu's house, I went back to mine to shower and change. But first, I poured fresh water into a bowl, opened a can of tuna, and topped it with Sam's favorite kibble.

I drank some cold sparkling water straight from the bottle and watched him gobble it down.

"What you did back there with the gnomes was amazing," I said. "Thank you."

Talking to my cat seemed like a perfectly normal thing to do these days.

Sam's head popped up long enough for him to blink a few times and give a brisk meow, as if to say, "No big deal."

When I was finally ready to leave, Sam was sleeping on the ottoman in the living room.

At Stu's, we ate sausage and mushroom pizza at the dining room table while Clare and I explained what had happened with the gnomes.

"It's my fault, Dad," Clare said repeatedly. "Maddy told me to stay inside the car, but I wanted to take some pictures of the gnomes and—"

"Your impulsiveness is going to get you into some serious trouble one of these days," Stu interrupted. "And next time, Maddy—or Sam—might not be around to save you."

Clare served herself another slice of pizza. Her mother refused to allow carbs, which meant Clare had to get her fill where she could. I finished my slice, feeling the tension in the room dissipating while we talked about other things.

We had just finished dessert—the chili-infused lemon sorbet Clare and I had made—when Stu said, "I have a surprise."

By the smug look on his face, it was a good one.

"You're going to propose to Maddy?" Clare blurted.

My body temperature went up a few notches, and it had nothing to do with the spicy sorbet. Stu's face turned red.

He stole a glance in my direction. The poor guy looked so horrified I almost laughed. Instead, I gave a little shrug.

Teenagers.

The moment passed. Stu went over to the double doors leading into the backyard. His place was a bit gloomy for my taste, with the kind of dark wood furniture that would have fit in at a mountain lodge. He threw open the doors with a "Ta da!"

In the backyard, which was three times the size of mine, was a hot tub. A large and fancy one with colored lights and a little fountain.

"I had it installed this weekend while we were in Pasadena."

"You went to Pasadena without me?" Clare cried. "Leaving me alone with Mom? Thanks, Dad."

Stu and I exchanged looks. Clare still hadn't forgiven her mother for cheating on Stu. In fact, Clare seemed angrier at her mother than ever.

Stu frowned but didn't say anything. For the first time that evening, he seemed troubled, and I wondered if he had gotten an earful from Vicki too.

He slung an arm around his daughter. "It just got filled today, so it's not hot enough for us to get in tonight. But how about tomorrow?"

Clare poked my arm. "The three of us?"

Stu cleared his throat. "Uh, sure. But listen, I heard from your mother. She's not happy with what happened today, and while it's not fair, she blames Maddy and—"

"She was *so* mean to Maddy!" Clare said hotly. "I heard her. She was such a b—"

That time, I cut her off. "That is not how we talk about our mothers," I said firmly.

"Thank you," Stu murmured. "Your mother is making some pretty serious threats, and I am concerned. She seems to have taken against Maddy, so we need to let her cool down. Which means…" His words drifted off, and he scrunched up his face.

My breath caught in my throat. Was he about to say we needed to take a break in our relationship?

"Dad, what?" Clare said, her voice rising.

"I really hate this," Stu continued, "but I'm afraid we're going to have to be a little discreet about the three of us hanging out together. Which means not talking about it in front of your mom. We don't want to risk aggravating her even more. I hate the deception, but your mom just isn't being reasonable about this. And Clare, I know how much you like visiting Maddy at her house, but I'm going to ask you to only see Maddy when I'm around. All right?"

By the thunderous look on Clare's face, it was far from all right. I quickly interjected.

"As much as I love having Clare over, I think that's a wise move. Discretion is our middle name, right, Clare?" I shot her a conspiratorial wink, trying to lighten the mood.

Clare scowled. The princess makeup was gone. She had showered and was now dressed in pajama bottoms and a tank top. "I guess. It's stupid, though. Why does my mom always have to get her way?"

Good question. And yet, I understood the gravity of the situation. The former Mrs. Wells might have been unhinged, but she could still stir up a lot of trouble for Stu.

Stu looked at me. "Hot tub tomorrow night?"

"It's a date. I'll bring some snacks."

He turned back to Clare, who looked like she was getting ready to either cry or protest. "I'm glad you understand. It's just temporary. Until things calm down with your mom. All right?"

Clare rolled her eyes, pecked me on the cheek, and stomped into the house, hands balled into fists at her sides. I gave a little shudder, glad all that teenage hostility hadn't been directed at me.

When Clare was around, there were no sleepovers. "Good luck," I said to Stu when he walked me to the door.

He gave me a lingering kiss that took me back to the hotel in Pasadena, and then, holding my hand, he walked me to my Jeep.

At home, Sam had moved into the bedroom and was sprawled in the center of the bed. I changed into a soft oversized T-shirt, nudged him aside, and crawled in.

And then came the weird dreams. Enormous ugly creatures whispered at me from high in the trees. Goats chased me through Elysian Park. A chirping monster swatted me with its big tail.

No, wait. *That* was real.

At three o'clock in the morning, Sam woke me up. His body was twitching, and his tail flicked me. He was making that weird chirping sound he used when he spotted birds.

Heart racing, I switched on the lamp. Sam was fast asleep, obviously dreaming. I wondered if he was having nightmares too.

Chapter 12

I had just poured myself a cup of French roast in my Palo Verde office and was settling into a cozy side chair when my phone shrieked.

It was a message from the command center. Two more dead goats: one outside Cora Bernal's house, the other on Charlie Perez's property. Was our goat killer targeting HOA board members?

As before, both animals had been drained of blood.

Before I could put my phone down, it rang. It was Steve Zhao, the Occult Affairs researcher I had hoped could shed some light on our blood-drained goats.

"The good news," he began without preamble, "is I'm pretty sure it's *not* the Cucuy. And it's definitely not a ghoul. There wouldn't be much left if it had been. We didn't find a match with chupacabras either…or anything else in our database. So, I'm pretty confident when I say it's not an entity. At least—"

I cut him off. "I know, I know. At least the entities we're familiar with."

The nerds at Occult Affairs never missed an opportunity to warn us about the possibility of new entities.

"Exactly," Steve said. "I'm sorry I couldn't be more help. I could send you the analysis, but it won't do you much good. We're sure whatever did it was a bloodsucker, but you already knew that. I can tell you it had needle-thin teeth. Lots of them. But here's the interesting thing…the wounds were so small we could only see them with microscopes, and the wounds appear to have sealed shortly after the feeding, which explains why you didn't notice any obvious signs of injury. It's almost like the punctures were cauterized."

Leave it to the nerds to bury the lead. I ignored the word "feeding." That would have been a whole different discussion. Instead, I focused on identifying the predator.

"What could do something like that?"

"No clue. Some sort of vampire probably. But not the sexy, rich kind." Steve gave an awkward laugh.

I stared at a map of Chavez Ravine tacked on the wall. There were lots of places where goats could graze and plenty of places where whatever killed them could hide.

"All right. Based on your experience, what sort of creature do you think we should be looking for?"

"Um, I don't know. With teeth like that, it could be small, but honestly, I have no idea. If they were ordinary incisors, I might be able to guess, but not with those things." He paused. "Sorry."

After we ended the call, my agitation level skyrocketed. Now that board members were involved, I needed to act. I called Bailey Nixon, filled her in, and sent her to Charlie Perez's house to brief him. As board president, Cora deserved an in-person visit from the woman she had hired to head up security.

Now that this was no longer an isolated incident and given what I had just heard from Steve, I scheduled an all-hands-on-deck meeting with my team for the early afternoon, then headed up the hill to Cora Bernal's house.

Cora lived in Bishop near Elysian Park, so it didn't take long to get there. When I pulled up, Cora was waiting for me in the yard, pacing.

"I was headed to the grocery store, but something was blocking my door," she said. "That's how I found it."

The board president was wearing a cream-colored tracksuit. Tears glistened in her eyes. "The poor thing. Why is this happening?"

I patted Cora's arm and crouched to study the animal. It appeared to have been thrown onto the porch. If that was the case, the goat had probably been killed elsewhere. Which meant Cora's house had been chosen for a reason.

"Give me a moment." I dialed Bailey's number.

She picked up immediately. "Just got here." Bailey sounded breathless.

"Where did you find the goat?" I asked.

"Front porch." Bailey cleared her throat. "Charlie's wife found it on her way to the gym. She's freaking out."

"Does it look to you like the goat was dumped there?"

"For sure. It looks like someone threw it on the porch, and it took out a bunch of potted plants on the way. This is really messed up."

"Yeah. Can you please call Ben Tomas and ask him to pick up the goats? As in, immediately. In the meantime, take as many photos as you can, then check out the property and the houses next door. See if you spot anything unusual."

"Sure. What am I looking for?"

A vampire with needles for teeth. "Not sure yet." I thought of the giant shadow Stu and I had spotted weeks ago. "But be sure to check the trees," I added. "It's possible whatever we're looking for has wings."

Bailey gasped. "Oh no. Please don't tell me it's that Camazotz thing!" I imagined the young woman reaching for a scrunchie to tie back her long, copper hair.

The Camazotz was an enormous bat-like creature with Mayan origins. We had found it in the equipment yard, and it had gone straight for Bailey's hair.

"I don't think so." The Camazotz had been part of an entity invasion I had ended by putting a protection spell around Chavez Ravine. Whatever was responsible for the goat deaths obviously had gotten past my spell.

By the time my call with Bailey had ended, Cora had collected herself and was seated on a wooden bench under the shade of a tree. A taxi drove by slowly, coming to a stop a couple of houses up the block. After a few moments, a familiar figure with a head of thick black hair stepped out. The driver hauled a suitcase from the trunk and set it on the sidewalk.

Cora squinted. "Oh. Hernan's home."

There was no sign of my mother. Which meant she had gone straight back to Beverly Hills.

Hernan pulled the suitcase up the walkway. When he neared the porch, he gave a cry of alarm.

Uh oh.

"Stay here," I said to Cora, then sprinted up the street.

Hernan was wearing dark blue linen pants and a rumpled white shirt. When I reached him, panting, a goat's lifeless eyes stared at us accusingly. I placed a hand on Hernan's shoulder.

"Not a very nice welcome home," I said. "As you can tell, we've had a bit of a situation while you were away."

He wagged a finger in my direction. "And this time, you can't blame me because I haven't even been here."

"No, you've been off galivanting with my mother, sipping margaritas by the pool."

Hernan sucked his cheeks in. "Gallivanting! At our age? It was a struggle just to get to the resort. But it was worth it, mind you." He smiled.

Oh, please stop. I absolutely do not want any details.

"But look what happens when I leave for a few days! The place falls apart."

I rolled my eyes. Then, even though I didn't completely trust the old brujo, I told him everything and watched him pale.

"This does not sound good," he muttered.

"It doesn't. But the truth is, I can use all the help I can get. The poor goats are piling up fast. Do you think you can do a little investigating? See if you sense anything that can point us in the right direction?"

Hernan threw up his hands. "You're supposed to be the powerful bruja! I'm just an old wannabe, remember?"

"I never said that!"

Hernan huffed, crossing his arms in front of his chest. A deep frown added to the creases on his forehead. "Fine. Fine. I'll do a reading. Consult Santa Muerte. But don't get your hopes up. My powers may be a bit rusty after all that *gallivanting*." He jerked his head at the goat. "What are you going to do about that?"

"Ben Tomas is on the way. He'll take care of it."

Hernan sighed. "Tell Cora I'll come by and see her later."

To my surprise, Hernan gave me a quick hug, then trudged around to the side of the house, suitcase in tow.

The hug was a first. I wasn't quite sure how I felt about it, but I had to admit, being hugged was better than being stabbed.

We were making progress.

Three board members had discovered dead goats on their porches. Three *Latino* board members. That was interesting, but it was best not to make any assumptions.

Besides, it was possible Eileen Simpson or Dan Berman had dead goats by their front doors but hadn't discovered them yet.

I called Justin Torres and, after quickly explaining what had happened, asked him to swing by Eileen's and Dan's places. Discreetly, of course. Less than fifteen minutes later, he called back.

"All clear."

Late that afternoon, I called a meeting with my staff. Justin had already clocked off, but he said he would come back in. When he arrived, he was out of breath and holding a baby. Justin had talked about his son, but I had never seen him before. He was a sturdy child of about eight months, with a serious expression.

"Sorry." Justin exhaled loudly. "I had to bring the kid. My wife had an appointment, and I'd promised to watch Tonio."

Everyone stared at Justin and Tonio as if a two-headed entity had just entered the room.

Some babies were blobby things with indistinct features. Not Tonio. Arched eyebrows topped discerning caramel-colored eyes. His wavy brown hair appeared slightly damp.

"He looks pissed off," Bailey said.

I would have been pissed off too if someone had dressed me in a pastel seersucker romper.

"I had to wake him from his nap, and then I had to wrestle him into his car seat." Justin walked over to Bailey and dangled the child over her lap. "Can you hold him while I get a coffee?"

Bailey reared back as if she had been offered a slice of rancid deli meat. "I'm fine, thank you."

Justin rolled his eyes, then turned to me. "How about you, boss?"

Tonio stared as if daring me to accept his father's offer. He didn't blink.

I shook my head. "I need to focus on the meeting."

Liam slapped his thighs. "Bring him over here. I'll take him." The yellow-haired former Occult Affairs officer, just off bike patrol, was wearing black Spandex shorts. He had muscles worthy of Thor.

"Really?" Justin tilted his head. "Are you okay with kids?"

"I've got three nephews." Liam held out his mitts. "I'm an old pro."

Justin frowned slightly and lowered Tonio into Liam's arms. "He's actually better with women than he is with men, so don't feel bad if he cries."

We all waited, expecting Tonio to holler, but the child appeared mesmerized by Liam's sheer size. The baby's eyes went wide.

Liam gently poked Toni's nose. "Boop!"

If a finger the size of a hot dog had booped me, I would probably have screamed my head off. Instead, Tonio squealed in delight.

More booping followed. More laughter. Bailey rolled her eyes.

Justin poured his coffee and fell into the chair next to Liam. "You should have one of your own."

"Then I wouldn't be able to give it back when it starts crying." Liam chuckled, ruffling Tonio's hair. "But you're not going to do that because we're friends, right, buddy?"

Tonio giggled.

As usual, I had no obvious symptoms of baby fever now that I was around one. All I felt was impatience to get on with briefing my team. Babysitting difficult kids during my teenage years had evidently killed any romantic notions of what it was like to be a mom.

Bailey coughed pointedly and loudly. "As fun as this playdate has been, maybe we can start our meeting, guys?"

Justin's ears turned red. "Sorry, Maddy. I hated the idea of not being here for this, but maybe I should have stayed home." The poor guy appeared mortified.

"It's fine, Justin. The entity wranglers of Chavez Ravine can handle a baby for a few minutes." I cleared my throat, then ran my team through the Occult Affair's lab analysis on the wounds made by whatever killed the goats.

"Could something really drain all that blood through those tiny teeth?" Liam rested his chin on the top of Tonio's head.

"Apparently," I replied.

"And are they sure it's not a chupacabra?" Ron Mendez rubbed his leg where a chupacabra had bitten him.

Bailey snorted. "If it was a chupacabra, it wouldn't be going after goats. It'd be going straight for you, knowing what an easy and tasty target you are."

Everyone laughed. Except for Ron, who scowled. Rafi sat a little apart, legs crossed, palms facing upward. He was a little older than the others, so maybe it was that, or maybe he was too reserved, but he didn't take part in the banter.

"The nerds ruled out chupacabras," I said hurriedly. "Maybe they'll be able to tell us more once they've looked at the latest victims." I turned to Rafi. "Have you had a chance to go through all the camera feeds yet?"

He nodded, his dark eyes serious. "Yes, ma'am. The camera on Mr. Perez's street was too far away to capture anything, and the one near the Frias home didn't show anything out of the ordinary."

"Rafi here is Mr. Efficiency," Ron said, tapping his foot. "I came in a bit early to help him out, and he'd already gone through everything."

The older man gave a slightly crooked smile. "It was easy enough."

"Rafi's always first in, last out, aren't you, Rafi?" Ron sounded irked by his co-worker's clockbusting habits.

Rafi swallowed. "Just trying to avoid the worst of the commute."

Ron *humphed*.

I jumped in. "Thanks for checking those feeds, Rafi. I appreciate the extra effort."

He had been with a small police force in eastern Los Angeles County and had impeccable references, so hiring him had been a no-brainer. And he was happy enough with his housing situation so had refused the subsidized housing in Chavez Ravine.

"All right. The board will be meeting this evening to decide whether to continue the grazing program. In the meantime, we need to keep a close eye on the remaining goats. We really need to catch whatever is attacking them in action. Anyone have any ideas how we can do that?"

Liam bounced Tonio on his knee. I would have expected the kid to be sick from all the movement, but he appeared perfectly content. "Yeah. We need to get more of us on e-bikes. They can get us close to where the goats are grazing, and they're fast. Good for chasing."

"Great idea," I said while the room erupted in groans.

Bailey stood, rubbing her backside. "There goes my ass."

"My butt's just recovering from all that riding around at the cactus festival," Justin said.

"You guys need to put some more meat on your bones." Liam slapped a hand against his sturdy haunches, and Tonio jumped.

My phone rang. "Okay, folks. Meeting adjourned. Eyes on the treetops, please."

I took out my phone and answered. It was Stu.

"Hey, Mads. Look, I had a thought today, and I wanted to run it past you. It might be a little crazy, but I can't get it out of my head."

Stu certainly knew how to get a girl's attention.

"Bear with me for a moment. Where were you when you cast the protection spell over Chavez Ravine?"

"In my backyard. Why?"

"And where were you when you made the Smoke Bombs that took out the Chupacabras? And the ones you used on the ghoul?"

"I made those at my workbench in the sunroom. Stu, what's this about?"

"So, every time you've used your magic successfully, you were in Chavez Ravine. Is that right?"

I thought for a moment. "Yes, that's right."

"But it didn't work in Pasadena or in Beverly Hills."

"No—"

"Maddy, what if your magic only works when you're in Chavez Ravine? Do you think that's possible?"

I sat down on the command center console. Stu was right. Every time my magic had worked, I had been in Chavez Ravine, and both times it failed, I was somewhere else.

"Yeah, I guess that's possible. Really weird, though, don't you think?"

"Yes, but maybe it's worth figuring out. Gives us an excuse for another weekend getaway too."

I *did* like the way that man's mind worked.

My phone chimed in my hand.

"Stu, I'm getting a message. I'll call you later, okay?"

"Okay. Maybe we can talk about dinner plans."

I ended the call and checked the message. It was from Clare.

I really need your help! Please call me as soon as you can!

Chapter 13

Cramps. A bad case of cramps.

That was Clare's big problem. I was not unsympathetic. When I was her age, I'd had periods from hell. It was just that I was positive there was nothing I could do that wouldn't get us into even deeper trouble with her mother.

"But you're a healer," Clare cried into my ear. "If you don't help me, you're practically denying me medical treatment."

"Have you tried over-the-counter drugs?"

"Yes!" she wailed. "They don't work. Like, at all. Please, Maddy. Please. I'm desperate."

She certainly sounded desperate. And she was a tough girl.

Lencha's notes contained several cures I was sure would help her. It did seem cruel to deny her help just because her mother was being unreasonable, and it wasn't like I was going to use any brujería on the girl. Just some simple, basic healing with herbs I grew in my backyard.

"All right. But I'm going to call your father first. I don't want to do anything that might rock the boat without his approval."

Clare wailed again. "This is so stupid! I can't wait until I'm eighteen because this is total, one hundred percent bullshit. It's my body. It's *my* pain. I should be able to do whatever I want to make it go away, and I *need* your help."

She made it sound completely reasonable. Too bad her mother was not a reasonable person.

I took a few deep breaths and continued calmly. "I understand, sweetie. You're feeling bad, and you just want some relief. Let me just double-check with your father, and then I'll go straight home and get cracking. Okay?"

A long silence followed, then a wobbly intake of breath. "Okay. But hurry, please."

Of course, my call to Stu went directly to voicemail. I tried texting.

A few moments later, he replied.

Sorry. Stuck in a meeting. You okay?

It's Clare. Bad cramps. She wants me to make something for her.

Shit. If Vicki finds out.

Exactly what I'm worried about.

Can you help her?

Pretty sure.

The hell with it. Go ahead. We'll just keep this to ourselves.

The list of things we were keeping to ourselves was growing. Oh well. Divorces and custody battles could get complicated, but what a shame Clare had to suffer for it.

At home, I dug out Lencha's journals from my fireproof safe while Sam swirled around my ankles.

The first page I flipped to sounded like the perfect solution, just not to the problem Clare was having. Lencha called it a *retiro*, and it was used to remove a person from your life. I wondered if I could use it to banish Vicki Wells from mine. Was that a good idea? It seemed fairly straightforward, but I didn't dare. With my luck, it would backfire, and I would remove myself.

One of Lencha's recipes called for tea made from the herbs I grew in my backyard. But one needed to drink it days before the period started.

I couldn't help myself from getting lost in the journals, discovering all sorts of fascinating spells, including one to punish a cheating partner and another to cause paralysis. Had Lencha ever actually used them?

I needed to focus. After a thorough search, nothing seemed quite right for poor Clare. The tea potion was the closest, but the timing was bad.

Still, maybe there was something there. I paged back to the remedy, trying to understand what each ingredient brought to the mix.

Sam jumped up beside me on the wicker couch and bashed his furry red head into my arm.

"Do you think I need to improvise?" I asked.

My cat meowed loudly and head-bumped me again.

I had an idea. The herbal tea might work, but it was too late. We could try that next month. But perhaps I could mix up the herbs and use them in a sort of poultice Clare could apply. If the magic were concentrated enough, it might make it through the skin to the problem area.

I grabbed a small basket and a pair of scissors and headed into the backyard, where I snipped some yellow mugwort flower heads, a half dozen yerba buena stems, and several other herbs whose names refused to stick in my head.

My mother and Hernan Frias would disapprove, seeing it as another sign I didn't take my craft seriously. How was I supposed to use my magic to keep the neighborhoods safe when I couldn't even remember the names of my herbs?

But I couldn't continue to beat myself up about that. I had only realized I had inherited powers from Lencha a few months earlier. While I might not remember the names of all my herbs, in that time, I had managed to rid Chavez Ravine of a bunch of nasty monsters, subdue a ghoul and some chupacabras, take out the Cucuy, and cast a protection spell over the whole area.

I figured I was doing okay.

After I ground the herbs in my stone metate, I paced in front of the wooden workbench. It was time for the next step. Unfortunately, I had no idea what that step was.

Sam sauntered to the far end of the counter, where the clay statuette of Lencha sat silently. For a moment, I thought he was going to try and wake her up for a consultation, but instead, he swatted a length of twine made from jute and sent it shooting in my direction.

I didn't remember leaving it on the workbench. In fact, I had never seen it before. I picked it up and studied it. The length of twine was knotted in the middle.

Sam meowed.

I held up the string. "Dude. You're going to have to be a little more specific. I'm not following."

My cat blinked slowly, as if he couldn't believe I was so dense.

Sam stomped over and batted the knot. It suddenly unraveled, the fibers loosening and separating as if by unseen hands. I watched in astonishment while the knot came undone and the string went smooth and straight.

Sam let out a triumphant meow, his green eyes gleaming.

While I stared at the knot-free string, a rush of understanding washed over me.

Knots. That's what cramps were like. Big knots of pain in the belly. Clare needed to get her knots untied.

That was the missing ingredient in my magical plan. My next steps were clear.

I needed something to bind all the ingredients. Something neutral. Something odorless, like Vaseline. I found a jar at the back of a bathroom drawer. When had I bought it? I couldn't remember the last time I had used it. No sign of an expiration date. Did Vaseline go bad? I gave it a tentative sniff. It was fine.

I spooned a generous dollop of Vaseline into the metate and mixed it with the ground herbs. The heady scent of sage, citrus, and mint filled the air while I stirred the concoction together. Sam watched intently, his tail flicking back and forth.

But it needed something more, something to symbolize untying the knot.

Sam picked up the jute string between his teeth and dropped it into a shallow metal bowl I used to hold matches.

"You're on a roll," I said. It no longer seemed odd to speak to a cat. In fact, it felt perfectly normal.

I grabbed a match, lit it, and dropped it into the bowl with the jute string. For a few seconds, smoke rose from the burning jute, and when there was nothing but ash, I scraped it into the paste and stirred.

Almost ready. The one thing I remembered from my short time with my grandmother Liliana was her love of the Virgin de Guadalupe. My mother had said Liliana was one of those Christmas and Easter Catholics. But later in life, she had developed a special fondness for the brown-skinned Virgin. Lencha had mentioned her in her journals too and had appealed to her several times to help others heal.

I took a candle in the shape of the Virgin from a shelf. Julia and I had picked it up during one of our trips to the botanica, and it was a pretty pale shade of peach. I lit it and let a couple of drops of wax drip into the mixture.

After I said a few quiet words and gave it a stir, my potion was ready.

I scraped the mixture into a glass jar and screwed on the lid. In the kitchen, I hand-fed Sam some of his favorite treats, refreshed his water bowl, and then headed out.

Chapter 14

Clare answered the door, the picture of misery. Her brown hair was greasy, and she had dark circles under her eyes. She wore a thin white camisole top and navy sweats.

Clare blinked at me, bleary-eyed.

"Did I wake you up?" I asked.

She nodded. "Yeah. I don't seem to have energy to do anything but sleep."

I held up the jar. "I brought you a little something."

Clare scratched her cheek. "I thought you said you couldn't."

"I said I needed to check with your dad first."

Her eyes widened. "He said yes?"

Tired of standing on the doorstep, I stepped past her into the large foyer. "He was fine with it, as long as we keep it quiet."

I could hear Vicki Wells's screechy voice in my head, accusing me of subjecting her child to witchcraft. The funny thing was, she wouldn't have been entirely wrong. It just wasn't the kind of witchcraft she imagined.

Clare stared at the jar in my hand and swallowed. "Okay. What do we need to do?"

"Let's go up to your room, and I'll show you."

Clare grimaced. "It's kind of a mess."

"I'm sure it's fine," I said, following her up the stairs.

While the first floor resembled a hunting lodge, the second floor was an expanse of cream-colored walls, pale wood floors, and barn-style doors. Large windows flooded the wide hallway with natural light.

"That's my dad's room." Clare pointed at an open door.

I peeked inside, curious.

Stu must have had some decorating help. It was much more sophisticated than all that blue, brown, and gold plaid downstairs. Unbleached linen bedding, gray pillows, and masculine, minimalist furniture. A stack of books on the bedside table. A few framed photos of Clare on the dresser. No clothes draped over the backs of chairs or a laundry basket of dirty clothes in sight.

Why in the world had he bought such a large house for just the two of them? And Clare wasn't even around full time. It all seemed like a waste of money to me. Then again, I had spent too many years in a run-down one-bedroom apartment, so what did I know?

Clare's bedroom was at the back of the house, overlooking the yard.

She had *not* exaggerated. Her bedroom was a mess. Dirty clothes strewn across the floor, piles of textbooks stacked against the walls, and a jumble of keepsakes, lip balm sticks, and half-filled water glasses on the dresser. The unmade bed was a tangled heap of blankets. The room smelled faintly of stale sweat and something sweet and cloying. A large coconut-scented jar candle squatted on the nightstand. That had to be the culprit.

Clare shuffled over to her bed and sat, her shoulders slumped.

The room's clutter was overwhelming. How could anyone relax surrounded by so much chaos?

My mother would never, ever have allowed me to leave my room in such a state. On Saturdays, no matter how humble our living situation, we cleaned from top to bottom, and I wasn't allowed to leave the house until it was spotless. Including my bedroom.

I sighed. Clare was going to hate this but so be it. There was no way she could get better surrounded by that mess.

"This will take just a few minutes," I said, getting to work.

Clare fell back against the pillows, clearly horrified. "You don't have to do that."

"Oh, yes, I do, missy." I snatched up the dirty dishes and glasses and set them outside in the hallway.

Clare wrapped her arms around her stomach and winced. "Come on, Maddy. Just...I don't know. Ignore it. My mom does."

The words were out before I could stop them. "I am *not* your mother." Yikes. Where had *that* come from?

Clare surprised me by laughing. "No, you're not. You're too young, for one thing. My mom's even older than my dad." She must have registered my surprise because she hurriedly continued. "Yeah, she is. Five years older. Which makes the whole thing with her cheating on my dad kinda weird, right?"

That made Vicki fifty-three to Stu's forty-eight. Very interesting. But I was not about to discuss it with their daughter.

"Mmm." I snatched up dirty clothes from the floor and quickly filled up a hamper. After I tidied the stacks of books, I swept the clutter of stuff from the desk and dresser into an empty box.

Clare's attention was focused on the jar I had set on the nightstand.

"My therapist says I shouldn't take sides." Clare reached under the covers and pulled out a purple notebook. "But I'm like, how am I *not* supposed to take sides? My mom betrayed my dad. She cheated. She lied. The therapist says I need to at least *try* to have a good relationship with my mom, but she's gotten so weird since my dad met you. Why should she even care? She's got Thad."

I stopped cleaning and looked up.

"Yeah, *Thad*. That's his name. He's so stupid."

I went back to wiping down her dresser with a rag, then stepped away and surveyed the results. Better. I could think again.

Clare's knees were pulled up to her chest. Her brown hair hung in clumps around her pale face.

I tossed the rag into the hamper. "Before we get started, you need to take a shower."

Clare frowned. "Is it part of your spell?"

"It's not a spell," I said automatically. "But you'll feel better afterward, and if you don't shower, we'll have to declare this room a biohazard."

Clare's mouth opened, then closed. Her neck and face flushed. "It's not *that* bad."

"It depends on who you ask. I'm going to change the sheets. Is there a linen closet up here?"

Clare swung her legs over the side of the bed with a martyred sigh. She shuffled into the hallway and threw open a door. "It's in here. The lady my dad hired to decorate the upstairs stocked it." Clare paused, giving me a sly look. "She was so into my dad. I was actually nervous. But nope. He wasn't into her. Which is a good thing because she was a total clout chaser."

Clare sauntered down the hall. I stared after her. She was just as fierce in life as she was on the soccer field. It was a miracle I had made it past the goalpost with her dad.

I grabbed a fresh stack of sheets, a blanket, and a beautiful muslin throw the color of oatmeal and made the bed.

Clare soon returned with her wet hair in a towel, wearing a pale orange robe covered in tiny green and purple flowers. Like everything on the second floor, it appeared expensive.

She hovered in the doorway. "You didn't have to do this," she said in a small voice. "Thank you."

I pointed to the bed. "Okay, lie down. The sooner you get started, the sooner you'll feel better." Hopefully. But I was feeling strangely optimistic.

Clare was wearing flannel shorts and a black camisole under the robe.

"Take this paste and rub it on your tummy. Concentrate on the areas where the pain is the worst."

I sat on the edge of the bed while Clare dipped her fingers into the herbal paste and began to gently massage it onto her abdomen in small, circular motions.

Within a few seconds, she went limp, and her eyes fluttered. "That feels amazing," she murmured.

I closed my eyes, imagining the cramps like knots of twine beginning to unravel. When I opened them again, Clare was fast asleep.

I closed her door as quietly as possible and went downstairs to wait for her to wake up. We would know soon enough if my cure worked.

Chapter 15

Stu called from the car on his way home. He wanted to get carry-out from Olga's Cantina because he was in the mood for Mexican food, but I said that was silly when he had someone who could make it from scratch at home.

"I don't want you to have to cook."

"Don't be silly. I love to cook." Besides, it would give me a chance to poke around his huge kitchen. Also, I wanted to use his fancy professional-grade stove with the red gas knobs and built-in griddle.

"If you're sure," he said. "Text me your shopping list, and I'll stop at the store on the way home."

And just like that, we had reached the phase in our relationship where we could eat at home instead of going out. The new phase had so many implications, including possibly spending the night. Except now I wasn't just cooking for Stu. I had a teenager to think about. One who would prevent any sleepovers, unfortunately.

Luckily, Clare was an adventurous eater, unlike her father, who preferred steak and potatoes. In fact, he had probably been thinking of the carne asada at Olga's. Which I could make easily enough at home. Except for the beans. Unless Stu had a pressure cooker.

Time to snoop around.

I found a pressure cooker in the pantry, which was three times the size of mine. Also in the pantry were a bag of pink beans, some medium-grain rice, and, to my amazement, several white onions in a bowl. No mold.

The refrigerator had all the makings for hamburgers, which explained the onions.

I put together a shopping list, including saltine crackers and ginger ale for Clare, in case her stomach needed settling, then added a box of popsicles before sending it off to Stu.

When Stu got home, I put away the groceries, guessing where each item went. Stu sat at the kitchen island and poured two glasses of red wine, then settled back to watch me cook.

I started chopping an onion. "So, I'm curious. I was upstairs with Clare and couldn't help but notice it's got a whole different vibe than down here."

Stu laughed. "Yeah. Well, I can explain that. When I was a kid, my parents used to take us on vacation to Montana. My dad was really into fly fishing. We would stay at this lodge, and I thought it was magical. So, when I got this place and had to start buying stuff, that's what I liked, so that's what I bought. And then Eileen Simpson stopped by, and she was horrified. And the next thing I knew, she'd talked me into hiring her decorator, and I turned her loose on the second floor. I have to admit, as much as she got on my nerves, she did a good job. Right? What do you think?"

"It's beautiful up there," I admitted, peeling the butcher paper away from the flap steak.

Stu laughed again. "But not so much downstairs?"

"It's a little...plaid," I said lightly.

Stu snorted. "I can read between those lines."

Clare was still asleep when dinner was ready, so Stu and I ate alone in the dining room, and I filled him in on the latest with the goats. Like me, he was mystified.

After finishing off his second helping of carne asada, Stu topped up my glass of red wine. "Your turn to sit while I do the dishes. And then we're inaugurating the hot tub." He swept the plates into the sink. "Do you think Clare will want to go in?"

If she was feeling up to it, the hot tub might feel good. "I'll go upstairs and check."

I tried to rouse her, but Clare stirred slightly, shook her head, and mumbled, "Nah. Wanna sleep. Gahead."

She was turned away from me, only her damp dark hair visible above the muslin throw pulled up to her chin. Clare sounded groggy, but I wasn't worried. Nothing in my cure would have made her drowsy, so it was probably just her period.

Fifteen minutes later, Stu and I were in the hot tub, and it wasn't long before he slipped off his swim trunks. There were plenty of frothing bubbles, so I might not have noticed if he hadn't slapped the wet trunks on the side of the tub.

I nearly choked on my wine. "We're not alone, you know."

"I'll behave. I just hate wearing trunks. They're too constricting, and I honestly don't see the point if I'm in the privacy of my own home. If Clare comes down, I'll put them back on."

I set my glass in a cupholder. "I will not be joining you."

"That's fine." Stu chuckled. "But why are you sitting way over there? I'm not going to bite."

I was sitting across from Stu, back to the trees, so I could keep an eye on Clare's window in case she appeared. "I remember what happened when you pulled that move in Pasadena."

Stu gave a wicked grin. "We will always have Pasadena. But seriously, come sit next to me. I promise to behave."

"All right, but let's keep it PG."

I needn't have worried. Stu was a perfect—if naked— gentleman. We chatted about whether the board should cancel the goat program while the stars twinkled above us in the indigo sky and crickets chirped somewhere in the distance. It was a beautiful moment. I felt peace and tranquility, with the steaming water soothing my tense muscles.

Above us, a window banged open. "Hey, guys," Clare called down.

Stu quickly reached for his swim trunks while I turned to look up at his daughter. She was leaning out of her window, her hair a wild tangle around her face.

"How are you feeling, kiddo?" I asked.

"Great! Fantastic! My cramps are gone! I swear, Maddy. You could make a billion dollars selling that stuff. Wait 'til I tell my friends."

Stu—shorts barely on—quickly stood and pointed a finger at his daughter. "You will *not* say a word. Because if you do, your mother will find out, and we'll both be in hot water."

Clare snickered. "You're already *in* hot water."

"I'm serious." Stu wagged his finger, but his mouth was curled up in a smile. "If you think your mom was mad about the cure Maddy made for your friend's twisted ankle, wait until you see how she reacts when she hears Maddy defied her request and whipped up a spell to cure your cramps. We'll all be back in court in a heartbeat—"

But Clare wasn't paying any attention to her father. She was looking past us, at the trees. Her eyes were wide and staring. Her mouth fell open, but no words came out.

My stomach dropped. I did not want to see what was behind us. I gripped Stu's arm and jerked my thumb over my shoulder. That was the best I could do.

He frowned. "What is it?"

Clare screamed. An ear-piercing shriek that made my heart jump into my throat.

Stu and I whipped around in time to catch a glimpse of something roosting in a tree. There was just enough light to discern its enormous size. As large as a person, with a body covered in dark feathers and a head hunched into rounded shoulders. It had to be the same shadowy thing Stu and I had spotted not long ago after a celebratory dinner at Olga's Cantina.

Clare continued screaming while the creature gazed back at her, unmoving.

"Shit," Stu muttered, scrambling out of the tub.

The creature had a human face, with leathery gray skin and the orange, forward-facing eyes of a predator. Its piercing gaze was locked onto Clare. And there we were, wearing nothing but our swimsuits, not a single weapon within reach.

"We need to get inside," I hissed.

The creature in the tree shifted position, wings fluttering.

I felt hot all over. My hands started to glow red, and I focused all my energy on the creature, willing it away.

"Shut the window, Clare!" Stu yelled, hauling me out of the hot tub.

Winged Thing unleashed a bloodcurdling screech that tore through the air. I should have been afraid, but I felt only anger. How dare this abomination come into my community!

"Vete de aquí!" My voice shook while I channeled my magic. I hadn't meant to tell it to go in Spanish. It had just come out that way.

The monstrous thing hesitated for a moment. Its glowing eyes shifted toward me. And then, with a frenzy of flapping wings, it took flight into the night sky and disappeared into the darkness.

Chapter 16

I was convinced we had found our goat killer.

My hair was still wet from the hot tub. Ron, Bailey, Liam, Justin, Brandon, and I paired off and began our search, while Rafi in the command center checked the camera feeds. He called back moments later, saying the cameras had caught what appeared to be a giant bird flying toward Elysian Park.

I asked Rafi to send the clip to my phone and stared at the video. There was no mistaking the massive bird-like creature with leathery wings soaring through the night sky. I told Rafi not to share the video with anyone else. The last thing I wanted to deal with was a bunch of freaked-out homeowners.

My team regrouped in the parking lot at La Loma Plaza, and I showed the video to everyone. Ron scratched his head, while Liam and Justin leaned in closer to get a better look.

"Shit." Bailey shuddered. "That thing is way bigger than the Camazotz that went after me. How big do you think it is?" It was the middle of the night, so none of us looked our best, but that was the first time I had ever seen Bailey without her signature eye makeup. She looked vulnerable without it.

Liam gave a low whistle. "It's gotta be almost six feet tall." He turned to me. "You saw it in person. Does that sound right to you?"

"'Fraid so."

"The wingspan is probably double that," Justin said. "So maybe twelve feet."

Ron cleared his throat. He was wearing a dark green T-shirt and camo pants that nearly blended in with the nearby foliage. "The question is, what is it, boss? It can't be an entity. Unless that magic barrier you put up isn't working anymore. But if that were the case, we would have been overrun with all kinds of entities."

I shot Ron a dirty look. He knew more than the others did about my skills and just couldn't keep his mouth shut, despite my pleas.

That was the first time the others had heard about my protection spell, and they whipped their heads toward me.

"Did you really do that?" Bailey asked, her voice rising.

I pressed a finger between my eyes. There was no point in denying it. It was also arguable it was something I should have told them sooner. They were my team, after all. But I hadn't wanted them to think I could wave my arms and solve all their problems. Because once anyone thought that, their next idea would be that Chavez Ravine didn't need such a large security team, and eventually, I would be forced to downsize. Just the thought of it made me queasy.

"Yes, I really did do that," I admitted. "But there's no telling how strong it is or how long it will last. And I'm not sure it would work against new types of entities."

Liam rubbed the top of his head. His hair appeared gold under the streetlamp. "Wow. I know you made those pouches that helped against the chupacabras and gnomes, but I had no idea you could do anything like that."

Bailey rolled her eyes. "Did you forget she took out the boogeyman?"

"With a sword," Liam shot back. "Not with a magic spell."

"She tricked out all our swords with magic," Ron said. "Nobody could have killed him without using some brujería. El Cucuy was one powerful, mean mother."

I needed to get the conversation back on track. "The question is, do we continue looking for our monster bird in Elysian Park?"

The group didn't hesitate. They shook their heads.

Justin said, "We won't find it. The park is way too big. There are thousands and thousands of trees in there. It could be hiding anywhere. And just because it flew over the fence doesn't mean it stopped in Elysian Park. It could be anywhere by now."

Fatigue had begun to settle into my bones, and my eyes itched. "Okay. Let's do one more circuit around Chavez Ravine. Bailey and I will take La Loma. Ron and Brandon, you take Bishop. And Justin and Liam take Palo Verde. It's a big bird and requires a big tree, so focus on those. Buddy up. One person shines the flashlight while the other stands by with a slingshot. Use the special ammo—the steel balls with the spikes."

Ron rubbed his hands together. "I've been dying to use those."

"No one is dying tonight." Bailey punched his arm.

We split up, each pair driving to their designated area of Chavez Ravine. Bailey drove while I stared out the window. I lost count of how many times we got out of the SUV to inspect the treetops. The eerie silence of the warm night wrapped around us like a suffocating blanket.

Over and over again, Bailey would shine her flashlight on a towering tree, alert for any movement or strange noises. We crept along dark pathways, the beam of the flashlight cutting through the shadows, the crunch of gravel sounding under our boots.

When we neared the new housing development, I caught a flurry of movement. I held out my hand, a signal to Bailey to stop, and I put a finger to my lips. She turned off her flashlight, and our eyes slowly adjusted to the dim moonlight.

We inched toward the fence surrounding the construction site. A faint rustling was coming from the back of the property. The houses in that part of the development were nearly finished, so they blocked my view of the area, but I could tell the sound came from the edge nearest Elysian Park.

I took a Smoke Bomb from my belt, and we peered through the fence, trying to spot the massive bird.

"Let's try to flush it out so I can hit it," I whispered.

"My flashlight might get its attention." Bailey put her thumb on the switch.

"Let's give it a shot. On the count of one…two…three."

Bailey turned on the light and waved it around the spaces between the homes. At first, all was quiet, but then came a screech that made my blood run cold. The rustling was replaced by a loud whirring, as though someone had turned on a giant box fan.

Orange eyes came toward us, its huge wings rising and falling. I drew back and got ready to hurl my pouch. The bird ascended high into the air, turned toward Elysian Park, and escaped into the darkness.

I let out a huge breath. Bailey and I climbed up the hill to the running path bordering the park, but there was no sign of Winged Thing.

I called off the search and sent everyone home to bed. After dropping Bailey off, I checked in with Rafi. No red dots on the heatmap. Nothing on the security cameras. He promised to call if anything changed.

Sam met me at the door, then followed me into the kitchen, where I chugged down a tall glass of water. He meowed several times, then bumped his head against my shin.

His tail flicked, a sign he was annoyed. I pulled out a treat bag, but for once, he wasn't interested in food. He stared at me while I washed my face, then watched me from the nightstand after I crawled into bed.

"What do you want?" I asked.

Sam gave a long, plaintive meow.

I propped myself up on an elbow. "Oh. Do you want me to tell you what happened?"

He just stared at me, which felt like a "yes." After all, he was mostly nocturnal, so he was in no hurry to go to sleep. Unlike me. If I didn't give him an update, he would find a way to torture me until I did.

So, I recounted the night's events to my feline companion. He listened intently, his gaze never leaving my face, as if he understood every word I said. When I finished, a purr rumbled in his throat, and he flopped down next to me, pushing into my side.

I immediately drifted off.

———⇥·–⇥·║║║║·⇤··⇤———

A heavy thump woke me out of a dead sleep. My heart pounded, and I glanced at the clock. Just after six a.m. My bedroom was still dark. A sharp crack sent Sam leaping off the bed. A harsh scraping followed, and then a heavy thud shook the house.

Sam pawed at the front door.

There was no way I was going to open it without knowing what was waiting outside.

After a moment, Sam dropped to all fours, back arched, his spine a ridge of red fur.

There were no more scrapes or thuds outside, just early morning sounds of people waking up and starting their days. But Sam was still vigilant, so there was something on the other side of the door.

And I knew exactly what it was.

I opened the door a crack and looked down. The unseeing eyes of a dead goat stared back at me.

Chapter 17

Five HOA board members and one head of security. Out of those six, four received unwelcome packages on their front porches.

I went back to the kitchen to get my phone and call Ben Tomas. It chimed as soon as I touched it. I was getting pictures from the command center, and I could barely believe what I saw.

Welcome to fascist Chavez Ravine

That was spray-painted on the La Loma and Bishop guardhouses.

These people are ruining Chavez Ravine
Abolish the HOA and its harmful rules
Return Chavez Ravine to la gente

Those graced the front of the community center in Palo Verde, where the HOA had its offices. My phone chimed again— a call from the command center number.

"Boss, did you see the pictures I just sent?" Ron Mendez was on the early shift.

"Yeah. Looks like an artist who has a major beef with the HOA. Have you checked the cameras?"

"I did, and they caught glimpses of someone dressed in black. And I mean, *totally* covered. Gloves, a ski mask, the whole works."

"What do you mean 'glimpses'? Can you tell if they're male or female? Approximate height?"

"Not really. It's like whoever it was knew where the cameras are. They never got close enough to pick up any details."

I fell into a chair at the kitchen table. Obviously, this was not the work of an ordinary tagger. They had chosen easy-to-reach, strategic locations to leave their messages. And the use of "la gente"—the people—suggested someone familiar with the troubled history of Chavez Ravine.

But the thing that bugged me the most was the security cameras.

The tagger seemed to know where the cameras were and where they were pointed. Which meant our artist was probably a resident of Chavez Ravine who could walk around without a disguise while they noted the camera locations.

And there was another meaning behind the graffiti: Chavez Ravine might not have been the idyllic community everyone seemed to think it was. There was a message of resistance in those painted words, a symbol of upheaval in our community. The HOA had always run a tight ship, starting with its first president, and someone decided they weren't happy about it.

I called a horrified Cora Bernal.

"Maddy, I can't remember the last time we had this kind of vandalism. And the anger! What on earth were they going on about?"

"I don't know, which makes me think I'm missing something. Was there a controversial vote recently that might have pissed someone off?"

A long silence followed. "No. The last controversial issue was Hernan's plan of expanding the legacy rules so more families with historic ties to Chavez Ravine would be eligible for properties. But that failed." Cora sounded uneasy. "Our rules are meant to maintain the standards of our community, and most people appreciate what the HOA does. I have no idea what 'returning Chavez Ravine to la gente' means. What people? Mexican Americans? If it wasn't for the legacy rules, we would be the minority here. It doesn't make any sense. We're just maintaining a wonderful community. This really gets my goat. We're not fascists!"

I winced. "Speaking of goats, I got one of those too last night." And since I couldn't put it off anymore, I told her about the giant bird with the human face I was sure was our goat killer.

"But what is it?" Cora gasped. "What are you doing about it?"

"It's very elusive. I haven't identified it yet. We spent most of last night hunting for it with no luck. Somehow, it knew where I lived because it tossed a goat on my porch just before sunrise. I chased it to Rory Tuck's new development up the street, but it flew off. So, it's still out there, somewhere. Maybe hiding out in Elysian Park. I plan to go looking for it today—"

"I hope you plan on using your magic," Cora interrupted.

I watched a uniformed groundskeeper scrubbing off the graffiti. "I do." But there was no telling whether it would work.

"I hope you can get rid of them. Before…" Cora's words drifted off.

She couldn't bring herself to say what had been lurking in the darkest corners of my mind.

Before it attacked a person.

"Should we warn the residents?" she asked.

I had requested that Stu and Clare keep what they had seen to themselves, at least for a while, to avoid a public panic. Ideally, we would eliminate the damn thing before it could cause any more trouble, and that would be that.

"Can I have a little more time before we do that?"

Cora didn't hesitate. She was in no hurry to freak out residents any more than I was. "Of course. Besides, we don't really know what we're dealing with yet, do we? I don't know what we could say that would help."

She made it sound like waiting was a perfectly reasonable option. Not at all like stalling.

After we ended the call, I checked in with the command center. Ron Mendez had been busy.

"I had a look at what little video we have of our tagger. He wasn't messing around. He was like a machine, tagging and getting out. He started at the Bishop gate, then moved east. Probably left through the La Loma gate. We have a camera at the bottom of the hill, but it didn't catch him. Which means he got off the road and walked down the hill through the cactus. Which also means he knew about that camera."

"Are you sure it's a man?" I asked.

Ron cleared his throat. "Now that you say that, boss, no. I'm not. It could be a woman. They wore bulky clothes. Hair and face are covered. I don't know. I'll send you some screen grabs. See what you think."

Just minutes later, I scrolled through the photos. The clothes were oversized, which concealed the figure's shape. The posture in one frame hinted at a slender frame, but it was hard to tell for sure. I zoomed in on the face, anxious for a clue, but it was obscured by the ski mask.

While I continued to scrutinize the images, I wondered if the graffiti messages weren't acts of defiance against the HOA, but something else. The tagger had struck while my team and I were out looking for the mysterious giant bird. Was that just a coincidence?

I paced around my office, trying to connect the dots. Goats drained of blood. A mysterious bird creature with needle-like teeth. And now, anti-HOA graffiti. There had to have been a link between them all. But what was it?

For once, Hernan Frias was off the hook. The old brujo had certainly caused his share of trouble, making monsters to scare some of the residents, but he seemed to have learned his lesson. Besides, he was much more interested in romancing my mother these days than conjuring creatures.

I needed to prioritize. At the top of the list: create something I could use to neutralize a big bird. Maybe find a way to supercharge slingshot ammo.

At my workbench, I started off with the ingredients I had successfully used before, the ones that had subdued chupacabras and gnomes. But I needed something specifically tailored for the flying beast. One of its feathers would be nice. Two would be even better.

Maybe it had left some behind in the housing development, where Bailey and I had discovered it.

I headed up to the construction site, not exactly looking forward to chatting with the developer, Rory Tuck. He was extremely wary of anything that might spook potential buyers, and I never brought him good news, so he could be a little prickly.

Lucky for me, Rory was nowhere to be found. The door to his trailer was closed, and his white pickup was gone.

I parked the Jeep and climbed out, walking confidently through the gate and onto the property. The construction workers were too busy to pay attention to me. I avoided the main driveway and hurried through the side yards of the homes along the edge of the development. The houses were larger than mine, well-made, and beautifully designed. Definitely not cookie-cutter.

It took less than five minutes to find what I was looking for. Behind a row of bushes was a gigantic nest made of sticks and animal hair. There was a faint but disgusting odor of guano and death. I breathed through my nose, trying to keep my breakfast down.

And there it was.

A feather nestled behind a bush, half-hidden by leaves and twigs. The feather was a monstrous thing, easily the size of my forearm—a dusky gray with an iridescent shine that shifted from midnight black to a deep purple. While the outside of the feather was soft as silk, the central shaft was hard as bone. I gingerly picked it up, and a shiver ran down my spine.

The feather was no ordinary avian specimen. Which I suppose was what one would expect from a creature with a human face and teeth capable of sucking the blood from a goat.

Feather in hand, I retraced my steps to the Jeep, once again ignored by the busy crew, and drove down the hill.

Sam met me at the front door and swirled around my feet, meowing loudly.

"Success, my weird little friend," I said triumphantly, heading toward the sunroom.

Sam dashed ahead, and when I arrived at the workbench, he was sitting next to Little Lencha. For one hopeful moment, I thought she might come to life and offer some guidance, but nope. The red clay figurine of my great-aunt remained still but somehow watchful.

Sam, on the other hand, sniffed at the feather, then batted it out of my hand. It landed in the molcajete.

Had it been an accident? But I was beginning to think Sam didn't do anything by accident.

I picked up the pestle and ground the feather until it broke up, then crushed it into a pile of shimmery gray dust. After adding it to the bowl with the herbs, I stirred in a bit of habañero chili-infused water for extra oomph. The result was a murky paste that smelled of eucalyptus mixed with the pungent, acrid odor of old blood.

It reeked, but it felt kind of perfect.

When chupacabras had emerged in Chavez Ravine, we had thrown magic-infused pouches at the creatures, and they had backed off. The flesh-eating ghoul that had popped up at La Loma Plaza had been more of a challenge. We'd had to apply super glue to the pouches so they would stick to the rare and extremely dangerous entity. It had worked.

But this time, we would be dealing with a flyer, and a bloodsucking one at that. Just because it had only attacked a few goats didn't mean the creature wouldn't eventually go for a tasty human.

I had once used a slingshot to take out some monster birds Hernan Frias created. They weren't as nasty as our giant flying vampire, but the principle was the same. If I could cover my slingshot ammo in that stinky goo, I was convinced I could at least slow the damn thing down.

I looked at the concoction in my bowl. It was too runny. I needed it to stick to the steel slingshot ammo, so I had to find a way to solidify the paste without damaging its magical properties.

A quick search through Lencha's journals was all it took. As it turned out, runny potions were an age-old problem. Lencha had noted several thickening agents, with different methods for different ingredients.

In my case, I needed some resin. Which just meant a quick trip to the hardware store in Palo Verde. Thirty minutes later, I was back at the workbench.

While Sam looked on, I dredged a steel ball through the goop, then dripped a few drops of melted resin on the coated ammo. It quickly hardened, forming a thin protective shell around the paste. My fingers glowed faint pink while I worked. My magic had kicked in, and I moved quickly to coat several steel balls, using a muffin tin to hold the deadly projectiles as they dried.

I had a good feeling about this plan.

Except for one thing: If my magic only worked in Chavez Ravine, I would be useless once I crossed the border into Elysian Park.

I drank a glass of iced tea on the wicker couch, thinking about my next move. If the creature was in Elysian Park, I needed a magical backup plan. And a lure.

I called Ben Tomas, the master landscaper. "I need your help. Can you meet me at my house in an hour? And can you bring one of the goats?"

"Um, I suppose I can. What for?" Ben sounded mystified.

"It's an emergency. I'll explain when you get there."

"An emergency, huh? All right. I'll see if I can round one up and head your way."

Ben sounded a little annoyed, so I quickly said, "Thank you. I owe you one."

When we hung up, I texted Marta, Hernan's home health aide and housekeeper.

Is your cranky old boss around today?

Sí. And your mother is here too.

A winky emoji followed.

Gee, it really was my lucky day. Well, Malena B. might as well come along too. If the thing turned out to be an entity, maybe my mother could put her psychic connection to good use and tell me what the hell it was doing in Chavez Ravine.

Chapter 18

Ben Tomas picked me up in an enormous double-cab pickup with a crate in the cargo bed. While he drove to Hernan's house, I explained what we were going to do, including the part about bringing Hernan along to backstop me in case my magic didn't work.

Ben listened in silence, and at the end, he gave a little nod. He didn't seem the least bit surprised when I described my plan to shoot magic slingshot ammo at a monster bird. I figured Julia had let him in on my little secret.

My mother's reaction was more dramatic.

"I don't see how we can help! And I was just about to start making mole for dinner. From scratch. You know how long that takes."

I did. It was why I rarely made it. Hernan was in for a treat, assuming we survived our jaunt into Elysian Park.

I had to push my words out through gritted teeth. "We don't know what we're dealing with. My magic may or may not work, and if this thing is some sort of new entity, you may have a connection with it and be able to calm it down until Occult Affairs can round it up."

Clearly, she was conflicted. On the one hand, her daughter needed her for the first time in decades. And on the other, she had planned a romantic dinner for her...boyfriend, I guess I would call him...and didn't want that plan derailed.

But, proving I was her daughter, I turned up the guilt. "Let's remember…you owe me, *big* time. While you were off gallivanting in Mexico, I had to clean up that gnome mess, which wrecked my weekend getaway with Stu. So now, mommy dearest, it's payback time."

Next to me, Ben snorted, then tried to cover it with a cough.

My mother gasped. "After all I've done for you, Madeline, I do not deserve this level of disrespect. Isn't that right, Hernan? Isn't she being disrespectful?"

I turned in my seat and glared at Hernan, daring him to take my mother's side.

He raised his hands in surrender. "I think I'll stay out of this one, Malena." He chuckled nervously. "I can't afford to have Maddy hex me or something."

My mother sniffed and crossed her arms in front of her chest. "Well, I just don't understand why my daughter thinks you'll be of any help either. She's been quite dismissive about your skills as a brujo."

Silly me. I had forgotten just how nasty my mother could be when backed into a corner.

"If Hernan could figure out how to put up a protection spell to keep out entities, then banishing a single creature shouldn't be that big of a deal. Assuming I can't, of course."

"But my spell failed when I got sick," Hernan stammered. "You had to create a new one. My skills aren't what they used to be, ever since the cancer."

Fair point. But Hernan had been well enough to fly to the Yucatan Peninsula and work his way through the buffet line while sipping a margarita, so he was plenty healthy to lend a hand in Elysian Park.

"Don't forget, you agreed to consult Santa Muerte for me. Come on. This is a team effort, people. Even if you're not much of a brujo these days, you know a lot about the supernatural. Maybe once you see this thing, you'll recognize it from a dusty old book and can tell us more about it."

Hernan huffed. "Team effort. That's the problem. You're using the wrong team. You've got your own security people. Why aren't you using them?"

Ben glanced in my direction. Clearly, he was wondering the same thing.

I scraped a hand through my hair. It felt greasy. *When was the last time I washed it? Did I even put on makeup?* I caught a glimpse of myself in a mirror in Hernan's entryway. Nope. Dirty hair. No makeup. I looked a wreck.

"My team is just getting used to the idea that I'm a bruja," I said. "If my magic comes with geographical limitations, then I need to figure that out and tell them. It's not something they should discover when we're facing a dangerous entity."

Ben shot me another sideways glance, his brow furrowed in concern. This was new territory for the master landscaper, and I wouldn't blame him for wondering what he had gotten himself into by agreeing to help me out.

In the end, I won. We all piled into Ben's truck and headed up to Elysian Park.

When we arrived, Ben pulled over next to a row of mature palm trees with squat, swollen trunks. "Where do you want to go?"

Before I could respond, my mother did. "You said the creature likes big trees. Remember the grove with the chaneques? That might be a good place to start."

How about that? My mother could be quite the team player when there were no cameras around. I nodded. "That's a great idea. Thanks, Mom."

We parked near the grove. I helped my mother and Hernan out of the truck while Ben opened the cargo bed. The afternoon air was warm and thick. Faced with the reality of what we were doing, Hernan had become distracted. The tension radiated off him, and he muttered under his breath.

Ben tied a collar around the goat's neck, attached a lead, and tugged gently. The brown and gray goat jumped to the ground. The animal let out a bleat and shifted uneasily, as if it could sense something amiss in the air.

"Looks like we're in the right place," Ben said.

Within minutes, we were walking along a narrow dirt trail flanked by tall, gnarled trees. My mother was wearing sensible sneakers instead of her usual bejeweled sandals. Yellow sunlight seeped through the treetop canopy. I walked alongside Ben and the goat, who took to his leash, behaving better than many dogs did. Hernan and my mother trailed behind, heads bent together, talking in low voices.

My eyes kept drifting upward, half expecting to spot a human face peering down at us from the branches. A few squirrels darted past. The goat's ears twitched at every rustle in the underbrush. Ben walked with a determined stride. I noticed he had a shovel over his shoulder.

"Doing some planting while we're up here?" I asked.

"This is the closest thing I have to a weapon. Just in case. If I'd been smart, I would have brought a chainsaw."

"I honestly don't think the monster would stay still long enough for you to use it."

Ben scoffed. "No, but it makes a lot of noise and looks impressive."

He had a point. A chainsaw might have been more reliable than my magic...or Hernan's.

We journeyed further into the grove, and my mother and Hernan grew quiet. I glanced over my shoulder to make sure they hadn't turned around, but they were there, Hernan gripping my mother's elbow while they slowly picked their way along the uneven trail.

I felt a little stab of guilt. My mother was fairly fit, but she wasn't the outdoorsy type, and Hernan wasn't exactly the picture of health. Their apprehension was like a dark cloud hanging over our group. But it was too late now. And I really did need their help.

Ben stopped and pointed. "Look. The new wall. We're just on the other side of La Loma."

A stone wall rose into view. Tall enough to deter newly emerged entities from climbing over into Chavez Ravine, though if they did, my protection spell would kick in and send them back. When the wall was finished, it would be topped with razor wire. But in the end, it was just a wall. It wouldn't keep out flyers, like the winged creature we were seeking.

Ben turned toward me. "Is this a good spot?"

I looked up into the trees—big enough to hold a huge vampire bird. "Good as any." The goat nuzzled my hand. "What's his name?"

"Her," Ben replied. "Her name is Dina."

Whoops. I shouldn't have asked. Once I knew her name, I felt bad about dragging Dina into all this.

We watched Ben tie the lead around the tree. Dina gave a few experimental yanks, but when she found herself still tethered, she gave up and began nibbling grass.

"Now what?" My mother's question sounded like an accusation.

I patted my front pack, which was heavy with the slingshot ammo. "Now, we hide and wait."

Chapter 19

The minutes ticked by slowly while we huddled together. Each snap of a twig sent my pulse racing. My mother's makeup had melted in the warm, humid air. Sweat beaded on Hernan's forehead. Ben gripped the shovel like he was ready to swing it at a moment's notice.

I took out my slingshot and dropped a dozen coated lead balls into the pocket of my trench coat.

Hernan cleared his throat loudly.

"Keep it down! You don't want to scare the thing away, do you?" I whispered.

But I wondered if that was *exactly* what he wanted. He had become quite the scaredy-cat lately.

Hernan pinched his lips together, his nostrils flaring. My mother patted his shoulder, her expression saying she fully understood how frustrating I was.

Ben ignored us. He was too busy watching the goat.

Several more minutes dragged by. My mother's breath hitched in her throat, and then she hissed like a snake. Hernan nearly toppled over in alarm.

"Something's here," she whispered. "I can feel it."

And then I could too. A sort of thrumming filled the air. A shadow passed overhead. There it was, flying over us, gaze fixed on the goat, which began frantically tugging at its lead.

Just when I plucked a lead ball from my pocket, Hernan stirred beside me. I put the ammo in my slingshot and started to pull back the elastic band.

Things began happening very quickly. My mother gasped, and when I looked up, Hernan was striding toward the clearing, his hands bunched into fists at his sides. The air smelled of eucalyptus and something dark and musty—a strong whiff of trouble.

"Shit," Ben said.

"Stop him!" my mother cried.

Ben lurched to his feet, but I grabbed his arm. Hernan was standing next to the goat, looking up at the creature, arms outstretched.

"What is he doing?" Ben whispered.

"Hell if I know." I squinted at the retired professor, who had stooped forward like he was bowing. Had Hernan lost his mind? I relaxed my slingshot and dashed toward him, with Ben close on my heels.

"Stay back!" Hernan shouted. For a moment, I thought he was talking to the giant bird, not us, until he said, "Whatever you do, don't shoot."

An icy prickle of fear raced down my spine. I half expected the creature to swoop down and tear off Hernan's face with its nasty talons. But it remained where it was, high in the tree, perfectly still, its expression one of curiosity rather than lethal menace.

Hernan was standing next to the goat, his hand absently rubbing its head. What was that old brujo doing?

Hernan spoke, introducing himself in Spanish, then asking the creature its name and where it had come from. There was no response, but the winged monster did cock its head. Hernan said something else, that time in a language I didn't understand.

113

My mother joined Ben and me. "Nahuatl," she whispered. "The language of the Aztecs."

"Some people still speak it," Ben said quietly.

What the heck was Hernan saying? I felt a flash of irritation. The man had gone rogue. I had assumed I would have to beg for his help. It hadn't occurred to me he would try to strike up a conversation with the thing.

A low rumbling reached my ears. Beside me, Ben and my mother startled.

"Is that…?" my mother hissed.

I nodded. "It's talking."

"It's saying it's sorry about eating the goats, but it was hungry," Ben whispered. "It's a refugee. From Mexico."

I turned to stare at Ben. "You speak Nahuatl?"

He gave a little shrug, like it was no big deal. "A bit. I have a bunch of family in Mexico." Ben leaned forward, listening. Moments later, he added, "It says it lived with the monarch butterflies, but it had to leave because humans are cutting down the forest to plant avocados."

My mother sighed. "Pobrecito."

I rolled my eyes. Leave it to my mother to sympathize with a vampiric creature the size of a refrigerator. Hernan and Winged Thing continued talking for another few minutes. Then he bowed his head and made his way back to us. The creature stayed perched in the tree, its golden eyes sharp, observing.

Hernan let out a ragged breath. He repeated what Ben had told us. "It's not sure how it ended up here, but it likes the trees. It was starving, and then it saw the goats. It's very grateful for the blood. It doesn't need to feed that often, so if we can just give it a goat every once in a while, that should do the trick."

I couldn't believe what I was hearing. "Are you kidding me? That thing can't just hang around Chavez Ravine forever. It'll freak out the residents. And you seem to be forgetting something else. It threw a goat on your porch. What the hell was that about?"

"I asked about that. It says it didn't do it. And honestly, I'm inclined to believe it." Hernan didn't look half as troubled as he should have been.

"Maybe it was whoever did all that graffiti," Ben suggested.

I glanced at the vampire bird, and it stared back at me. It blinked several times, as if attempting to seem as innocent as a monster with a human-like face could manage. I wasn't buying it.

My mother was nervously biting her lip while studying the creature in the tree. Her face was flushed and moist from the heat.

I tried to read her expression, to sense if she was connecting with the thing. "Are you getting anything, Mom?"

My mother swiveled her head toward me. She wriggled her index fingers above her head. "Let me check. No. Nothing." She paused, frowning. "I guess that means it's not an entity."

I wasn't about to let her off that easily. "You're a psychic. Can't you at least tell me what kind of vibe you're getting? You know. Looks scary but has a heart of gold, except for the occasional need to bleed a goat dry. That kind of thing?"

My mother huffed, clearly annoyed by my irreverence for her famed abilities. "Fine, fine. Let me concentrate." She closed her eyes and took a deep breath, hands clasped together. After a few moments of silence, she opened her eyes and shook her head. "I can feel its presence, but otherwise, nothing. You can't say I didn't try."

I let out a frustrated sigh.

"It's very old," Hernan said. "Ancient. It speaks Nahuatl and Mayan. People used to make sacrifices to it."

That got my attention. "Well, I hope it didn't get too used to that because we're *not* doing that here." I couldn't believe Hernan, the HOA board member, would even suggest it. "We need to get rid of that thing."

Hernan's eyes slid away from my face. "It's immortal. You can't kill it. At least, not easily. So yes, I say we do what it's asking and sacrifice the occasional goat."

The heat had shortened my fuse. "Oh, yes...I'm sure that will work out just fine. I can see it all now. We'll just build a stone altar in front of the community center. People can come for happy hour and a ritual sacrifice. They'll love seeing a giant vampire bird flying through the community, maybe perching above the playground."

Ben sniggered. My mother was beginning to look decidedly uncomfortable.

"Hernan. Can you even trust it?" my mother asked.

Hernan threw up his hands. "How am I supposed to know? I'm just telling you what it told me. I'd say dealing with a vampire refugee from Mexico puts us in uncharted territory."

I glanced at my mother, wondering if she would snap at him. She certainly would have snapped at me. But no, she merely nodded. Whatever they had gotten up to in Mexico had lingering, positive effects.

She turned to me, her expression a mix of worry and curiosity. "So, what do you want to do now, Madeline?"

I wanted to aim my slingshot at the thing and kill it hard. Except the magical coating I had applied to the ammo was melting, leaving a sticky, gooey mess at the bottom of my pocket. I picked up a steel ball. Nothing. No tingling in my fingers. No pink glow.

Suspicion confirmed. My magic was dead outside of Chavez Ravine.

Though if Hernan was right and the damn thing was immortal, it probably wouldn't have made any difference.

Ben was staring at me, eyebrows raised.

I turned to Hernan. "We need to cancel the goat program. Immediately."

He opened his mouth, then closed it. "It's not going to like that."

Had everyone lost their mind? "Sorry. It's my job to keep creatures out of Chavez Ravine, not invite them over for dinner. Imagine what our residents would say! And if Rory Tuck finds out, we'll be in court the next morning."

Hernan raised his eyebrows. "I don't think you comprehend exactly what we're dealing with."

"It's a spoiled little vampire bird used to getting its own way," I snapped. "Well, boo hoo. It's dealing with a former Occult Affairs officer who doesn't negotiate with scaries."

"She took down those chupacabras," Ben said.

"And El Cucuy," my mother added.

Hernan closed his eyes and took a deep breath. "All right. I'll go and give it the bad news."

He had taken a few steps when I realized the bird might blame the messenger. Hernan was annoying, but I didn't want to watch a monster suck his blood. However, the creature listened impassively. The air vibrated with the whoosh of its massive wings when it flew off, away from Chavez Ravine.

Chapter 20

During my private chat with Cora Bernal, the board president immediately agreed to cancel the goat program. Ben Tomas and his crew rounded up the animals by that evening and whisked them away.

My mother surprised me by extending an invitation to join her and Hernan at eight for a mole dinner—"I had hoped to be serving dinner at seven, Maddy, but *someone* seemed to think a little hike in the woods was more important"—but I had already promised to meet Stu for dinner, so I declined.

When I arrived at Olga's Cantina, freshly showered and wearing a navy-blue linen dress and white sneakers, I ordered a glass of pinot grigio, then explained what had happened with the bird and my non-magical ammo in Elysian Park. Stu stared at me, his electric blue eyes radiating unease.

"You were right," I said, keeping my voice low. "My magic doesn't seem to work outside Chavez Ravine. I'm not sure why, and I don't know if it's even possible to fix it."

Stu dipped a corn chip into a bowl heaped with guacamole. "Can you try asking your great-aunt? Maybe she can light up and explain it."

"She's gone silent on me. Yet another mystery. My mother and Hernan keep saying I need to quit relying on Lencha and figure things out for myself."

"That's a little unfair." Stu chewed thoughtfully. "I mean, you've not been at this very long. It all kind of got dumped on you when you moved in. Every student needs a mentor."

I sighed. "It's silly to think I need a mentor at my age."

"No, it's not. Age doesn't matter when you're learning something new. You need help, plain and simple. I like your mom. She's a hoot, but she's wrong on this one, and so is Hernan. You said he's a brujo. He should be supporting you."

I nearly choked on my wine. "Hernan? Please. We've just reached the point where he's not trying to kill me anymore. Besides, he's my mother's boyfriend." I shuddered. "He's actually trying to play nice, but I think it's an act. From what his granddaughter said about him, he's way too self-centered to help me. Plus, his magic is iffy."

"You met his granddaughter?" Stu sounded surprised. "Wow. Things must be moving fast between Malena and Hernan if you're meeting his family."

I dragged a chip through the restaurant's signature thin red salsa. "Nothing like that. I was actually stalking her at the hospital when Hernan was sick, trying to get some information on him."

"Why am I not surprised?" His blue eyes darkened. "Are you sure getting rid of the goats will get rid of that monster? Clare was so terrified by what she saw she actually begged me to take her to her mom's." Stu sipped his margarita. The ice clinked against the glass.

"I'm not sure. I'm hoping without the goats around it'll go somewhere else. Like the zoo. But I wasn't about to bargain with it. I'm pretty sure if I agreed to give it the occasional goat it would ask for a herd and then a virgin or whatever."

"Geez." Stu paled. "Let's hope it's gone, then. Did you tell your team?"

I nodded. "Yeah. I've got everyone out patrolling and two extra people in the command center, watching the feeds."

"For how long?"

I shrugged. "For the next several days at least."

Stu reached across the table and squeezed my hand. "You've got this, but let me know if there's anything I can do."

From the way his thumb lingered against my wrist, I knew he had something else in mind besides his trove of rifles. But that's where my mind went. Stu had once come to our rescue with a rifle to take out an especially pesky supernatural creature. I wasn't above asking for that kind of help again if things got desperate.

After stopping at the command center to reassure myself everyone was on task—they were—I headed home just after eight o'clock. A dark veil of purple and blue descended over Chavez Ravine, long shadows across the pristine lawns of the houses in La Loma. The house next door was completely dark. Leo was at an out-of-town conference, and Toby had joined him. I wondered what Julia was up to and thought briefly about inviting her over for a nightcap in the backyard, but I was too tired for that. An early bedtime was shouting my name.

I stepped out of the Jeep. The muggy night air wrapped around me like a moist blanket. A faint sound caught my attention—a distant melody drifting from the new development up the street. Today had been move-in day for some of the residents of the new neighborhood Rory Tuck had called Phase I—charming homes at the rear of the property that backed up against a wooded ravine. By the time I approached my front door, laughter had reached my ears.

Rory must have been thrilled. He had sold more than ninety percent of the houses, all above asking. The development was for people fifty-plus who wanted to live in Chavez Ravine and enjoy luxurious amenities but who didn't need a lot of square footage.

Rory had wanted to buy me out and expand his development, but he hadn't stood a chance, thanks to the complicated rules of legacy in Chavez Ravine.

I unlocked the front door and stepped inside, grateful for the cool, dry air that greeted me. Sam was waiting in the small foyer, his tail swishing back and forth. I fed him a few of his favorite treats, poured a glass of wine, and went into the backyard, nervously scanning the trees.

While I paced the garden, my sense of unease grew. The encounter with the creature played on a loop in my head. The new development was right next to Elysian Park, where we had found the vampire bird.

Even with Stu's reassuring words and support, I couldn't help but be overcome by a sense of foreboding. Almost a full moon. Well, technically, it was a "waxing gibbous," but that sounded wrong, more like a monkey trying to get rid of its leg fur.

The twilight bathed the garden in an eerie glow. Sam stopped prowling around and stood up on his hind legs, his fur bristling.

My heart thumped in my chest. "What is it, Sam?"

He let out a guttural howl that lifted every tiny hair on my body. Seconds later, a bloodcurdling scream pierced the night, followed by a cacophony of frantic shouts.

Shit.

My heart went into overdrive, and I dashed inside the house, grabbed my slingshot and several magic-coated ammo balls from the workbench, then locked the door behind me. I sprinted up the street, pausing long enough to call the command center. Rafi picked up immediately.

121

"Bailey and several others are on the way, ma'am."

I had to take a couple of deep breaths to get the words out. "Did you see anything?"

Rafi paused. "No, ma'am. A resident called it in. We'll check the feeds—"

I ended the call and continued running. The chain link fence was gone, and so was the gate. The development had officially opened. In their place was a tall, wooden arch surrounded by cascading greenery.

More screaming.

I sprinted up the driveway, the last few magic ammo balls clutched in my hand, which had begun to itch. A good sign.

A full stomach and a stitch in my side were slowing me down. When I rounded a corner, I spotted the vampire bird swooping above a small grassy park, knocking over tables and chairs. The ground was strewn with plates and glasses while people fled. Tiki torches added a surreal touch to the mayhem.

Watching a vampire bird roost in a tree was one thing. Seeing it in action was another. It was a terrifying sight to behold. How could something so big fly at all?

The creature's wings whooshed in the air when it circled overhead, screeching loudly. Backup would arrive any moment, but I didn't dare miss my chance at such a clear shot. My hands were glowing red, which meant my magic was working.

I loaded a lead ball into my slingshot and stepped out into the open.

"Hey, you pinche cabron," I yelled. "Over here!"

That got its attention. It wheeled around, gave another one of its earsplitting cries, and sped toward me. It wasn't exactly graceful, but it was intimidating. Its golden eyes glowed with recognition. Or was it anger?

My hands trembled while I took aim.

Before I could get off the shot, there was another screech behind me. My fingers went cold. I whipped around. Another of the giant birds was coming at me, its gray human face set in a determined grimace, talons outstretched.

There were *two* of them. Correction. Three. There was another two off to my left. And yet another coming from over a rooftop.

Five of the damned things were headed straight for me and my little slingshot.

I turned on my heel and dove into the bushes. Pressing myself against the ground, I struggled to catch my breath. The vampire birds circled overhead.

I pulled out my phone and called Bailey.

"Almost there," she wheezed.

"There are five of them."

"What?"

"They are seriously pissed off," I said. "Grab your helmets before you head in."

We ended the call, and I waited. My heart felt like a hamster running around in my chest.

Across the way, I spotted a group of women huddled behind a bar, one of them in a white shirt and black pants, clutching a tray as if it could shield her from harm. A canopy hid them from view when a bird flew past.

I wished I could duck out long enough to give them a reassuring wave and tell them help was on the way, but I didn't dare move.

My phone rang. Rory Tuck.

"Where the hell are you?" he shouted into my ear. "Do you have any idea what's happening up here?"

The developer was cranky at the best of times, and I had learned that a quick, clear response was the best way to deal with him. But for some reason, at that moment, I chose snark.

"Hey, don't you come from a long line of Irish witches? Why don't you see what *you* can do?"

"Are you serious? That is not the point! You're getting paid big bucks to deal with this shit, so deal with it. And fast!"

I ended the call. Moments later, footsteps pounded on the fresh sod.

"Oh, thank God," a woman cried.

Bailey, Justin, Liam, and Ron had arrived, helmets on their heads, wearing leather jackets despite the heat. They fanned out. The birds' cries were deafening, blending with the screams of trapped, terrified residents.

I did my best to shut it all out, to focus on preparing my shot. Then I took a deep breath and stepped out of my hiding spot. The largest creature—the one from Elysian Park—snapped its head toward me. With glowing red hands, I aimed at the bird's chest and let loose the magic-infused ammo.

It struck the beast, and a burst of intense blue light flashed at the point of contact. The vampire bird shrieked, its wings flapping wildly while it spiraled downward. There were cheers and shouts from the women behind the bar. But just before it hit the ground, it recovered and shot straight up into the air. It flew off over a two-story Craftsman-style house.

I grabbed another steel ball and ran after it, zigzagging along the paths. It was too late. It skimmed the ridge of trees along the border with Elysian Park. I retraced my footsteps to the grassy area, where my team was fending off the other birds with their batons.

"Our ammo isn't working, boss!" Ron shouted.

Mine had some effect, so I fired off the rounds I had, which sent three of them squawking away.

That left one.

Justin grabbed a bar stool, turned it legs-out, and used it as a shield. The others followed his example and clustered together, backs touching. They kept it at bay while it repeatedly plunged toward them, talons out. I had run out of ammo and was looking around for something long and pointy I could use as a weapon when someone shouted behind us.

It was Stu, running toward us in his pajama bottoms, gripping a shotgun.

The vampire bird swung around to face him. I watched in horror as it careened toward him, mouth open wide, revealing needle-like teeth.

Stu's face went white, but he took aim at the fast-approaching creature. I couldn't watch.

The crack of the gun was deafening.

When I opened my eyes, Stu was breathing heavily, still gripping the rifle while the bird flapped away.

Chapter 21

I actually felt sorry for Rory Tuck. The grand opening of his dream project in Chavez Ravine had been ruined by a flock of nightmare birds.

Rory was too busy fending off their angry questions to come after me, but by the way he kept casting furious looks in my direction, it was just a matter of time.

I took in the scene, and my heart sank. What had been a festive celebration had turned into a scene of destruction. Tables were overturned, and debris littered the ground. Lights blazed from the nearby houses, and figures stood in the windows, too frightened to step outside.

Stu gave shotguns to Justin and Liam—the only two members of my security team who had proper training. They had placed themselves in strategic positions around the development. If Hernan was right and the birds were immortal, all they could do was scare them off again. The job of eliminating them would be mine.

Somehow, in all the chaos, I remembered I would need more feathers so I could mix up another batch of ammo goo. When people started to disperse, I kept my eyes on the ground.

While I searched, I called Cora to let her know we would need shotguns for the next few days. The board didn't like the idea of my team having firearms because that gave the impression Chavez Ravine was a dangerous place, so Cora called a short emergency meeting and got the board to approve the temporary use.

She confessed that Eileen and Dan hadn't been told the entire truth, that Hernan had told her and Charlie about the ancient beings in search of…new blood. Only the Latino board members understood Chavez Ravine's supernatural past, so they had agreed it was best to leave all that out of the discussion.

Still, the board agreed to let my team carry their shotguns.

"But only until you can solve this problem, Maddy. Which I trust will be soon."

Message received, boss. No pressure.

"Also, please do what you can to calm poor Rory Tuck."

Poor Rory, indeed. The new owners had him surrounded and were demanding refunds. While Rory appeared genuinely upset about the bird blitz, he was also a hard-headed businessman. He quickly pointed out everyone had signed a document clearly stating there was no guarantee the community would always be entity-free.

Since they didn't have shotguns, Bailey and Ron decided they needed to have compound bows. They kept pulling up photos on their phones of fierce-looking weapons with ridiculous names like "Maxima Striker" and "Deploy King."

"Seriously, boss." Ron held up his phone. "We need these. They're light and killer fast. It'll take those bad boys right out of the sky."

With a sigh, I glanced at the picture of the Maxima Striker. It didn't look like any bow I had ever seen. The general shape was familiar, but it appeared strangely industrial, made of a connecting series of malformed oblong rings. Weird. Also, scary and powerful-looking.

Not to be outdone, Bailey chimed in, "I bet Chad at the Slingshot Academy can do the training."

Of course, he could.

"Okay, let's put this on the agenda for our next staff meeting. Why don't you two do your research and put together a recommendation? But for now, I need you to help me find as many feathers as possible."

Bailey stared at me. "Feathers? Like, from those birds? Why do you want those?"

"Yes, those feathers, and never mind why I want them. Please, just see how many you can find."

After Bailey went off in search of feathers, Ron's eyes met mine. "Are you going to use them in your brujería?"

"Yeah. I am."

"I knew it! That's awesome."

"Yes, but Ron, please, let's keep this between ourselves. We've already talked about my magic *way* more than I am comfortable with."

"You got it, boss." Ron moved to the edge of the park, his eyes on the ground.

A voice rang out across the grassy area. "Madeline Madrigal! Our newest residents would like to hear from the head of security about the association's plans to keep them safe."

Rory Tuck. Of course. Hands on hips, a murderous expression on his face.

I took a deep breath and strode toward the nervous crowd. It was my least favorite part of the job, but there was no avoiding it. We'd had so many supernatural problems and freaked-out residents, it was actually getting easier.

———>·→·||||||·←·←———

Stu was snoring in my bedroom while I crushed feathers at my workbench. I was still too wound up to sleep, and it felt good to keep busy. Though I wished I could conk out like Stu. My mind just had other ideas.

Stu had insisted on staying over. He thought the bird we had encountered in Elysian Park might hold a grudge, so he slept with his rifle on the floor next to his size twelve sneakers.

I had finally sent my team home around midnight and had arranged for extra guards from an outside agency to help patrol the housing development.

A community-wide alert was also sent out, asking residents to shelter in place until seven o'clock the next morning due to a "concerning incident of supernatural origin in the new housing development in La Loma."

That creative writing class I had taken freshman year was finally paying off.

I also sent all the footage from nearby surveillance cameras to Steven Zhao, my nerdy BFF in Occult Affairs. With a CC to Jo, of course.

Jo replied immediately.

Since when do entities of the same type arrive in multiples?

Smaller types like gnomes? You're up late, BTW.

Oh, please. Gnomes are an anomaly and you know it. Call me in the morning.

The vampire birds weren't entities, new or otherwise. At least, I was ninety-nine-point-nine percent certain. But I couldn't afford to rule anything out, and publicly suggesting the creatures might be entities would buy me some time with the residents of Chavez Ravine. It was a more palatable explanation than admitting ancient vampiric creatures were moving into our gated community.

One thing had gone right. If I had given in to Hernan's request that we provide his bird friend with a sacrificial goat, we would have been setting up a goat buffet hours later when his pals arrived.

Sam seemed miffed he had missed his chance to chase the big birds. He sat stiffly next to Little Lencha and pouted. For her part, the figurine didn't seem the least bit interested in what was going on.

"Feel free to offer any advice," I said. "I could use some help."

Nada.

The clay figure's painted eyes didn't even seem to follow me like they used to. Maybe my mother was right. Maybe Lencha was more interested in resting in peace than bootstrapping a pesky new bruja.

I finished the batch of my special bird-fighting concoction, scraped the goopy paste into a glass jar, and stuck it in the refrigerator. Stu didn't even stir when I crawled into bed at three a.m.

When my alarm went off at six-thirty, Stu was in the shower. He had started a pot of coffee and fed Sam, who didn't even bother to look up when I shuffled into the kitchen.

I sank into a chair and scrolled through a blizzard of messages.

From the command center: *No more bird sightings*

From Cora: *Do you plan to extend the shelter in place?*

From Eileen Simpson: *What are you going to do if your birds start attacking people?*

"My birds." She was a piece of work.

Then a few minutes later, also from Eileen: *Residents need to get to work and go about their business. The shelter-in-place must absolutely end at seven. No excuses!*

Then about a minute later, Eileen again: *Why aren't you responding? My clients in Chavez Ravine are asking questions and they deserve answers right now!*

About a dozen frantic texts from Hernan, all saying I should have agreed to the goat sacrifices and avoided all this trouble. He offered to talk to them and negotiate a deal.

That one I could answer: *We do not negotiate with monsters*

His answer surprised me: *That's what your mother said*

Well, how about that? My mother had taken my side for once.

Nothing more had happened overnight to justify extending the shelter-in-place. When Stu got out of the shower, I asked him to arrange for a half dozen sharpshooters he had on contract to help patrol the grounds. It wasn't exactly what the board had authorized, but I could always ask for forgiveness later.

I didn't expect Stu's people to take out the creatures if they were immortal, as Hernan claimed, but the shotguns had scared them away the previous night, and that was good enough until we could figure out a more permanent solution.

At seven o'clock, as planned, I tapped out an update to the community. The shelter-in-place was ending. Caution advised, report any unusual activity, etc., etc.

Stu sauntered into the kitchen, a towel wrapped around his waist. The sight of his well-muscled back was normally enough to drag my thoughts toward the bedroom, but my limbs felt heavy, and I could have sworn my head was a balloon attached to my achy neck.

"Don't take this the wrong way, but you look terrible." Stu poured a mug of coffee, added a splash of cream and a half teaspoon of sugar, and set it on the table in front of me. He left the room and returned moments later wearing a white T-shirt and plaid boxers.

After getting his own coffee, he lowered himself into the chair opposite and continued.

"What time did you go to sleep?"

"Two," I lied.

"Mmm. What are you doing about the shelter-in-place?"

"Cancelled it." I glanced at the clock on the microwave. "As of ten minutes ago."

Stu sipped his black coffee. I had no idea how people could stand it, and I had long given up trying. The extra calories from a splash of cream and pinch of sugar were a small price to pay for smoothing out the bitterness and bringing out the hidden flavors.

"We're thinking about trying out hunting bows," I said. "Ron and Bailey's idea."

"Good idea. Those should work. I'm afraid I can't help you. I've never used them myself."

I glanced at the window. Another bright Los Angeles morning, the sun warming my face. "They're putting together a proposal." I gave a tired sigh. "Just the idea of learning a new weapon feels exhausting. They'll probably mean we can send the sharpshooters home, which will make the board happy, but it's unlikely they'll take those things out for good. I wish I could just wriggle my fingers, and *boom*, they'd be gone."

"Have you tried that?" Stu sounded dead serious.

"No. That's the movie version. My brujería is a lot more complicated." And usually involved chilis, a long list of ingredients, and the occasional third party, like Santa Muerte. She made me nervous, so I had given the statuette of Our Lady of Holy Death to Hernan, but I could always ask him to see if she could shed any light on the ancient vampires from Mexico. In fact, those things seemed right up her alley.

132

"So that's what you were up to last night? Making something magical? For what, exactly?"

I took another sip of coffee. "Yes, I was making some stuff for my slingshot ammo. Like what I used last night but stronger. Among other things, I added extra feathers to give it a boost."

Stu nodded thoughtfully. "The feathers representing their essence?"

"Pretty much."

That seemed to satisfy him, which was fine by me. I was glad he was interested, but I wasn't yet comfortable talking about the specifics. It somehow felt wrong, like sharing an old family recipe with an outsider.

He got up and topped up my coffee. "Well, if it works half as well as whatever it was you made for Clare's cramps, then we're in good shape because that stuff was miraculous. I reminded her not to tell her mother, but she's already blabbed about it to her friends, so I'm sure they'll be all over you once it's safe to come back to Chavez Ravine."

Stu kissed the top of my head and strode out of the kitchen.

Chapter 22

Julia invited me to her shop for an open house she was hosting showcasing her latest pottery collection. I almost said no. My giant bird problem was so distracting, and it felt impossible to spend time on anything else. But then I reminded myself Julia had been a great friend, and she deserved my support. A couple of stupid birds weren't going to keep me from showing up for the woman who had decorated my house and stocked my closet.

When I arrived at her shop in Palo Verde Plaza, Julia was attending a clutch of customers. She looked fashionable, as always, wearing a mustard-colored top and bright green pants, her auburn hair in a French braid. I browsed the shelves, waiting for her to break free, but couldn't stop myself from eavesdropping.

A fortyish man with a mop of curly dark hair was in the process of explaining he needed something special for his girlfriend—oops, not his girlfriend, his sister—who was having a birthday. He had heard so much about Julia and had to come check out her shop.

Julia stiffened. "You've heard about me? From whom?"

"Pardon?" The man lowered his eyebrows.

"Who told you about me?"

The man scrunched up his face in a parody of concentration. "Um, my friend Seth, I think."

"Seth Abrams?" Julia's tone was as sharp as a knife's edge.

She rarely sounded so disapproving, so I moved in a little closer. The man wore expensive-looking jeans and a vintage acid-washed T-shirt proclaiming his love for heavy metal.

His gaze dropped to Julia's cleavage. "Yeah, Seth. We're friends. Well, neighbors, actually, and when he found out I was looking for a gift, he suggested I come check you out." He gave her a not-so-sly leer. "And I like what I see. The shop, I mean."

Julia crossed her arms in front of her chest and glared. Her reaction didn't seem to have much effect on him. He licked his lips and winked. What a loser.

Julia cleared her throat. "I know Seth. As in, Seth the Stalker. We went out a few times. Ever since, he likes to send his friends to harass me. Are you here to harass me? Or are you actually going to buy something?"

Julia wasn't talking loudly, but the shop wasn't that large, and the other customers had stopped mid-browse to stare.

Heavy Metal blinked rapidly, clearly caught off guard. He grabbed the closest item from a shelf—a beautiful, glazed bowl painted in indigo and white swirls. "Oh, I'm here to buy something. Definitely. For my girlfriend."

Julia wasn't about to let him off the hook. "I thought you said you were looking for your sister."

"Oh yeah. Of course. My sister. It's her birthday this weekend. My girlfriend and I broke up, and we'd been together forever, so I'm kinda preoccupied, you know?"

Julia snatched the bowl from his hand. "I don't really. This is one of the more expensive pieces in the store. Did you check the price?"

The man shook his head, biting his lip. I could almost see the wheels in his head churning. Julia wasn't at all what he had been expecting. Seth had probably described her as a gorgeous airhead, someone who would give him a good story to take back to his dipshit friend.

"No, I didn't," Heavy Metal said. "It's fine. I mean, whatever it costs, it's fine. I mean, I like it."

Julia flashed a chilly smile. "I'll ring you up, then." She stepped behind the counter, peeled the price tag from the bottom of the bowl, rolled it up between her fingers, then flicked it into a trash can. She pressed a few buttons on the white mobile card reader and held it out.

Heavy Metal gave a little hiss when he glanced down at the screen. "Oh. Well, okay. It's handmade, right?"

Julia ripped off the receipt and slid it across the counter. "Yes. I make everything here in my shop. Each piece is one-of-a-kind. Would you like me to gift-wrap it for you? It's included in the price."

"Uh, no. Thank you."

Julia wrapped the bowl in plain brown paper and slid it into a teal shopping bag. She flashed a fake smile. "Well, thank you for coming in."

Heavy Metal snatched the bag from Julia's outstretched hand and hurried out of the shop. The bell over the door tinkled. I had almost forgotten about the other customers until they laughed.

"You showed him," an older woman said.

"Good for you! I am totally inspired!" a younger woman chimed in. "He was so gross. Totally creepy."

Julia placed two hands on the counter and took a few wobbly breaths. "I can't believe I just did that, but I am so sick of Seth's shit."

In a few steps, I was standing in front of her. I grabbed her hands and gave them a little shake. "Who the hell is Seth, and why didn't you tell me about him?"

Julia gave a sidelong glance at the two women, who were now debating which set of mugs to buy.

"I met him at Olga's about a year ago," she began in a low voice. "He's really good-looking and totally rich, yeah? Stocks or something. And he seemed nice. Really nice. At first. We went out a few times, and then *bam*, he became incredibly controlling, so I said nope. Not doing this anymore. But Seth doesn't like being told no. He started texting, calling, DMing constantly. So, I blocked him, and then he started showing up at my house, here at the shop, even a gallery downtown where I was having a showing.

"Once, he followed me around Palo Verde Market. I started shouting at him in the parking lot and kind of made a big scene. Which *really* pissed him off. And not long after that, guys started showing up here, pretending to want to buy stuff, but then they'd start hitting on me, and I found out Seth was telling them I was a sure thing. But I guess word got around Seth was an asshole because it stopped. For a long time. Until that idiot."

While Julia talked, I ground my teeth, and my body temperature shot up a few degrees. How dare Seth and his minions harass my friend like that? Julia had dealt with Heavy Metal just fine, but that wasn't good enough. I needed to make sure Seth got the message.

"I'll be right back." I banged out the door and sprinted into the parking lot, where I found Heavy Metal standing next to a sports car the color of the Hulk.

Of course, he would drive something so ridiculous.

"Hey." I wedged myself between the driver's side door and the driver. "I happened to be in Julia's shop and overheard your conversation. I have to say, I'm a little concerned."

Heavy Metal's head snapped back. He squared his shoulders. "Pardon me? Who are you?"

"I'm the head of security for Chavez Ravine." I adopted the brisk tone I reserved for difficult members of the public. "Julia Suarez is a valued member of our community. She's also a legacy resident, which entitles her to certain protections." I wasn't making that part up. People rarely read their HOA documents. "Our association is committed to providing a safe and respectful environment for legacy residents and protecting them from harassment." I paused. "What's your name?"

Heavy Metal raised the teal shopping bag and wagged it a few inches from my nose. "I was just doing some shopping. I don't see why you need to know my name. I didn't do anything wrong." He paused and cleared his throat. "My name is Austin Renfrew."

Talk about pretentious names. "Did Seth Abrams tell you to go 'check out" Julia?"

Austin stared down at the bag in his hands. "Of course not. He just mentioned her store when I told him I needed a gift."

I shook my head. "That's not what you said inside, but okay. So, here's what we're going to do. You're going to stay out of Julia's store, and the next time you see your friend Seth, you're going to give him a message for me. Stop harassing Julia, or I'll be paying him a personal visit and dragging him in front of the HOA for violating the rules. And believe me, that's not a fun process. Got it?"

The sneer returned to Austin's face. "This is bullshit. Don't you have better things to do? Like protecting us from whatever the hell flying monster shit is attacking us?"

I shot him my best professional smile. "My team is committed to protecting the community from all sorts of monsters. Supernatural or otherwise."

He stared at me for a moment, then squished his lips together. I stepped aside, watching while he got in the car and drove away.

When I returned to Julia's shop, we were alone. She threw her arms around me and gave me an enormous hug. She smelled amazing. Like lavender and bergamot. "Thank you. For whatever you just did."

I patted her back. "Nothing too exciting. Just some preventative threats. But, Julia, I've seen you in action. When we first met, you took out a hairy monster dude with a rolling pin, remember?"

Julia pulled away with a laugh. "That was different, yeah? I can't go around hitting guys with rolling pins just because they make me mad."

She had the most infectious laugh, so I giggled too. "Well, okay. Point taken. But I've got to ask. How much did you charge that guy for the bowl?"

Julia flicked her brown eyes up to the ceiling. "Four hundred dollars. Two hundred extra for being such a dick." She grimaced. "I actually can't believe he paid it."

I glanced around the store and at all the beautiful things in it and pecked her smooth cheek. "I can. And in my humble opinion, he got a deal."

———›··›·᠁⊹᠁·‹··‹———

Ron and Bailey put together a very persuasive presentation on hunting bows. They had compared models and had chosen one they felt could help us deal with the birds but could also be used for other kinds of supernatural intruders.

Bailey had taken the extra step of investigating training options. So, armed with their recommendations, I went to the board and made my case.

It turned out, when giant flying vampires invaded the expensive neighborhoods of Chavez Ravine, the board became quite cooperative. I got enough money to buy five expensive bows plus training.

In return, the board got something they could talk about when confronted by irate homeowners. It was a win-win, except I knew it was just a delaying tactic.

The hard work was still ahead: figuring out how to kill things that couldn't die.

Blackwood's Archery Camp lay at the far end of the San Fernando Valley. Given the heat, I had been hoping for an air-conditioned warehouse, but Blackwood's was too old-school for that. We were to train outdoors in a vast field of dry, patchy grass under the sparse shade of a few spindly trees.

Tally Blackwood ran the organization. Wildlife hunting expert. Outdoor enthusiast. Winner of countless awards in bowhunting competitions. People came from all over to train or level up their skills with the world-famous Tally.

We hopped out of the SUV and into the blistering heat. I had pictured Tally as a fit young woman in camo, with no makeup, so when an older woman came barreling out of the Quonset hut, I figured it had to be her mom.

"I'm Tallulah, but you can call me Tally," she drawled in a Southern accent.

Tally was somewhere between fifty and sixty. Her age was hard to pin down because her skin was deeply tanned, with wrinkles around her eyes and mouth. Apparently, she had omitted sunscreen from her beauty regimen. The chunky highlights in her short brown hair had turned brassy. Medium height. Large chest. Skinny legs.

"Thank you for seeing us so quickly," I said, trying to hide my surprise.

But I had gotten one thing right: Tally wore a camo-print nylon tracksuit and a stars and stripes headband.

"Glad to oblige. Sounds like you're dealing with quite the situation in your fancy-pants community." She frowned. "I will say, I'm not exactly comfortable with the idea of using the kind of bows we're talking about to neutralize entities, as dangerous as some of them may be. I thought that sort of thing was against the law."

My team turned and stared at me expectantly. I would need to choose my words carefully. "Yes, I would say killing entities is against policy in most cases. I used to work as an officer in Occult Affairs, and I still have strong ties with the agency's research department. We're fairly sure we're dealing with a new type of entity, one that's immune to the non-lethal weapons we normally use. But these are dangerous, vampiric creatures who have already killed several animals, so the usual policies don't apply. Safety first, you know."

Tally eyed me with suspicion, then offered a curt nod. "If you say so. We've got everything already laid out." She pointed at Ron. "Why don't you come with me, young man? I've got water bottles and some energy snacks in a cooler. You can help me bring it out."

While we waited for them to return, I looked around, wondering why Tally had chosen LA to set up her business instead of someplace like Alaska or Montana.

Bailey must have read my mind. "Tally's husband inherited this property from his parents. They've got a big house on the other side of those trees."

That explained it. And flying into Burbank airport was easy. Besides the heat, there wasn't much bad weather to worry about.

The former Occult Affairs officer in me was a little concerned about the giant field. There were some distinctive mounds no one had bothered to tamp down.

When Tally and Ron walked up, carrying the cooler between them, I asked, "Do you get many entities popping up around here?"

Tally set the cooler down, and a frown came to her face. "Darlin', you have no idea. But they've given us a break for the last six months or so. Before that, we had a bunch of gnomes that ran off before Occult Affairs could get here. Last I heard, they'd moved into the Japanese garden in Lake Balboa, and they've had a devil of a time trying to clear them out." Tally paused long enough to gesture around the field. "Now, that's one type of entity I wouldn't mind sticking around. I've never been one for gardening, and it would have been nice if they'd stayed long enough to make it all pretty, like they do."

I laughed, thinking about the gnomes running amok in Beverly Hills. They never seemed to choose places that could use their help. Instead, they gravitated to the lushest, wealthiest locations, where residents were easily frightened. Not even my mother had been able to convince them to move to places where they might have been useful.

I turned to Justin. "Why don't you go and grab some Smoke Bombs? Just in case."

Minutes later, Tally was running through an introduction to the equipment. There was some discussion about the types of arrows that would be most effective against the monster birds after I explained their feathers were able to deflect steel balls.

Tally gave a dismissive sniff. "Steel balls aren't arrows, are they? But point taken. You'll want high-penetration arrows, the kind used on tough hides. Sounds like the arrows designed for aerial shooting won't work for your targets."

Liam raised a giant hand. "I have a question. Shouldn't we be practicing on flying targets instead of those things?" He pointed at the row of large bags painted with the familiar bullseye target.

"You're getting ahead of yourself, young man," Tally said. "You need to be able to hit those before we move on to moving targets."

The bows were much more complicated than my humble slingshot, what with releases, sights, and broadheads. I found them awkward to handle, and the steady posture required for accurate shooting was hard to hold for any length of time.

Liam, with his powerful shoulder muscles, had the easiest time of it. Then again, of all the members of my team, he was the one who seemed to have a natural gift for weaponry.

Ron Mendez was the slightest built, but I was surprised by how quickly he learned the basics. Maybe that was because, for once, he wasn't his usual showboating self. He followed Tally's instructions with rapt attention and had excellent results.

Of course, that seemed to annoy Bailey, who, like me, was struggling with the awkward equipment. She was not only athletic, but damn good with a slingshot, so she had expected hunting bows to be fairly simple. Her face had turned bright red from exertion, frustration, the heat, or all three.

I handed her a bottle of chilled water and patted her shoulder. "You're doing fine," I said quietly. "It's hard."

Bailey chugged her water and wiped her mouth with the back of her hand. "Then why isn't that idiot having a problem?" She jerked her chin in the direction of Ron.

"Never mind him. And this isn't any easier for me. We just need to double down." I held up a hand. My fingers were red from what Tally called "string slap." It hurt like hell. By the end of the day, I would have some serious bruises.

"We're probably just tired," Bailey grumbled.

Exhausted, more like it. We'd had little sleep the night before, and we were trying to learn something new outside, with the sun beating down on our heads. I was cranky too. And I was beginning to feel resentful about the vampire birds making it all necessary. Dealing with normal entities and gnomes seemed like a snap compared to the creatures with scary teeth.

I checked my phone again for messages from the command center. When we left Chavez Ravine that morning, everything had been fine. No giant birds swooping in to attack people while they hurried to their cars. No pets carried off. And no more anti-HOA graffiti.

Yet my unease only grew while the training session progressed. Tally demonstrated drawing and anchoring and the more difficult art of controlled releases. By one o'clock, we were sweaty and thirsty.

"I'm starving," Liam announced. His yellow hair was damp with sweat and plastered against his forehead.

"It's time for lunch, then," Tally replied.

The woman had thought of everything. She had sandwiches and chips ready to go in the air-conditioned Quonset hut. We ate surrounded by trophy mounts, their glass eyes watching us from the walls.

By the time I had finished my sandwich, my eyes were hot and itchy, and my body felt brittle with fatigue. I wanted nothing more than to crawl onto the chaise lounge in the corner and take a nice long nap. But that was not an option. Bosses didn't nap.

I guzzled a bottle of espresso cold blend, and we went back outside for target practice.

The heat was even more intense, and my target seemed to swim before my eyes while my hands trembled. But the caffeine eventually kicked in, and my aim improved. The espresso worked its magic on Bailey too, and soon, we were whooping and hollering when our arrows hit their marks.

Ron complimented Bailey for hitting the bullseye three times in a row, and she slugged him in the arm, but I could tell she was pleased.

Justin groaned. "My hands are cramping up, and my shoulders are killing me. Am I doing something wrong?"

"Your form is fine, son." Tally gave a good-natured chuckle. "Just remember, no pain, no gain." She turned toward me. "I've got some time tomorrow morning. We can pick up with the aerial practice then, if you'd prefer."

My body was begging for mercy, but I shook my head. "There's no telling when the vampire birds will return. We can't really afford to wait. We'd better keep at it."

This was met with groans all around. Tally beckoned Liam and Ron to follow her into the Quonset hut, and minutes later, they were back, carrying a metal barrel between them that vaguely resembled R2-D2. Tally plugged it into a battery.

"All righty. This little piece of equipment will shoot off foam discs every five seconds. Your job is to take them down. We'll be starting off with short-range flu-flu arrows until you get the hang of it."

Easier said than done. Once again, Bailey and I trailed the guys. This bothered me less than it did Bailey, who was maybe a little too competitive. Falling behind her co-workers, even just a bit, rattled her.

Another two grueling hours passed. By the end, we were able to hit the flying targets, but not consistently enough to satisfy me.

"But, boss, those discs are tiny compared to the monster birds. The real things should be much easier to hit," Liam said.

Tally laughed. "Do you really want the vampire birds to get that close before you can hit them? Flu-flus are just for beginners.

Now we'll try the carbon-aluminum slims. They're small in diameter, and they should give you the range and penetration you need."

Bailey's competitive spirit went into overdrive, and she focused on hitting the flying discs. After another hour, my concentration began to flag, and my arms felt like noodles. The discs blurred together with the blue sky.

I set my bow down. It was time to call it quits. "I think we've got the basics," I said.

The others let out loud sighs of relief.

"How do you think we're doing?" I asked Tally.

She shrugged. "We managed to pack in a full course today. You all could use some extra practice. Then again, that's true of everyone." She jerked her head at Liam and Ron. "Those two are your best shots, for whatever that's worth."

Beside me, Bailey bristled.

"C'mon back into the office. Chad had your order delivered here, so I'll get you set up with your new equipment."

Back into the air conditioning we went. Tally stepped into a closet and took out six large boxes.

"Five Maxima Strikers and seventy-five carbon-aluminum slims. Most hunters only carry five arrows at a time, but I guess your boss wants you to have extras."

Their boss was planning to put a resin-hardened potion on them, so yes, she wanted her team to have extras.

Bailey and Ron each grabbed two bow boxes, and Liam picked up the arrows. They put them into the back of the SUV, and we headed home to Chavez Ravine.

And whatever was waiting for us there.

Chapter 23

Liam carefully dipped an arrow tip into the magic-boosted paste. "What if this stuff throws off the trajectory of the arrow?"

Bailey leaned closer and squinted at the tip. "Just make sure it's not too thick." She turned to me. "There doesn't need to be a lot of it to work, right?"

Like many questions about how my magic worked, I wasn't sure. "I don't think so. Just make sure there's enough to completely cover the tip. A thin, even layer will hopefully do the trick."

We were gathered in the back room of the command center, coffee cups scattered around the long table.

Justin sniffed the paste. "What's in this stuff?"

"Hey, you guys, we don't ask questions about brujería," Ron said.

Justin chuckled. "Oh, come on. We're in the Latino club, remember? Maddy will tell us."

Bailey snapped her head up. "Hey, there's only one club around here, and that's Chavez Ravine Security Club."

I thought that was a funny thing for her to say. There was an edge to her voice, and it took me a minute to figure out why.

Ron had grown up hearing stories about Chavez Ravine's unusual history and had been the first to figure out I used brujería. The others hadn't been thrilled with Ron's inside scoop and had confronted me about it, pointing out the unfairness of being kept in the dark. I saw their point and had promised to be more open with the entire team.

And for the most part, I was. But my Mexican witchcraft was like a giant puzzle with quite a few missing pieces. Why did my magic only work within Chavez Ravine? Why could I ward off danger with my hands sometimes, but not always? The journals Great-Aunt Lencha had left me from beyond the grave were filled with instructions for cures and spells, but that was pretty much it. Apparently, Great-Aunt Lencha had never needed to take out giant flying vampires.

Liam stood, rubbing a shoulder. "I'd sure like to give these a test run before we're face-to-face with one of those things. Do you think we should take a run out to Phantom's Pass? Shoot a few of these at a target to make sure they still work right?"

Phantom's Pass was the closest wildland and had a convenient entrance from the Bishop neighborhood. I thought for a moment, then shook my head.

"Better not. If anyone sees us with a hunting bow, they'll call the police. Plus, we don't want to accidentally hit anyone."

Liam shuddered. "I sure wouldn't want to be hit with one of these bad boys." He frowned. "It's too bad we didn't take some of this stuff with us to Tally's place. We could have tested them out there."

"We really don't want too many people to know what we're up to." I got to my feet and winced when my lower back twinged.

The night before, my entire body had ached from our bowhunting session. I had slept through the night without waking once. Then in the morning, it had taken several cups of coffee, an espresso, and a pan dulce from Muertos Cafe just to make it into the shower. Which had been gloriously long and hot, but I still felt like I had been run over by a truck.

Bailey carried her arrows to a smaller table next to a window. "How long will these take to dry, do you think?"

I placed my arrows next to hers, then cranked open the window. "It's a sunny spot, and with the fresh air, they should dry soon enough."

"Do you think those things will come back tonight?" Ron sounded nervous. He had lost a little of his swagger from the day before.

"We got lucky last night," Justin said. "Man, I couldn't sleep, thinking my phone would blast an alert and wake up the baby."

Bailey pulled a face. "I don't know how you deal with that baby on your schedule. I couldn't even handle a cat."

"I couldn't do it without my wife. She's amazing. But Tonio is getting to the phase where if he knows I'm around, he wants to play. Doesn't matter if it's three in the morning."

Bailey smirked, "What kind of name is Tonio, anyway? It sounds like you made it up?"

"It's short for Antonio. Us Mexicans are big on nicknames."

I remembered the nicknames the first monster hunter of Chavez Ravine had mentioned in her journals. Ripper. Junie. A pang of regret hit me over the loss of Trini Duran's diaries, which had been destroyed in a fire ignited by Hernan Frias. But that was back when he was trying to get me fired. How far we had come.

Ron cleared his throat. "But seriously. Do you think the vampire birds will come back tonight?"

Liam added his arrows to the table. "Maybe they had to go elsewhere to feed. Who knows. Maybe they'll even stay there? And they're not like vampires from the movies. Maddy saw one during the day in Elysian Park, so sunlight doesn't bother them. Which means they can attack whenever they want."

"But they showed up after dark at the new development in La Loma," Ron said.

Liam realigned the arrows until they lay in a perfect, orderly row. "Yeah, well, military strategy basics. Catching the enemy off guard. Cover of darkness. And there's a psychological aspect to it too. The dark makes it scarier, doesn't it? They're going for maximum impact."

Justin's dark eyes widened. "You talk about them like they're intelligent."

"That's because they are. They've got human faces, right? So, they've probably got human-like brains. Which makes them smart. And Maddy said they're ancient. They've had hundreds of years to refine their techniques."

Everyone stared at Liam, including me. The guy was full of surprises.

"You didn't study military strategy, did you?" I was only half-joking.

Liam straightened, his broad chest jutting out. "As a matter of fact, I did. I went to a military college in South Carolina. Mostly because my father and grandfather went there. It wasn't for me, but I graduated, then pissed off my dad when I moved out here to join Occult Affairs."

I was taken aback by the information. Clearly, I hadn't read his job application thoroughly enough. Otherwise, I would have known this. He and Justin had come highly recommended by Bailey, and that had been enough for me.

Bailey seemed impressed. "Wow. To think you could have been off fighting wars instead of entities and the freaks we're dealing with now."

"Exactly," Liam said. "But honestly, when I first heard about the LAPD starting up Occult Affairs, I knew that was the job for me. It took a while to make it happen, but I did it." He grinned.

"And then you met the asshole chief who treated us all like crap," Justin said. "Even the boss."

"Even the boss," I repeated with a smile. "If the chief had treated you all better, you might not be here today. His loss. My gain."

In the next room, Brandon cried out. Now what? I leapt to my feet and was the first across the threshold.

"Everything all right in here?"

He was standing behind the huge console, his fingers tapping the keys. A moment later, a video appeared on a wall monitor. It was from one of the surveillance cameras on a residential street in Palo Verde, not far from Stu's house. I recognized the area immediately. It had some of the largest, most opulent homes in Chavez Ravine.

Behind me, Ron said, "Oh shit."

My heart sank while I watched the video. People were running in all directions. A vampire bird swooped into view, its jaw opening impossibly wide, and closed in on a stylishly dressed woman. Her heels were slowing her down. She abruptly stopped, changed direction, and bolted toward a Spanish-style house, then disappeared inside.

Brandon pulled up another camera angle. A burly man in a suit shimmied under an SUV when one of the giant birds approached.

I recognized him. It was none other than Charlie Perez, HOA board member and real estate investor.

And then it all clicked into place. It was Tuesday, the usual day for brokers' open houses, when real estate agents toured properties coming on the market.

The others had already fetched the arrows from the backroom and were stuffing them into their new quivers. Liam handed me mine. I hoped the magic-boosted paste had dried enough to do its job.

"Where are we going?" I asked Brandon.

He glanced down at the console and rattled off an address. Luckily, it wasn't far away.

Liam was already striding toward the exit. He stopped abruptly, turning. "Should we call Stu for rifle backup?"

I snatched a set of keys for the largest SUV from a hook on the wall. "He'll be at work. Let's wait and see what it looks like when we get there."

We arrived at the scene of the attacks within minutes. Justin parked in the middle of the street. It was sheer chaos. People screamed. Creatures shrieked.

Liam jumped out first. We had arrived without a strategy. There hadn't been time to talk it through on the short ride over.

We took a moment and put on our gear—the chest and arm guards that had come with our bows. Bailey and I tied up our hair before putting on our helmets.

While Liam targeted one of the massive birds flying directly at him, a woman dashed out of the Spanish house, screaming and gesturing wildly. "What took you so long?"

I recognized her immediately. Board member and realtor Eileen Simpson. Eileen was wearing a navy-blue jumper, her layered hairdo a mess, as if she had crawled through the landscaping. She probably had.

"Get back in the house," I shouted.

But it was too late. Eileen had dashed straight into the path of an incoming vampire bird. The collision knocked her across the yard. The impact threw the thing off course, wings flapping frantically while it struggled to regain altitude.

Liam aimed and fired an arrow. It struck the monster's backside with a flash of purple light, causing it to screech in pain and veer to the right. Another bird was descending toward Eileen, who had realized her mistake and was lurching toward the house. Justin and Ron were busy firing at two birds circling low above the street, trapping people inside the vehicles. More flashes of purple light, but no feathered bodies fell from the air.

Bailey had managed to get inside the house and was on the second-floor deck, aiming at another bird heading for Eileen. It was the largest one—the one I had seen in Elysian Park—and probably the leader of the flock.

Her arrows missed their mark, but the monster was furious. Its gray human face was contorted with rage when it flew past. As it wheeled around, I sprinted toward Eileen.

A manicured hand shot out and grabbed my ankle. "Do something!" she cried.

With Eileen's nails digging into my ankle and her floral perfume invading my nose, I unslung the Maxima Striker from my back. I ignored the ache in my muscles and the weight of the bow, then notched an arrow coated with the magic-boosted paste.

The monster was zigzagging toward us almost playfully, as if it had all the time in the world. Bailey's arrows whizzed past. Its mouth was opening, showing rows of yellowed needle-like teeth.

If its mouth opened any wider, its lower jaw would drop off.

"For God's sake, Madeline, shoot!" Eileen shouted.

I took aim at the creature's broad chest and released the arrow. The projectile soared through the air.

To my amazement, it went exactly where I had intended, striking the creature's chest with a burst of intense purple light. The giant bird faltered, its golden eyes widening. It began to fall toward the ground but righted itself and rose into the air.

It took a moment to register what had happened. The arrow had struck, then ricocheted as if it had hit a metal plate.

Time seemed to stand still. The monster gave me a disgusted look, then wheeled away.

I looked around. The other birds were following.

Five terrifying creatures flying confidently into the distance.

Chapter **24**

After the daylight attack, I had no choice but to start another lockdown. It was inconvenient, but I needed to keep residents safe. Until we figured out a way to kill or banish the vampire birds, normal life would need to be put on hold.

"But what *are* those things?" Eileen cried. "Why are they here? What do they want?"

Cora Bernal had invited me to an emergency HOA board meeting, and we were gathered around the long wooden table in the conference room. All five board members appeared rattled, but Eileen was the most upset. She had scratches on her face and arms from crawling through the bushes to escape the creatures.

I stuck to my story about the possibility our vampire birds were a new, more lethal type of entity. For once, Hernan kept his mouth shut.

"I can't say what the creatures want." I chose my words carefully. "But they appear to be targeting specific individuals."

Eileen opened and closed her mouth like a fish. She appeared to be having trouble catching her breath. "Are you saying those things came after *me*? Specifically *me*?" She swiveled in her chair and glared at Charlie. "I was just sitting the open house for Charlie. It's his listing, except he couldn't stay the entire time, so I said I'd stay and help him out. Isn't that right, Charlie?"

Eileen appeared desperate to distance herself from the creatures. Not that I blamed her.

Charlie frowned, then nodded. "That's right. I arrived early to open up the property and meet the caterer. I had pastries delivered from Muertos Cafe."

I wondered who else had known about the open house. The command center would have. We received a daily list of all activities throughout Chavez Ravine that would involve people from outside the community. It was a protocol I had set up after taking the job as head of security.

"But surely the open house was just coincidence," Cora said, clearly flustered.

Hernan was staring at me, his bushy eyebrows raised. "We killed the goat program, so they might see us as an alternate food source. Or there could be some other motive behind their attacks."

That was exactly how it was beginning to feel to me.

"But that doesn't make any sense," Dan Berman said. "You talk about these things like they're capable of having a motive." He snorted derisively. "They're *monsters*."

"Unless someone else is commanding them," Hernan replied, then clamped his mouth shut, laying a hand on his chest.

I nearly choked on my water. That idea had been bouncing around in my head, but I wasn't ready to openly discuss it. And certainly not in front of Eileen and Dan Berman, who had been kept in the dark about most of the supernatural goings-on in Chavez Ravine.

Eileen gasped. "Like some kind of puppet master?"

More like a witch. The thought sent a shiver down my spine. Cora gave Hernan a withering look.

Hernan held up a hand. "I shouldn't have said that. I'm sorry. That's ridiculous, of course. I'm not sure what possessed me."

I had never heard the retired professor back down before, and it caught me by surprise.

Eileen and Dan looked relieved at Hernan's apology. Cora and Charlie did too, although for a different reason; they knew as well as I did it was a distinct possibility someone was behind the birds' attacks.

Cora cleared her throat. "Well. We can't just let these creatures terrorize our community. What's your plan, Madeline?"

I knew what she was doing. Cora wanted to change the subject before Eileen and Dan realized Hernan might have had a point.

I got to my feet. "The birds have feathers that deflect the arrows. We need to figure a way around that, and we need to seriously consider allowing the use of rifles. Stu Wells can help us find marksmen, but all of you will need to decide if that's something you want to do. More immediately, I need to deal with the lockdown. We're going to offer escorts to residents in the shopping center parking lots, and we'll assign guards to protect Ben Tomas's landscaping crew. Otherwise, we're going to ask people to stay in their homes or, when commuting, in their cars until we get this problem solved. That includes all of you, of course."

After the meeting, Hernan followed me down the stairs into the lobby. He grabbed my elbow. "I'm sorry about back there."

"Do you really think someone could be commanding those things? Is that what Santa Muerte told you?"

Hernan tutted loudly. "No. That's not how it works. We're not on those kinds of terms yet, but I'm sure she's trying to communicate something through the cards. And through my dreams…" His voice drifted off.

"And that is?"

Hernan scraped a hand through his thick black hair. "She's telling me they are immortal and that they can't be killed by ordinary means. If that's right, then arrows aren't going to work, and neither will bullets."

"I created a little something special for the arrows," I admitted. "It had some flash bang to it that surprised them, but that was about it. It didn't help the arrows penetrate their feathers. But do you really think we can't take them out? El Cucuy was immortal, wasn't he? We got him with a magic sword."

Hernan glanced over his shoulder to make sure we were alone before he continued. "The stories about El Cucuy suggest immortality, but they're not conclusive. I'd say he was more of…an enduring presence."

"You make it sound like there's a difference." I rolled my eyes. "All right. If these things are actually immortal, how are we supposed to get rid of them?"

"You mean *you*. How are *you* supposed to get rid of them? I'm not in the business of hunting monsters."

"Just *creating* them when it suits you," I muttered. "You managed to conjure up some scary birds of your own."

Hernan crossed his arms in front of his chest and huffed. "I assure you, I had nothing to do with these vampiric creatures. I'm much more interested in matters of the heart than in the dark arts."

My eyebrows seemed to have a life of their own. I was pretty sure they had reached my hairline. "Meaning my mother?"

"Yes, of course. She's an amazing woman. I never thought I'd meet someone like her and have the feelings I have at my advanced age. Life is a miracle, and aging is its poetry, as the saying goes."

"Mmm" is all I managed to say. Not all that long ago, Hernan couldn't resist bashing my mother. Now, he was probably bonking her.

I took a moment to wipe that image out of my head.

"Hernan, there aren't that many people who could have summoned those things. You could have, and maybe I could have, though that's debatable. Rory Tuck has some hereditary skills, but there is no way he'd do anything to jeopardize his new development. He was genuinely furious when the birds showed up at his grand opening party. Are there any brujas or brujos unaccounted for in Chavez Ravine?"

Hernan uncrossed his arms and shoved his hands in his pockets. "No. No one that I know, anyway." He frowned. "Do we have any new residents in Chavez Ravine that we should look into?"

Was it possible the guy was becoming a team player?

"That's actually a very good question. I'll get a list of new arrivals from the past six months. If we can find whoever summoned them, maybe they can help us kill them."

"You can't *kill* them. That's what I've been trying to tell you. You need to think about the problem differently. You'll need to unmake them, erase them, or lock them away."

"All right. So how do I go about 'unmaking' them?"

Hernan's expression changed. His eyes seemed to lose focus, as if he was trying to remember something.

"Hernan? Are you okay?"

I couldn't tell whether he even heard me, but he began to slowly nod his head.

"I understand now. This is what Santa Muerte was trying to tell me in the cards. This isn't something you can do alone, Madeline. You're going to need help. Undead help."

Outside, a horn blasted. Liam had arrived to drive me to the command center. It was only across the plaza, but he didn't want me to risk getting swooped by a giant bird.

Hernan went back up to the conference room, and I went outside to Liam in the SUV.

For the rest of that long and exhausting day, Hernan's cryptic words played over and over in my head.

Chapter 25

What the hell is going on with Chavez Ravine?

Is it cursed?

Were the goats just appetizers?

I loved my neighbors, but sometimes, I wished they didn't have my number. Leo and Toby were out of town, but that hadn't stopped the Chavez Ravine grapevine from reaching them with the latest gossip.

LOL! No, everything's under control here

Bullshit! We're friends. Tell us the truth. Puhleeze!

I sighed. *Love ya but I'm kinda busy handling DRAMA*

Another notification popped up on my screen. It was from Jo in the Occult Affairs command center.

What the hell is up with Chavez Ravine?

I quickly typed out a response detailing the attack in Palo Verde.

OK, stay safe. They really need you up there. We all do.

When I was trying to think of a snarky response, a call came through from Steven Zhao. I answered immediately.

"I got the analysis back on that feather you sent over. Interesting stuff. Want to hear what it said?"

I put him on speaker and massaged my temples. "No, I want you to hit delete and then empty your trash can."

"You're kidding, right?" Steven said with uncertainty.

"Of course, I'm kidding. I'm waiting with bated breath."

"Okay. So, this is kinda cool. The feather structure is totally, one hundred percent unique. It's not like anything we would see in a normal avian species or even in any of the flying entities we've documented. It's dense and made from keratin, with metallic-like filaments woven in. The outer layer is coated with something we're still trying to figure out. A couple of layers of those things are strong enough to resist ballistic forces."

I fell back in my chair. "Well, crap. That explains it. Is there anything that could get through those things?"

"I'm afraid that's not my department," Steven said. "Do the feathers cover their legs too?"

"All the way down to their feet." I drummed my fingers on my desk. "Is there anything else?"

"That's all I've got, I'm afraid." Steven paused. "Except...I don't think this is an entity two-point-oh." He cleared his throat. "I think it's more along the lines of that Cucuy thing in Phantom's Pass." Steven had encountered him, briefly, when the boogeyman tried to drag off his co-worker.

"Yeah, I think so too." My voice sounded flat.

"What are you going to do?"

Man, I was getting tired of that question and even more tired of not having an answer. But I liked Steven, so I told him the truth. "I have absolutely no idea."

My phone chimed once again. That time, it was Julia.

"Maddy, I hate to ask this because I know how busy you are, but is there any chance you can pick me up at the garage on Broadway? The Volvo died, and they won't be able to fix it until the morning."

I would have done anything for Julia, and it wasn't like I was in the middle of a big plan to take down our vampire birds, so I happily agreed.

Broadway was just down the hill from the La Loma gate, so I hopped in the Jeep and picked her up, with a Maxima Striker bow on my lap just in case.

Julia shifted in her seat and cleared her throat. "Those don't work, from what I heard."

That grapevine again. "Well, they scare the things off, but that's about it."

The guard at the La Loma gate was wearing a helmet. He waved us through.

Julia reached over and squeezed my knee. "I'm not complaining. And thank you for coming to get me. I tried Ben, but he didn't answer."

"Well, he works with a lot of noisy equipment, or I'm sure he'd have picked up."

"Yeah, maybe."

I glanced over at her in surprise. "Are you not telling me something?

"Oh, I don't know." She sighed. "Ben's really great, but he doesn't seem to be into me as much as I'm into him."

Julia was a 'shout-it from the rooftops' kind of girl.

"Ben's just quiet. Some people aren't so…demonstrative."

Julia peered out the window nervously. "I know. I mean, things are good, but I thought we would have reached the 'I love you' stage, but that hasn't happened."

"You just started going out!"

"Yeah, I guess I'm being silly."

"And impatient," I said sternly. "Give the guy a chance. You don't strike me as the clingy type anyway."

Julia ran a hand through her auburn hair. "Ooo. Maybe I am a little clingy. My therapist says I'm afraid of abandonment because my parents died while I was young, so maybe that's it.

I'm working on it, but I think I have freaked guys out before. Plus, I'm a kind of a loud person. Maybe I'm just not Ben's type."

"You're smart and creative and funny and beautiful. If you're not his type, he's an idiot, but I actually think you may just be rushing things a bit. Do you think you could adjust your expectations and just enjoy getting to know him?"

Julia laughed again and punched my arm. "Maybe you should be my therapist."

I laughed. "I think I'll settle for being your friend."

The moment we arrived at Julia's house, the front door opened. Ben appeared holding a chain saw, his hair damp from a shower. He glanced at the sky while he strode toward us and opened the passenger door with a flourish. "Señorita, may I escort you inside?"

Julia glanced my way, sheepish.

"Dummy," I said, giving her a little push.

Ben gave me a friendly wave before slinging an arm around Julia's shoulders. "Thanks for delivering my girl safe and sound."

With Clare at her mother's, Stu asked me to stay at his place. As usual, I didn't want to leave Sam alone, so I invited him over to my place instead. But that meant I was on the hook for dinner.

I changed into shorts and a thin cotton shirt. Not exactly sexy, but comfort was more important while cooking. I had a nice cut of skirt steak in the refrigerator, so I took it out, along with some vegetables.

While I seeded the jalapenos, another message arrived. Rory Tuck. I had wondered why I hadn't heard from him earlier, and his text explained it. He had spent the day dealing with complaints that he had defrauded new buyers with false promises of security. Given his short temper, I thought he was about to blame me, but to my surprise, he didn't.

I made no such promises. Ridiculous!

It was like we were old buddies who had gone through hard times together.

I washed my hands in hot water and then tapped out a message: *Bummer. Would it help if I met with the new residents? Let them know about everything we're doing?*

That sounded about as fun as a root canal, but it was part of my job, and Rory had saved me from his evil cousin. I owed him one.

Nah, they're too hysterical to hear reason right now. But ty. Tell Hugo hi for me.

Before Sam had run away from Rory and moved in with me, Rory had named him Hugo. A winking emoji told me all was finally forgiven.

And that was it. Just some nice friendly venting.

I went back to chopping vegetables while Sam patrolled the windows. If anything unfriendly showed up, my cat would be the first to spot it.

My phone calmed down long enough for me to concentrate on my steak guisado. It was my mother's signature dish, and it had taken me years to figure out how to prepare it without the vegetables going mushy. Of course, she could have shared her recipe, but she was odd that way. All her Mexican recipes were stored in her head, and none came with specific amounts. It was all, "a little of this" and "a little of that." No cooking times either.

I sauteed the chopped onion in olive oil and then the green peppers separately, boiling chunks of potato until they were barely done. The green beans went into the steamer.

After dredging the steak in flour, I threw it in a sizzling pan, and when it was just cooked through, I removed the meat, added chicken broth, tomato sauce, and jalapeno, gave it a good stir, put the beef back in, and set the pan to simmer.

When Stu walked in, he was wearing a blue suit, holding a rifle in one hand. He sniffed the air. "It smells amazing in here." He set the rifle down on the kitchen table, wrapped his hands around my waist, and nuzzled my neck.

I leaned into him and wondered why I hadn't started dinner until *after* he got home, which would have left us time for other things. "Hello to you too."

"We could have ordered in," he said into my hair. "You didn't have to cook after the day you've had."

I turned around to face him. He seemed tired. The crinkles around his blue eyes were deep, and so were the smile lines around his mouth. Stu wasn't the type to complain about his business, but running a security company with high-profile, demanding clients wasn't easy.

"Actually, it's why I needed to cook. It helps me relax."

"Lucky me. Most people would just order in pizza." Sam swirled around our ankles, and Stu glanced down with a wince. "He's either welcoming me or figuring out where to take a chunk out of me. I can never tell which."

I gave him a little shove. "We're on lockdown, remember? No unnecessary outdoor activities, and that includes food deliveries. I've already heard from some of the restaurant owners, and they're not happy. Olga's Cantina does a big takeout business, and Olga wants us to provide escorts for her drivers."

Stu grimaced. "I've met Olga. She's tough. What did you say?"

"I said she'd need to take it up with the board." I grinned. "She wasn't too happy with that. The next time we go to Olga's, they might not give us a table."

Stu gave a theatrical sigh, then went to my bedroom to change. We had begun leaving a few items at each other's houses, like toothbrushes and extra clothes.

Stu came back into the kitchen in bare feet, shorts, and a T-shirt, holding a bottle of red wine. "Do we dare?"

An occasional glass was one thing, but splitting a bottle felt risky. That was the thing about our jobs. They both required that we have clear and sober heads in case something happened off-hours. In Chavez Ravine, that meant most nights.

I checked out the label. It was the good stuff. "I think we deserve it."

"Hell, yeah, we do." Stu uncorked the bottle and poured out two glasses while I dished the steak guisado into bowls.

I lit a candle and set it in the center of the table. We might have been in lockdown, but there was no reason we couldn't enjoy a nice, romantic meal at home while we waited for whatever the vampire birds had in store for us next. Maybe we would get lucky, and they would fly over Beverly Hills and discover gnomes were much tastier than we were.

Stu speared a potato dripping in red sauce, chewed, and then rolled his eyes in the back of his head. "If you ever decide to open a restaurant, Olga would be in serious trouble."

That made me laugh. "No, thank you. My first job was at a taqueria, and I quit after six months. The customers were jerks, and the stress was unbelievable. Compared to that, Occult Affairs was a snap."

Stu held up his glass. "Here's to a quiet night."

"To a quiet night." As soon as the words left my lips, I wished I hadn't said them aloud. It felt like I had just jinxed our evening.

The feeling continued to nag at me even when we crawled into bed and switched off the lights.

Chapter 26

One moment, I was dead asleep, and the next, I was wide awake, trying to figure out why my heart was beating so hard. I swung my legs over the side of the bed, listening.

Over Stu's light snoring, I heard something hissing. It had to be Sam.

I padded down the hall and into the sunroom, which was brighter than it should have been at that time of night, but I immediately understood why. The fancy lighting in the backyard was on. It could have been triggered by movement, which meant there was something out there.

Sam was pacing in front of the sliding glass door, eyes locked on something outside. I crept toward the sunroom and peered around a wall to see what was out there.

Golden eyes stared back at me.

My insides went cold. A vampire bird was standing there, taking up a lot of space and pissing off my cat.

"It's okay, Sam," I lied.

Sam stopped pacing long enough to stare up at me, his green eyes blinking. A moment later, he stood on his hindlegs and began chittering and scratching frantically at the glass. The massive bird's eyes never left my face. My thoughts were going in a dozen different directions, pondering my next move.

A noise behind me made me nearly jump out of my skin.

"Stay there, Maddy," Stu whispered. "Keep it busy. I'm going out through the garage."

I wanted to scream, "No!" but I didn't dare. Stu wouldn't have listened anyway. I hadn't told him about the lab analysis on the feather, which was idiotic since he had arrived carrying a rifle and I had said nothing to set the record straight. There was nothing I could do about that now. Stu was already slipping out the door to the garage, probably toting a loaded gun.

There was something else I could do, and that was to keep the monster focused on me.

I flipped it off. Its ugly features got all pinched, and its feathers puffed out. Interesting. It might have been an ancient creature, but it seemed to understand the gesture well enough.

"What's the problem? Haven't met a chingona before?" Probably not. Smart-mouthed women with bad attitudes had probably been the first to be sacrificed back in its day.

Sam hurled himself at the glass again, but the creature's gaze was locked on me, the corner of its nasty mouth curling up in a sneer.

Up close, there was nothing majestic about it. It was just enormous, intimidating, and weird. Hernan had claimed it was immortal, and he seemed to think the thing deserved our respect. But from this distance, I could tell it was just another supernatural pain in the ass demanding too much of my attention.

Through the glass, I heard Stu shout, "Hey."

Vampire Bird gave me a long, hard look and then slowly turned its head to the left. I pictured Stu lurking in the shadows, clad in his blue silk boxers, clutching his rifle.

I half expected the bird to open its jaws and take off toward Stu. Instead, it pivoted and began to hop away from the door.

Sam howled.

A deafening shot boomed through the night. Stu shouted something. Sam clawed my bare legs.

What the hell had just happened?

With shaking hands, I rushed to unlatch the sliding door. I made it outside just in time to watch Vampire Bird take to the air with a powerful thrust of its wings. The downward draft sent a small patio table skidding across the pavers. I ran to Stu and clutched his arm. He was all right. I sagged against him, my muscles weak with relief.

"Damn, those things are big," he gasped.

Sam raced up the hill and vaulted over the fence in pursuit.

I gripped Stu's bare arm. "Did you hit it?"

Stu shook his head. "I did, but I don't know what that thing is made of. The bullet just bounced off."

"My buddy at Occult Affairs ran some labs." I squinted at the night sky. "It's impervious to whatever we shoot at it."

Stu's hand went around my waist. "And you didn't tell me before because?"

"I was cooking? Plus, I didn't expect you to go all Dirty Harry on me."

Stu squeezed my side. "Fair enough." He looked pointedly at the hill. "Should we go look for Sam?"

"He could be anywhere. Besides, I think he can take care of himself." Those were brave words, but truthfully, I wanted to shout Sam's name and jump in my Jeep, like any normal pet owner.

"One of these days," Stu said, "we need to have a conversation about your cat."

"Yeah, I'm not sure how helpful I'll be—"

My phone blasted to life. It was Rafi at the command center.

"Ma'am. We have several reports from around Chavez Ravine. I have dispatched guards, but I just wanted you to know. A resident in Bishop reported one of those birds walking around their second-story deck, tapping at the windows. We have a similar report from Palo Verde." He paused. "And all of Bishop is without power. The cameras showed two of those things flying into a transformer." Another pause. "It appeared intentional, ma'am. And they were able to fly away after that."

Hell. Those things were smart. "I had one show up at my house too. Don't send anyone. It's gone. Did you call out the team with the bows?"

"As you requested, yes."

Not that the arrows would do much good, but Liam, Bailey, Justin, and Ron had the most experience with the things.

"Do me a favor, Rafi, and call the power company. Tell them we have an entity problem and that we need emergency service but not to send a crew until daylight."

"Will they do that, ma'am?" Rafi sounded uncertain.

"Yes. Entity clusters get priority service."

The power company had adopted that policy after several shapeshifting Boggarts emerged during a high school football game. It would have been a simple cleanup, but the power went out, and Occult Affairs had spent the next several hours trying to manage the chaos while the entities lurched among the crowd in the dark.

"There's one more thing," Rafi said. "Two, actually."

My heart sank. "Oh?"

"The resident in Bishop who called is the president of the board. Cora Bernal. And the homeowner that called in from Palo Verde is Charles Perez. Also on the board."

I scraped a hand through my hair. First the goats dumped on their porches, and now this. Obviously, it wasn't a coincidence. But how would those ugly things know Cora and Charlie were on the board, and why would they care? I thought back to the anti-HOA graffiti. Were the birds and the vandalism connected? It seemed like they were, but why would ancient creatures from

Mexico take an interest in a gated community's homeowners association?

Because they were being directed was the obvious answer. But by whom?

"All right, Rafi, thanks. I'll give them a call in a bit to check in with them."

Stu sat on the couch, staring at me. Before I could explain what happened, my phone went off once again, the vibrations sending a jolt through my body.

It was Julia.

"Are you okay?"

"I'm fine." Her voice was high and thin. "But we've had some excitement here. You're not going to believe this, but we woke up because something was scratching at the glass door in my bedroom, and when we pulled back the curtains, one of those hideous things was outside. The security lights had come on, so we could see it perfectly. It was just standing there. That's creepy, yeah? And the next thing we knew, Sam was in the backyard too, and I was yelling at him through the glass to get away, and then that monster turned to look at Sam, and that's when Sam went at him. Straight at him. He launched himself and head butted it and knocked it over! So, I totally freaked out, and I'm screaming, and then Ben grabs the chainsaw, goes outside, and fires it up. But he couldn't do much with it because he didn't want to accidentally hurt Sam. The bird flew off, but Sam's here with me. He's got some cuts. They're not too bad, though, considering. Should we take him to a vet?"

I couldn't imagine subjecting an unsuspecting vet to an agitated Sam. "No. We'll be right over."

Any normal person would realize that, amid a vampire bird attack, a better idea would be to wait until morning. But since I had become a certified crazy cat lady, all I could think about was rewarding Sam's bravery with salmon delite, so off we went, helmets on our heads.

Twenty minutes later, we were back home. I had used a thick towel to carry him, and when I unwrapped the squirming bundle on my workbench, there was blood on the towel.

"Poor guy," Stu said over my shoulder.

Sam licked his left hind leg, which had been sliced by a talon. There were red, matted spots on his back.

"Are you sure you don't want to take him to a vet?" Stu paced behind me. "It looks pretty bad."

I shook my head. "I think I can make something that will work better and faster. Can you take my phone so I can concentrate? Go ahead and answer it if anyone calls."

Stu kissed my shoulder. "Of course. I'll let you know if there are any emergencies. Otherwise, good luck."

He padded out of the room. A few moments later, he returned with a bottle of chilled sparkling water for me and a fresh bowl of water for Sam. The wounded furball gulped it down thirstily. I took that as a good sign.

I gingerly parted Sam's red fur, searching for more cuts. By the time I was done with my inspection, I had counted eight, the one on his leg being the worst.

I grabbed clean rags from a shelf, dampened them in the kitchen sink, and began cleaning his wounds. Other than a few miserable meows, Sam didn't protest. I ground herbs in a metate, then scraped them into a bowl. The salve would need a binding agent.

"Don't move," I told Sam sternly. "I'll be right back."

I could have sworn he nodded. In the kitchen, I heated beeswax and olive oil in a pan until it was just the right consistency—thick but spreadable—then added the ground herbs to the mixture, saying a few words under my breath.

While I waited for the salve to cool, I massaged Sam's head. His eyes closed, and he began to purr. "Sam, I know you are gnome boss, but those birds aren't gnomes. They're dangerous. Really, really dangerous. You could have been killed."

Sam's green eyes flicked open.

"Don't look at me like that. I'm serious. Hernan says they're immortal. Attacking could get you killed, and then what will become of me? I'll be a sad, former cat lady, that's what."

Sam rubbed his large head against my hand.

I got to work applying the salve to his wounds. When I was done, Sam was limp and relaxed. I carried him into the bedroom and crawled into bed next to a sleepy Stu, who mumbled, "The command center called. No sign of the birds. Everything's fine. How's Sam?"

"Recovering," I said, exhausted.

Sam nestled into the backs of my knees. All three of us immediately fell asleep.

I began to have one of those dreams, the kind where I knew I was dreaming and I could wake myself up if I wanted to, but I didn't because I dreamed Trini Duran's notebooks had come to life. But instead of Trini and her crew facing off against the terrifying monsters she called "jumpers," it was me leading a ragtag team through the gully heading to Phantom's Pass. Except it wasn't my team, it was Trini's, the tough guys from the Chavez Ravine of old. Ripper and Junie were at my side, carrying medieval-looking chains with spiked balls at the end. Other men were behind us, moving with the menace and grace of panthers, scanning the landscape for threats.

The air was thick with tension while we approached a clearing where the vampire birds flocked together, waiting, their golden eyes glinting in the darkness. Ripper and Junie rushed forward, swinging their weapons. Other men lunged past me, brandishing machetes, knives, and clubs. A vampire bird went down and stayed down, and then another.

Trini's gang was once again doing battle to save Chavez Ravine.

And then I woke up, fully alert, heart pounding.

The sun was coming up. Sam was still asleep, but Stu was moving noisily around in the kitchen.

When I passed the sunroom, a light caught my eye. It was Little Lencha, the clay figurine glowing a bright yellow. My heart did a little dance of joy. She hadn't done that in a long time, and I realized how much I had missed her.

"Que pasa, tia?" I said.

The light gave a jaunty pulse in response. An old, yellowed piece of scrap paper lay next to the statuette. Names were scrawled in a familiar hand. Lencha's.

Ripper
Junie
Pete
Ruben
Chito
Lalo
Cowboy
Richard

I only recognized two from Trini's journals: Ripper and Junie. She might have mentioned more, but the journals had burned in the fire, so I would never know.

The other nicknames had to have been those of the men who fought alongside Ripper and Junie. But why had Lencha written them down? All the men were long dead.

Dead. Dead fighters who had battled the monsters of Chavez Ravine. Dead fighters with valuable experience. Men who couldn't be killed because they were already dead. Men perfect to help me "unmake" immortal creatures.

The implication took my breath away. Lencha had written down those names because she knew I would need them.

But could she mean…

I was cold all over and whispered, "Do you want me to raise these men from the dead?"

The figurine turned bright green. And then it went dark.

Chapter 27

How the hell was I supposed to resurrect a bunch of dead guys? I didn't even know their real names. Or where they were buried. Or how to bring them back to life.

I needed to take things one at a time. First, find out their real names.

Luckily, I knew exactly who to ask for help. Hernan Frias, the unofficial historian of Chavez Ravine, who had access to all sorts of records.

I called Ron Mendez and asked him to swing by Hernan's house and drive him to the community center in Palo Verde, where I would meet him. Then I messaged Hernan and told him I needed his help. I figured the old egomaniac would be flattered.

I was wrong.

But your mother made chilaquiles!

My mother was certainly spoiling him.

Tell her to stick them in the oven. This is an EMERGENCY. What in tarnation is going on?

Hernan was the only one I knew who used words like that.

When I see you, I'll explain

Which took a long time after we met in the library because Hernan kept interrupting. I handed him the scrap of paper with the names and explained what Lencha was telling me to do.

"You don't know how to do something like that!" Hernan sputtered. "You're not a necromancer!"

We were alone in the historical records room. I sat in a chair and folded my hands on the table.

"You're right. I'm not. But I am a bruja, and since Lencha left me a list of dead fighters, she apparently thinks I have enough skill to do the job." I sounded confident, but inside, my stomach was quivering like it was made of jelly.

Hernan paced in front of the table. "You don't know that's what she meant."

"What else could she have meant?"

He threw up his hands. "I don't know! I just can't believe it. Revenants are serious business, Madeline. Okay. What if you somehow manage to do this? To reanimate the dead? What if you lose control of them? What if they don't want to do what you want them to do? What if they won't go back in the ground when all is said and done? Have you thought about any of these things?"

"What's a revenant?"

I got exactly the reaction I was hoping for.

Hernan exploded. "Madre mía de Dios, you don't even know what a revenant is, and you're about to bring dead men up from their graves. Lord help us!"

I smirked. "Come on. I know what a revenant is. I've watched movies about them, and there's this really good French series about—"

Hernan stopped pacing and pounded a fist against the table. "Stop! This is no joking matter, Madeline. When we speak of the dead, we speak of them con respecto. Especially the hombres you're talking about." He shuddered.

I sat up straighter. "You've heard of them?"

"Of course, I've heard of them." Hernan sniffed. "Ripper was famous in Chavez Ravine. He was friends with Lencha and a woman named Bertita. She had a big house in Palo Verde, and everyone used to gather there. Ripper spent some time in jail for petty offences, but he was mostly a good man. I say mostly because he ran a crew that defended Mexicans when they started getting pushed around and hassled in Los Angeles. That used to happen a lot back then. If someone got beat up bad enough, Ripper would go after whoever did it. Eventually, Ripper ended up at Folsom State Prison. He didn't last long. Some guys thought he belonged to a rival gang and killed him."

I thought for a moment. "Junie died fighting to save Chavez Ravine from the monsters the Irish sorcerer conjured up, right?"

Hernan shot me a dark look. "You know that story?"

"I would know more if you hadn't set Trini Duran's journals on fire."

A pained expression crossed Hernan's craggy face. "I regret that. Sincerely and truly."

Amazingly, I believed him. And in a weird way, I could understand why he had done it. He had long resented the Bantacortes for their reputation as the go-to brujas in the tight-knit community. Then I showed up, the granddaughter of Liliana and the great-niece of Lencha, the most famous bruja of them all, and he had completely lost it. For a while, he had been determined to get rid of me any way he could. But all of that felt like it had happened a long time before.

I tapped the sheet of paper. "So, do you know where these men are buried?"

"It shouldn't be too difficult to figure it out. In the sixties, someone started an oral history project, collecting stories from the people who nearly got evicted. It's very thorough." Hernan crossed the room to a built-in bookcase and started poking through the dusty stacks of books.

After a few minutes, he snatched a notebook from the shelf and waved it over his head.

"Here it is!" Hernan sat across from me at an old wooden table and flipped through the pages. "We're in luck. The fellow who collected these stories wrote their full names besides their nicknames. Slide that paper over, will you?"

I did as I was told, resisting the urge to come around the desk and hover over his shoulder.

Hernan retrieved a pair of black-framed reading glasses from the pocket of his pressed white shirt and started reading. "All right. Here we go. Are you ready to take notes?"

I snatched up my phone and tapped on the Notes icon. "Ready."

Hernan shook his head. "I don't know how you can use that thing for something so important." He cleared his throat. "There's only one Chito on the list, and his name is Manuel Vargas." He glanced at the paper, then flipped through the pages of the battered notebook. "There are two Lalos, but it looks like one died in childhood, so it's the other one we're interested in. And here it is. Lalo is Eladio Flores."

Within a few minutes, we had a complete list of first and last names. Hernan sat back in his chair, looking pleased with himself.

"Well done, señor. Now, how do we find out where they're buried?" I asked.

Hernan clasped his chin. "As it happens, I have access to a genealogy website that has cemetery records." He shoved his chair back and, with a grunt, used the armrests to push himself into a standing position. Hernan rubbed his lower back. "Your mother says I need to be more active. Maybe she's right."

Hernan logged onto a computer terminal on the counter, then began tapping away. After a moment, he waved me over.

"Come and read me those names. It'll go faster that way."

Less than ten minutes later, he sat back in his chair and crossed his arms across his chest. "How about that. They're all buried at Evergreen Cemetery."

"I've heard of it, but I've never been there. Where is it?"

Hernan rolled his eyes. "You've never been there? It's the oldest and largest cemetery in Los Angeles. Many of the early white settlers of Los Angeles are buried there, but there's also lots of Japanese, Mexicans, and Armenians. There's even a fascinating section called Showmen's Rest, where circus performers and carnival workers are buried. Your mother never took you as a child?" Hernan made it sound like an amusement park.

I shook my head. "No. My grandmother Liliana was buried at Calvary Cemetery."

Hernan frowned. "But not Lencha. She was buried next to Bertita at Evergreen. They were best friends, you know."

Once again, I wanted to know more about Lencha's untimely death. One of these days, I would. But at the moment, I had other things to worry about.

Like how, exactly, was I going to reanimate the corpses of fighters who had been dead for decades?

Chapter 28

Evergreen Cemetery was less than five miles from Chavez Ravine. There was plenty of time for me to do some reconnaissance while it was still daylight.

I hadn't yet told Stu what I had in mind, and I was afraid he would try to talk me out of it. He was the one who had figured out my magic might not work outside Chavez Ravine, so it only made sense he would worry things might not go well at Evergreen. Hell, I was worried things might not go well.

And if my magic *did* work? While he had been incredibly supportive of my brujería, I wasn't sure he could handle my raising the dead to fight vampire birds. That might have been pushing it.

Besides, there was a good chance my crazy plan wouldn't work, and then, for the rest of our relationship, Stu would be able to say, "Remember that time when you tried to resurrect some dead guys?"

No, I didn't see anything good coming out of a conversation with my boyfriend. At least, not yet.

However, Hernan had gone back home and told my mother. Of course, she called and had plenty to say.

"Oh, Madeline, why must you always take things too far? Did you think through all your options? Did you consult with me? Did you do everything in your power to get rid of those awful birds? Of course not. As usual, you're taking a shortcut."

"A shortcut? You think resuscitating dead people is easy? I don't recall you ever trying it."

"Don't be rude, Madeline. You know what I'm saying. What you're doing should be considered a last resort. I can only imagine what your grandmother Liliana would say. She'd say you're bringing disgrace to the Bantacorte name and putting the family legacy at risk."

When she went on rants like that, it was hard not to tune her out. "Mmm, it's a risky plan," I mumbled.

"Pendejadas is what it is," my mother said, then hung up.

"Bye, Mom. Nice chat." I returned my phone to my pocket.

After dressing in comfortable shoes suitable for staking out a cemetery, I checked on Sam, who was curled up on his favorite ottoman in the living room.

All the blinds and curtains in the house were closed, just in case the creatures decided to pull their Peeping Birds routine again.

I typed out a message to residents, explaining the lockdown would continue for the next twenty-four hours, at which time the head of security—me—and the HOA board would reevaluate the situation.

The lockdown was becoming very unpopular, and I could understand why. The people of Chavez Ravine were used to being outside, enjoying the parks and running paths, dining on patios, and lounging in their beautifully landscaped yards. I needed to restore order, to get people back to their routines as quickly as possible, and the shortest path to doing that ran through Evergreen Cemetery.

Sam's wounds were healing nicely, but I still reapplied the salve to the worst of the cuts. He didn't even stir.

Before heading out the door, I grabbed some Smoke Bomb pouches from a box stashed in my closet and carried them into

182

the garage, where I had left the Jeep. For unknown reasons, entities had never appeared in cemeteries, but the way things had been going, I wasn't going to take the risk.

In less than twenty minutes, I was driving past the stone pillars on Evergreen Avenue and into the cemetery. Hernan had drawn a simple map marking Ripper's grave. He and the others had been buried in the Mexican section at the southeastern end of the property.

If I hadn't known about its rich history, I would never have guessed there were so many important people buried there. The hard, dry ground had patches of crabgrass. Tombstones tilted drunkenly in various states of disrepair. Willow trees appeared starved for water and provided scant shade.

In the distance, people walked and jogged along a rubberized pathway around the perimeter of the cemetery.

One day, I would have to come back and find the spot the circus performers were buried in.

I parked near the area where Hernan had assured me I would find Ripper and his buddies.

The heat of the afternoon was unrelenting. The air was still and heavy, with the musty scent of old earth. Dry grass crunched under my boots. I made my way through the rows of gravestones toward the Mexican section, where pinwheels, flags, and a mix of faded plastic and wilting fresh flowers beckoned.

My search was complicated by crabgrass growing over the stones. I pushed it aside with my shoe so I could read the names. Finally, I found the first one: "Ripper Cuevas." The letters were barely visible, nearly erased by time and neglect. He had gone to his grave with only his nickname.

Despite the heat, I shuddered.

Within ten minutes, I had found the others too, including Ruben "Cowboy" Rodriguez, Julian "Junie" Lopez, and Eladio "Lalo" Baca.

I sat cross-legged on the scratchy grass and looked around. About fifty yards away lay the jogging path and a large gap in the chain link fence, like a car had driven through it. That was handy. Easy access for my late-night activities.

I turned my attention back to the gravestones. Ripper had died at the age of forty-nine. Junie had been only twenty-three when he was killed fighting monsters alongside Trini Duran in Chavez Ravine. The other six had died between the ages of thirty-five and nearly seventy. I wondered if they did return, what age would they be?

Time seemed to stop while I sat there. Traffic hummed in the distance, but otherwise, it was quiet and strangely peaceful.

I didn't know how I was going to lure these poor men from their graves. It felt like I should have been bothered by that, but I had the strong sense that something would come to me. It had to.

There was one thing I could do to prepare the way. Hernan had said the dead deserved our respect, so I could start by cleaning their gravestones. I got back in my Jeep and drove to a hardware store, where I picked up a bucket, a small container of soap, some bottles of water, and grass shears. At a florist shop, I used my company credit card to pay for eight bunches of red carnations.

Back at the cemetery, I spent the next hour trimming the grass from the gravestones and carefully washing them with soapy water. I dropped the carnations into the in-ground vases, added water, then stood back to survey my work. It seemed like I should say something, like a prayer of some sort.

I bent my head and said the only prayer that was appropriate for a gravesite. My mother had taught it to me when my grandmother Liliana died.

Grant them eternal rest…

I had spoken just a few words when the irony struck me with the force of a bat hitting a piñata. In a few hours, I would be back to interrupt their peaceful slumber.

I only hoped they would forgive me.

Chapter 29

On the drive home, I stopped at a Mexican market in Boyle Heights famous for its fresh roasted chicken. I wasn't in the mood to cook, for once, but I needed protein to fuel me up for the night. After dropping my groceries at home, I checked on Sam—still sleeping on the ottoman—and headed for the command center.

On the way, Stu called to say he needed to help his brother, who was recovering from surgery, so he would spend the night there.

"But I'm not crazy about the idea of leaving you alone, with everything going on," he said.

He would have been even less crazy about it if he had known what I was up to.

"I'll be fine."

Brandon was on duty and reported a crew had fixed the transformer in Bishop. But they had demanded protection services, so he had dispatched Bailey and Liam, who stood around with their bows. Of course, it was more for show than anything else. The team knew my magic-boosted arrows had only scared the vampire birds off. But it was better than nothing.

Brandon stared at a camera feed showing a nearly empty La Loma Plaza. "Is there a plan for tonight?" He shifted in his chair.

Yes, there was, but I wasn't ready to share it. Yet. There was a decent chance my magic wouldn't work outside Chavez Ravine, what Stu would have referred to as an operational weakness.

"I'm putting the entire team on standby overnight. Just in case. I want someone stationed outside the new housing development. The new owners are nervous, and so is Rory Tuck. I want them all to see we're paying special attention since they've already had a problem."

"Sounds good." Brandon took a swig of water from a canteen flecked with muted forest colors. His passion for camo knew no bounds.

At seven o'clock, nerves had killed my appetite, but I shredded some chicken, threw it in a salad, and forced it down. Sam was awake and prowling around, so I mixed bits of chicken into his dry food.

The salve I had whipped up for Sam was doing even better than I had hoped. Even the deep cut on his leg was mending fast. He was nearly back to his noisy, judgy self.

After brewing a pot of coffee, I took my mug into the sunroom. I stared at the workbench, wondering if I had anything that could help me raise the dead.

In the garden were ingredients for healing an injured cat and easing the pain of cramps. I could put together pouches to subdue surly gnomes and hungry ghouls. But for raising the dead? Nada. That was a whole new level of magic.

The reality of my situation seemed to grow grimmer with each passing minute. I looked at Little Lencha, hoping one last time she might be able to offer some help. But her clay eyes seemed to be avoiding mine. Had she really meant for me to reanimate the fighters from their graves, or had I misinterpreted her message?

Despite getting the cold shoulder and because I didn't know what else to do, I started talking to her.

"Tia," I began. "I'm not sure what to do. I thought El Cucuy was bad, but these things? They're not only scary; they're a complete mystery. Not even Hernan Frias knows much about them. There are five of them. Five! Weapons don't hurt them, and my magic only slows them down. Hernan seems to think only the dead can help me 'unmake' them, whatever that means, and I'm just reminding you that you seemed to agree because you left me a list of names of guys you knew back in the day. And I know I'm still very new to all this, but I think I've done a pretty good job learning the craft. I mean, El Cucuy! But like any serious student, I need the occasional help of a mentor. So, could you at least point me in the right direction? Is that too much to ask? Because while I hardly ever agree with Hernan Frias, he's right. I don't know diddly about necromancy."

I was breathless when I finished. That had been a long speech to give to an inanimate object.

I got no reaction from Little Lencha. Sam jumped up on the workbench and began licking the wound on his leg.

I leaned over and pushed his paw away. "Dude, knock that off. Or I'll get one of those cone things, and I don't think you'd like that."

Sam's head snapped up, his green eyes widening.

"I am totally, one hundred percent serious. You keep that little piece of sandpaper you call a tongue away from the boo-boos."

Sam scooted a little closer to Lencha, as if expecting her to protect him.

"I wouldn't count on her if I were you."

The alarm on my phone went off, and my heart nearly stopped. It was my reminder. Time to head to the cemetery and hope inspiration would strike.

My throat felt like it was closing. I drained the last of my coffee, stood up, and leaned over until I was eye level with Little

Lencha. "All right, if you're not going to tell me how to do this, then you're coming with me."

I snatched up Little Lencha and strode toward the door to the garage.

Sam raced ahead of me and stopped next to the Jeep. His ears were bent forward, and his tail was flicking from side to side. I sighed. If I didn't let him tag along, he would probably find a way to break out of the house and follow me anyway. Also, it was entirely possible I would need his help. Plus, if things went sideways, he would keep his mouth shut.

The area around Evergreen Cemetery looked entirely different at night, and I had to circle the cemetery twice before I found the gap in the fence. With Little Lencha in one hand and a flashlight in the other, we crossed the uneven ground toward the freshly cleaned graves. The full moon cast an eerie light over the cemetery, illuminating the crumbling tombstones. The wind had picked up too.

Sam trotted beside me, his tail held high, as if he sensed the gravity of our mission.

When we reached Ripper's grave, a chill ran down my spine.

What the hell was I doing?

At that moment, I wanted nothing more than to go home, pour myself a glass of wine, get in my jammies, and watch a British mystery on TV.

The silence of the night was broken only by the distant sounds of traffic and the rustling of the dry willow leaves.

I gently set Little Lencha down on the grave marker. The clay figure stood out against the dark gray of the stone. Sam sat nearby, watching intently, while I took a deep breath and closed my eyes, picturing the names on the yellowed piece of paper my great-aunt had given me. She had done it for a reason. I needed to trust her. Trust myself.

"Ripper Cuevas, Junie Lopez, Pete Chavira, Ruben Baca, Lalo Flores, Chito Vargas, Cowboy Sifuentes, Richard Figueroa," I began. "Please forgive me, but I call upon you to help Chavez Ravine in its time of need. A great, immortal evil is threatening our people, our homes, our way of life."

Little Lencha began to glow purple. My skin prickled all over. Blood whooshed in my ears.

I repeated their names and then said them again, louder still. Sam howled and began to scratch frantically at the crabgrass. There was no one around to hear, so I shouted their names. The figurine seemed to pulse with energy, its glow intensifying with each repetition. A gust of wind blew my hair and raised a twisting column of dirt and twigs, spiraling upward.

Heat was coming from the glowing statuette.

When I called out the names of the street fighters once more, the ground beneath me began to thrum. Little Lencha's glow expanded, illuminating the tilting tombstones around us. I held my breath, heart thudding, while Ripper's gravestone loosened from the earth and lifted into the air.

Sam leapt away. I grabbed the figurine before it could fall over, stumbling backward and landing on my backside, with Little Lencha clutched to my chest.

Around us, the ground heaved and buckled. A heavy mist descended, making it impossible to see anything beyond my boots.

A few moments later, someone coughed, and a man's hoarse voice came through the fog.

"Who we fighting?"

Chapter 30

When the mist cleared, eight men stood before me. They looked like they had just walked out of a picture from the library at the community center.

Slicked-back hair. Baggy, high-waisted trousers. Pointy-collared long-sleeved shirts rolled up to the elbows. A few guys wore white T-shirts. And their clothes were clean.

Amazement and relief washed over me. They didn't look like zombies. And they didn't appear to be ghosts. They seemed like regular, solid people.

Confused, solid people. A bit like newly emerged entities. Except for one guy with a pencil mustache who stared at me expectantly.

Possibly because I was still sitting on my butt in the dirt, clutching a clay statuette.

I scrambled to my feet and took a deep breath. "Are you Ripper Cuevas?"

"That's me. Who are you? What in the pinche hell is happening?"

A distant meow reached me from somewhere off to my left. Sam must have been spooked, but he would come back soon enough.

I cleared my throat. "My name is Maddy Madrigal. I think you knew my great aunt, Lencha Bantacorte. This is all a little hard to explain, but I'm a bruja too." I straightened a little when I heard myself saying those words aloud. "You've all

191

been…deceased…for a long time, but Lencha tells me you and your friends can help me with a problem we're having in Chavez Ravine. It's a big one."

I paused to let that sink in. Concern replaced confusion, and the men exchanged looks and muttered among themselves.

Ripper rubbed the side of his face. "So, you brought us back from the dead? Oh man. You must be some bruja mas loca to do something like that."

The men standing behind him laughed. It wasn't a very nice thing to say, and I wasn't sure how I felt about that.

"I prefer chingona, thank you." That got a reaction. I lifted my chin and placed my hands on my hips. "And as you'll see for yourselves soon enough, Chavez Ravine has changed. A lot. And I'm head of security for the community."

"You?" A handsome young man in a white T-shirt, with a scar above his lip, stepped forward and eyed me suspiciously. "What does that mean? You the police or something?"

"I used to be. But now I'm responsible for protecting the people who live in Chavez Ravine. Except, as I mentioned, we're having a problem that I believe only you can help me with. What's your name?"

"Pete Chavira. I live in La Loma. Or I guess I used to live there. I'm a boxer." He jerked his head at Ripper. "Ripper taught me."

The short fellow standing next to him snorted. "You make it sound like you were a pro. You worked at the brickyard, tonto."

Pete bristled. "Hey, Chito. I fought La Luz Mala, remember?"

The men laughed again. "You mean, the bad light burned off half your face," another said. "Lencha had to make something special to fix you up."

Ripper narrowed his eyes and pointed at my hand. "What's that? That's not Santa Muerte, is it?"

I had forgotten I was still clutching Little Lencha. "No. It's a sculpture of my great-aunt. A friend made it for me."

Ripper held out a hand. For a guy with a name like that, he wasn't as intimidating as I had expected. Medium height. Sturdy build. I reluctantly placed the figurine into his hand. He held it up to his face and squinted at it.

"Shine that light over here so I can see it better."

The men gathered around, curious.

"Oh, yeah. This is real good. It looks just like Lencha, don't it?"

The men nodded.

Ripper said, "You never wanted to get on her bad side."

"She looked mean, but she was pretty nice when you got to know her," Pete said. "That stuff she put on my face after the bad light saved me from having a bunch of scars."

"And going blind," Ripper added. "La Luz got one of your eyes too."

It all felt so normal, just a bunch of guys standing around, reminiscing. I could have almost forgotten they were revenants I had summoned—with Lencha's help—and we needed to get to work.

When I held out my hand, Ripper gently placed Little Lencha in my palm.

"What we're dealing with at Chavez Ravine, I'm afraid, isn't anything you've seen before. They're giant birds—"

"Like the ones that flew into Bishop?" Pete's voice went up an octave.

I shook my head. "I don't think so. They're bloodsuckers. Vampires, actually, and they're ancient. From the days of the

Mayans. They started out killing some goats, but they're going after humans now."

"They just, what? Showed up one day? I don't think so." Ripper shook his head. "Someone sent them. Like that damn fool on the city council, with those jumpers and the rest of those freaks."

Ripper might have been a revenant, but he was quick, and so were the others, by the way their heads were bobbing up and down in agreement.

"You're right. Someone must have summoned them, but I don't know who yet." I cleared my throat. "And here's why I'm here, talking to you now. Those things are immortal. That means I can't kill them with guns or arrows or magic. I need someone like you to take them down."

Ripper balled his hands into fists. "Someone like us? What's that supposed to mean?"

In their time, these men had faced some pretty awful treatment. Those wounds were still fresh for them, so I understood why they were sensitive. I needed to choose my words carefully.

"I summoned you because, well, you're experienced monster fighters. There's nobody alive who has your kind of experience. And there's something else. Nobody alive can kill these things, but you can. Because you're not alive. Do you understand what I'm saying?"

Ripper turned to look at his friends. A silent conversation passed between them. He thumped his chest.

"We understand enough. Let's go find these pinche vampires, then."

Easier said than done. I had been so worried about how I would revive these fighters that I hadn't considered how I would get them up to Chavez Ravine if I succeeded.

Now I needed help, and there was only one person on my team who would understand what was going on. And who would hopefully keep his mouth shut. Ron Mendez.

I held up a hand while I dug into a pocket for my phone. "Hold on a sec," I said to the group.

Ron picked up immediately. "What's up, boss?"

"I need you to bring the Suburban and meet me as soon as you can." I rattled off the address.

A short silence followed. "Why are you over there? Isn't that near Evergreen Cemetery?"

"Yeah. I'll explain when you get here. But hurry, okay?"

"Of course."

When we hung up, eight pairs of eyes stared at me. Oh, of course.

"Phones are a little different than they were back in your day. A lot of things are going to be different. You should be ready for that." I shoved Little Lencha into the deep side pocket of my trench coat. "I have a ride coming. Why don't we wait near the street until he gets here?"

Ripper shrugged. "You're La Jefa. Whatever you say."

That was more like it. *Woman boss* was much better than *crazy witch lady*.

There was still no sign of Sam. Funny, vampire birds with teeth six times larger than he was didn't scare him, but revenants made him nervous.

I didn't have any treat bags in the car I could tempt him out with, so I gave a low whistle. "Hey, Sam. Come on out. It's fine."

The men looked around, confused. "Is Sam your novio?" Ripper asked.

Before I could answer, Sam emerged from behind a nearby tombstone and strutted toward me, ignoring the men staring at him as if they had never seen a cat.

"That's Sam?" Pete asked. "Is he yours? What do you feed that thing?"

The young man with hooded, sleepy eyes hurried to walk next to me and stuck out a hand. "My name is Junie. What kind of cat is it?"

Junie's hand was dry and very, very cold. "He's a Bengal. It's a large breed."

"I always wanted a cat," Junie said wistfully. "I would have liked to have one of those. He looks like a tiger."

Sam rubbed his head against Junie's calf. Oh, brother. Five minutes ago, he was hiding, but there he was, getting cozy with a dead guy.

"Weirdo."

Junie clucked his tongue. "Ai, you shouldn't call him that. Animals are very sensitive."

It was going to be a very interesting night.

We had almost reached the gap in the fence. I figured it wasn't too smart to stand on a dark street with a bunch of tough-looking guys, even if they were dead, so I held up a hand.

"Let's wait here."

We stopped under a scraggly tree.

Ripper stood next to me. "So, you can talk on the little telephone outside? There's no wire."

I decided to keep things as simple as possible. "Yeah. Phones are a lot smaller...and portable."

Pete pointed at a passing car. "Looks like cars got smaller too. And uglier. I like that red one, though." He jerked his chin toward my Jeep parked at the curb, and I felt a flutter of pride.

"That's mine. It's old but gets me everywhere I need to go."

"If it needs work, let me know," Junie said. "I'm good at fixing cars."

Ripper reached behind me and slapped Junie on the back. "Hey, we're not here to fix cars. We're here to—"

He was interrupted by Pete shouting. Movement across the street caught my eye. The other men started shouting too.

Ripper grabbed my arm. He had a very strong grip. "What the hell is that?"

It was an entity eruption in progress. Right on the front lawn of a bungalow across the street. Crap. Occult Affairs would send a team, and if it was a slow night, they could be there soon. Which would mean complications. Too many OA officers knew me, and there was no way I could explain what I was up to.

"Everything is going to be okay," I said hurriedly. "We had some big earthquakes, and ever since, we've had all kinds of entities coming up out of the ground." I glanced across the street. "Like that thing that appears to be...oh hell. It's a banshee. It's going to make a lot of noise, so maybe plug your ears. I'll go take care of it. Don't worry. I used to do this in my old job. Seriously, don't move. Stay right here."

Ripper's grip tightened. "What the hell's an entity?"

"Things that don't belong in our world." I shook him off. "Do not follow me. I'll be right back."

The banshee was trying to climb out of the ground. A porch light came on. An older couple appeared in the window of the bungalow. I grabbed a Smoke Bomb from the Jeep and darted across the street, then gave the homeowners a friendly, reassuring wave.

When I glanced behind me, the men had moved out of the shadows of the cemetery and were standing on the street. I waved my hand at them. "Get back!" I yelled.

They didn't budge. Did being dead affect one's ability to follow directions? I needed to move fast.

The banshee had long red hair and a pale face. She was young but with sunken, desperate eyes. While I ran toward her, her mouth opened wide, and she began to wail.

The banshee was out of the hole, crawling toward me on all fours, her gown stark white against the grass. I slammed down the pouch and gave it a good stomp. Purple mist exploded into the air, and from behind me came the collective gasps of the revenants. The banshee collapsed and went completely still.

The front door of the bungalow opened, and a small bandy-legged man stepped out. "It's lucky you were around. Gracias." He looked past me, his expression shifting to disapproval. "I don't like the looks of those guys. Want me to call the police?"

Oh, hell no. "It's fine. I'm former LAPD, and I know them. They're just curious. That's all."

The man shrugged. "I guess I should call Occult Affairs, even though half the time you call them, it takes forever for them to respond and—"

I interrupted him. "I'll call Occult Affairs so you don't have to."

The man nodded. "If you can, tell them to fill the hole. That's another thing about those people. They leave all the mess for us homeowners to clean up, but that's not right. Not with the taxes we're paying." His eyes shifted again toward the revenants. "Go home. It's too late for a pretty lady like yourself to be out at night. But thank the Lord you were here." He made a sign of the cross and disappeared inside.

I dug my phone out of my trench coat pocket and called the command center. The guy who answered was someone I recognized.

"I just happened to be in Boyle Heights and dealt with that banshee that popped up. She's down, so whenever you can, send a team to collect her. No rush, though."

"Wow, okay," Tim said. "I saw that on the heatmap, but I've got everyone on the West side at Will Rogers Park, trying to round up some freaky lizard that looks like a Komodo dragon. I was just about to call someone in to handle it, but you know how much the chief hates OT, so thanks for the favor."

"No problem. Tell Jo she owes me one."

I gazed at the redheaded banshee on the ground. The purple mist was dissipating around her. Right then, a white Suburban came racing down the street and stopped in front of the bungalow.

The driver's side window rolled down, and Ron stuck his head out. He had a shallow crease on his cheek from his pillow.

He gestured at the banshee. "Is that what you wanted help with?"

I shook my head. "Nope." I pointed at Ripper and the other men, who had stepped off the curb and were staring open-mouthed at the enormous vehicle. "We need a ride back to Chavez Ravine." I dug out my keys and handed them through the window. "You take my Jeep. I'll drive those guys."

Ron's eyes widened. "Who are they?"

He already knew too much, so I let him in on the rest.

"Remember the stories you heard Cora tell about monsters that showed up in Chavez Ravine? Those are the guys who fought them."

I waited for that to sink in. Ron shook his head, frowning.

"They can't be. They'd be dead." He opened and closed his mouth. His eyes bulged. "Oh, tell me you didn't. You like, what? Brought them back to life?"

"I did." With Little Lencha's help, of course. I was pretty sure I was smiling.

Ron crossed himself. "I hope we don't go to hell for this." He got out of the SUV, his eyes darting to the men walking toward us. "Hey, guys." He stepped aside to give them a wide berth and sprinted for my Jeep. "I'll follow you. Where are we going?"

That was a very good question. We needed a private place to talk things through with my new undead recruits. I couldn't very well troop them into the command center or bring them into my home.

"I get shotgun," Ripper said, climbing into the passenger seat.

No one argued with him. The other revenants climbed into the back.

"Let's go to Lencha's house," Ripper said.

I started the Suburban. "I don't think her house exists anymore." I cleared my throat. "Besides, I don't know where it was."

Ripper shifted in his seat to stare at me. "You don't know where your own tia's house was?"

I shook my head. "No." It came out like a croak.

"I can find it." Ripper crossed his arms in front of his chest. "We used to meet outside her place. You know, near the mailboxes."

Ripper was in for a big surprise. The clock on the dashboard read twelve thirty. It was going to be a very long, very weird night.

Chapter 31

My undead passengers stared silently out the windows of the Suburban. When I glanced in the rearview mirror, Junie was holding Sam against his chest. My cat seemed perfectly content to play emotional support animal for the young man who had just emerged from his grave.

I wasn't quite sure how I felt about what I had just done. It didn't exactly seem wrong. I wouldn't have done something so extreme if circumstances hadn't been so dire. But it didn't feel right either.

It was too late for hand-wringing. I had made a choice, and now I needed to make it work. And the faster the better. I forced my shoulders back and continued driving.

When we reached the road leading to La Loma, Ripper leaned forward, both hands on the dashboard. "There's a street now? It used to be a dirt path."

"Yeah, we had to carry groceries and everything up there," Pete said from the backseat. "A lot of people never came out of the neighborhood because it was so hard coming and going."

The middle-aged man at the guard station recognized the vehicle and waved me through. He squinted into the Suburban while we passed.

Even in the darkness, the men gasped and cursed when we crested the hill.

The bright moon, streetlamps, and landscape lighting illuminated the lush gardens, the beautiful, spacious homes, and the meticulously maintained path winding its way up to Phantom's Pass.

"This isn't Loma, is it?" Ripper sounded stunned. "All the open hills are gone."

"It is," I said. "I know. It's a lot to take in."

"What happened to this place?" Junie asked.

I cleared my throat. "Money. People left their homes to their kids just in time for property values to go up and up and up. The schools got better, and people were able to send their kids to college, so they were able to get better jobs. They made more money and bought houses in Chavez Ravine too. Then, the city was very generous to the people they'd evicted and gave special protections to the Latinos."

"How about that," Ripper muttered.

"Look!" Pete cried.

I hit the brakes, my heart racing.

Pete's head and shoulders emerged between the two front seats, gesturing toward a house on our right. For one terrible moment, I was afraid he had spotted a vampire bird, but it was just a massive Spanish-style mansion with a fountain so grand it could have belonged to Las Vegas.

"That one's a bit too much," I said.

"Es muy bonito." Pete sounded close to tears. "I think that used to be my house…and the ones next door too. It must have all got torn down. I just can't believe it."

"I can't believe I'm alive," Junie said.

"You're not," Ripper replied. "We're all on borrowed time here. Isn't that right, Señorita Madrigal?"

I shuddered. Yet another thing I hadn't considered. How would I send them back to the afterlife? Presumably, with Little Lencha's help.

My hands trembled slightly, and I gripped the steering wheel.

"Yes, borrowed time." My voice wobbled. I continued to drive.

Ripper poked my shoulder. "So where do you live?"

I cleared my throat. "La Loma."

"People used to say the girls from Palo Verde were the prettiest," Ripper said. "But the girls from La Loma were all right too."

I didn't know what to say to that.

"Trini Duran was real pretty," Pete said from the backseat. "She was from Palo Verde. She was kind of tough, you know, and she wasn't curvy or anything. But I always liked her."

Ripper snorted. "You didn't have a chance in hell with Trini. And La Jefa here is better looking than Trini. More womanly, you know."

Pete smacked the back of Ripper's seat. "You just think that because La Jefa's older. Trini was my age. Young. Not old, like you."

"Hey!" Ripper and I cried out at the same time. The whole let's-compare-Trini-with-Maddy was getting a little embarrassing. And super inappropriate.

I glanced over at Ripper, who was staring straight ahead. We passed under a streetlamp, and I could make out his profile clearly. Back in my twenties, when I had been in my bad boy phase, he would have been my type.

Had I just thought that about a dead guy? I shuddered. But to be fair, the men didn't appear dead and didn't act it either, so the whole thing was a bit confusing.

"Ripper's just a big flirt," Lalo said. "Don't mind him, Señorita Madrigal. You're not married, are you?"

"No," I said briskly. "I'm not."

"Got any kids?" Ripper asked.

"She just said she's not married!" Lalo protested.

Ripper shrugged. "She can be a widow. Or had kids without a husband. It happens."

"I do not have children." Honesty seemed like the easiest and fastest way to change the subject. "My great-aunt Lencha didn't have children either."

So there.

"Neither did Catalina, the bruja from Palo Verde," Lalo said. "Now, she was a real beauty, wasn't she, guys?"

"She was, she was," the men murmured in the backseat.

"A very wonderful, kind lady." Ripper crossed himself. "It was terrible what happened to her."

Now it was my turn to be surprised. "I never heard about another bruja in Chavez Ravine besides Lencha."

"That's probably because Catalina Montez was killed. By some idiot who thought she was the Night Lady killer and murdered his brother. But he was wrong. Catalina had nothing to do with it."

The conversation was spinning out of control. I had never heard the story about a killer named the Night Lady either. But at the moment, I had more important things to worry about, like figuring out how we were going to unmake the vampire birds.

"Can you drive us to Duran Market in Palo Verde? Trini used to work there with her father. I'd really love to see it. Remember how we used to hang out there, guys?" Pete seemed so wistful a lump rose in my throat.

"Not me," Ruben's voice sounded scratchy. "I used to hang out at Genaro's."

I gripped the steering wheel harder. "Duran's doesn't exist anymore, but we can drive by the new market in Palo Verde. It's pretty fancy." I pointed it out while we crept past it.

Pete gave a low whistle. "That's a market? It looks like an office building. Is the Palo Verde School still around?"

Finally, I was able to deliver some good news. "It is. And so is El Santo Niño Church."

I made a U-turn and headed back toward La Loma. Voices overlapped in the backseat. The revenants gawked while they looked out the windows, and I was reminded they had been friends, brothers in arms, who had banded together in life to help Trini Duran fight an invasion of monsters.

Hands grabbed the back of my headrest and shook it. "That's my old church. Can we go? You know. Say a little prayer? For tonight?"

I was torn. Though I desperately wanted to get on with things, it seemed cruel to deny the revenants a chance to see the strange new Chavez Ravine they found themselves in.

Ripper spoke before I could. "No way, Chito. We cross that threshold and who knows what might happen to us." That shut Chito up.

We had just reached the bottom of a hill when Ripper's hand smacked the dashboard. "Stop!"

With my heart beating wildly, I slammed on the brakes.

Ripper jumped out of the SUV and dashed down a narrow road marked "Dead End." The other guys hopped out too and disappeared after him.

Crap. I had no choice but to park the Suburban and follow.

The street was lined with newer two-story houses that were modest by La Loma's usual standards. The road dipped and ended at a gully.

Ripper and the others stood in front of a wooden fence about halfway down the street, where a wide palm tree stood sentinel.

I was panting when I caught up with them. "What is it?"

"This is it," Ripper said. "This was Lencha's house."

I couldn't seem to catch my breath. "Are you sure?"

Ripper nodded. "Of course, I'm sure. I used to come here all the time."

In the deep pocket of my trench coat, something vibrated. Little Lencha. My fingers closed around her, and she was warm in my hand.

I sighed. Any other time, I would have been excited to find out where my great-tia had lived, but with the vampire birds hanging over my head, it felt like an enormous distraction. Yet I could understand the men were probably hungry for a landmark from their past. They had all known Lencha, and they wanted to see where she had lived, where they had gathered in times of trouble. We could spare another few minutes.

I went over to the fence. It had a sturdy lock with a keypad. I punched in the universal HOA code, and a moment later, I was standing in one of Ben Tomas's landscaping equipment yards. The men pushed past me and walked through the rows of potted palms and flowers.

"The house is gone!"

Feet pounded in the darkness while the men ran toward the back of the property.

"Look!" Ripper shouted. "Her shed's still here."

I couldn't believe it. My great-aunt's shed, where she had cured her neighbors and worked her magic, had managed to survive all these years. I followed the men to the back of the yard, where a small, wooden shack still stood, but barely. Ripper yanked open the door. I stood just behind him, pulled out my flashlight, and flicked it on, illuminating an ancient workbench and a few empty shelves, all covered in grime.

"She was always in here, cooking up something," Ripper said.

Pete gave a sad little laugh. "Remember that stuff she used to make to rub on our throats when we had a cough? It smelled so bad."

"It worked, though," said a tall, skinny young man with a long, narrow face.

Junie followed with Sam, who leapt from his arms and perched on a mound of earth. Sam meowed loudly and pawed the ground.

That got my attention.

I aimed my flashlight at the cat. Sam blinked but didn't budge. The mound was the same reddish-brown shade as the clay in Little Lencha.

Ripper joined us. "I remember that stuff. Lencha swore by that red clay. Once, we were drinking tequila, and she told me that clay was the secret to her magic."

Butterflies beat their wings against the insides of my stomach, and hairs lifted on the back of my neck. I handed the flashlight to Ripper and crouched, pulse racing while my fingers brushed the dirt. A surge of energy shot through me. My skin tingled. The clay beneath my touch felt alive, as though it was pulsing with magic. I closed my eyes, listening to a faint whispering in my ears. It felt as if the land itself was trying to communicate with me in a language all its own.

If the red clay was Lencha's secret ingredient, then it could be mine too.

From somewhere deep in my mind, an idea was squirming to get out. I could almost feel it, getting bigger and bigger, and then, I could understand it.

Lurching to my feet, I pulled out my phone and called Julia. After a few rings, she answered.

"Maddy...you okay?" Her voice was thick with sleep.

"I'm sorry to wake you, Julia, but I need to ask you something very important. Where did you get the clay to make Little Lencha?"

A long silence followed, then she mumbled something to Ben. He must have stayed the night.

"I got it from one of Ben's storage yards in La Loma. It's amazing stuff. Perfect for my pottery. Better than anything I've been able to buy."

No surprise there.

"Ask Ben if the property where you found the clay used to belong to my great-aunt, Lencha Bantacorte."

More mumbling. After a few moments, Ben came on the line.

"Hi, Maddy. Yes, that storage yard used to belong to Lencha. It's one of the reasons no one has been able to build on it. The association owns it, and they've let me use it temporarily, but they're holding it for Lencha's heirs. From what I understand, she didn't leave a will, so they have the HOA lawyer working on getting the property transferred. Cora and Charlie will kill me if they find out I'm telling you this, but it's coming to you, Maddy."

Tears blurred my eyes. "Okay."

I was stunned. By the generosity of the HOA, by the undead street fighter who had brought me to that place, by the knowledge that Little Lencha had been made from the magical earth in her own backyard. This was a new kind of confidence. For the first time in days, I was certain that we—this crazy band of undead men and a chingona security chief—were going to take out the deadly, ancient threat terrorizing my neighbors.

I apologized again for waking them up, stuck the phone back in my pocket, and sniffed. Junie lowered himself onto the ground, sat cross-legged, and pulled Sam onto his lap. Soon, we were all sitting in a circle, the red mound of clay in the middle. I scanned the inky expanse of night sky and the shadowy silhouettes of the trees, searching for any sign of the vampire birds, but there was nothing.

Pete was the first to break the silence. "I was thinking. About your monsters. You know what we could do to take those things down? And I think we can use that thing that almost got me. La Luz Mala."

I turned to look at him. Once again, I wished I still had Trini Duran's journals. The parts I had read hadn't mentioned any "bad light," nor an attack on Pete. "What is La Luz Mala, exactly? And was it here? In Chavez Ravine?"

Pete shoved his hands into his high-waisted trousers. "Yeah. The evil light. It's like a bad omen or something."

"It was worse than that," said the short guy named Chito. "My mother said it was a trapped spirit, and when they went to Bakersfield to pick grapes in the summer, a bunch of families would drive together in a convoy in case any cars broke down, and once, they saw a floating light on a side road at night. It was real dark, and the driver at the front turned to follow it, but the truck ended up in a ditch. My mom swore it was La Luz Mala. It tries to trick travelers so something bad happens to them."

"And it was here?" I repeated.

Pete nodded. "We found it in an old store near Duran's Market. It must have come out of the well with the other monsters. I hit it with a bat, and it burned me good. Maybe it would burn up those birds you keep talking about. Send them back to hell." He shrugged.

Junie groaned. "And how are we supposed to call La Luz Mala? Whistle? Even if we did, how are we supposed to use it against the birds without burning ourselves?"

Ripper clapped Pete on the back so hard he almost toppled forward. "Pete, you're not such a dummy after all. That's a good idea. We've got La Jefa right here. If she could bring *us* back to life, she can call La Luz Mala. And Junie, it can't burn us because we're already dead, remember?"

For a few moments, the men talked among themselves in low tones, and then all eyes turned toward me.

Sam stretched out a paw and flicked red dirt at my face.

I wiped it away with the back of my hand. "I get the point, Sam."

The cat jumped back into Junie's lap. His green eyes blinked innocently.

I took my flashlight from Ripper's hand and swept it around until I found what I was looking for: a spigot and a watering can. After running some water into the can, I sprinkled it on the red clay. When it was just moist, I used both hands to form a ball, then carried it into the shed.

I closed my eyes and imagined the menacing red glow of La Luz Mala. My fingertips tingled, and Little Lencha vibrated in my pocket. When I opened my eyes, the shed was full of a crimson light. The red clay had transformed into a pulsating ball of dark energy. My hands stung, and I quickly pulled them away.

The ball continued to float in the air. I stepped back outside the shed, my eyes never leaving La Luz Mala. To my relief, it moved through the air, following my footsteps as if tethered to me by an invisible thread.

The men gasped, their faces illuminated by the red glow.

Ripper scrambled to his feet. He reached out a hand and gingerly touched La Luz Mala. "It doesn't hurt."

He snatched it up like a ball and flashed a wide grin. Pete sprang to his feet and held out his hands.

"Over here." His voice was filled with anticipation.

La Luz Mala zipped through the air toward Pete, who caught it neatly. The revenants played a lively game of catch, the glowing orb darting between them. Each player handled the radiant ball deftly without feeling its searing heat.

Junie grabbed La Luz Mala from Ruben and held it against a prickly pear cactus. Its skin began to blacken and blister, crackling and steaming where the red orb had touched it.

Junie yelped.

"Keep it down, will you?" I hissed. We have strict rules about noise after ten o'clock."

Junie pulled La Luz away from the cactus.

Ripper clapped his hands together. "Let's go get those birds."

Chapter 32

Undead fighters? Check.

Magic that actually worked? Check.

A deadly floating light ball? Check.

A cat who preferred a revenant to the owner who fed and cared for him? Check.

Five giant vampire birds coming to meet their doom? Not a sign of them.

We had moved to the top of a hill in La Loma and were hiding out in the gully. It provided cover, but the location had its challenges. Namely, making sure the hot molten orb didn't start a fire.

"How long are we supposed to wait around for those things to show up?" Lalo cracked his knuckles.

"As long as it takes," Ripper snapped. "You got someplace better to go?"

"Back to that cheap pine box his cheatin' wife put him in," Ruben said.

"She cheated on him with you, pendejo," Ripper noted.

Lalo shot Ruben the middle finger. "I'm never gonna forgive you, man. We were friends."

"Guys," I said sternly. "Can we please stay focused? For all I know, you all turn to fairy dust when the sun rises, so the clock is ticking."

"Chingona," Ruben muttered.

I was about to respond—not very nicely—when my phone vibrated in my pocket. It was Ron Mendez.

"Are you seeing the birds?" I asked.

"No, boss. But we have a problem. A serious one." Ron's voice was urgent and barely above a whisper.

And why not? Hiding in the dark with a bunch of dead men and a lethal light ball didn't seem like enough trouble already.

"What is it? And can you talk louder? I can hardly hear you."

"No, I can't. I don't want Rafi to hear me. He's just outside, and I'm babysitting the heatmap and feeds."

My knees were beginning to hurt from crouching. I sat down on a flat rock. Still uncomfortable but less distracting. "Why don't you want Rafi to hear you? I'm confused. What's going on?"

Rafi was one of our newer but most reliable staffers, willing to take shifts no one else seemed to want.

"He's up to something," Ron whispered. "He's been…spying on you. I just found out. He's outside, talking on the phone with someone, and he'll be back soon, so I need to hurry. But when I walked in, he was watching the camera feed that's near your house. He closed it real quick so I wouldn't see. So, I got curious. I've been checking to see what feeds he's been accessing, and it looks like he's been trying to track your movements. And not just tonight. He asked me, real casual and everything, if I knew where you had gone and if you had anything planned for tonight to deal with "the threat." That's what he called it. And I lied. I said I had no idea, but I had decided to come in on my own because I couldn't sleep and might as well get some OT."

My thoughts scattered in a dozen different directions. Why was Rafi so curious about my movements? What did I really know about the guy? Only that he had come with good references from the sheriff's department out in the far reaches of Los Angeles

County. Of course, I had ordered a background check on him, like I did with all employees, and it had come back clean. No flags. Stellar credit too.

"Is he back yet?" I asked Ron.

"He's still out there. I can see him through the window. He looks nervous."

That didn't sound like Rafi. He was usually calm and businesslike.

I glanced over at the guys. They had finally stopped arguing and were scanning the sky.

"Do you have any idea who he's talking to?"

"No," Ron said. "But it looks serious. Whatever is going on, he doesn't look too happy."

"I'm going to check something, and if I find anything out, I'll message you."

When we hung up, I pulled up my work portal and logged in, grateful for the fast community Wi-Fi. It took less than thirty seconds to find Rafi Alarcon's personnel file. His address showed he lived in Pomona, which meant he had about a seventy-mile commute. Long, even by Los Angeles's standards. The job paid well, but it wasn't worth that kind of a drive. I didn't know anyone who lived that far out.

No, that wasn't right. I did know one person. Hernan's granddaughter, Valeria Torres.

Something niggled at me. A vague unease. When had I last seen Valeria? At Muertos Café, not long before. Had there been something slightly off about her behavior that day? Maybe she wasn't quite as friendly as the time we had chatted in the hospital cafeteria. It was probably nothing, but still.

"Sorry," I said to the guys. "There's just something I need to check."

Ruben snorted. "We're waiting to fight some monsters, and she's on her baby phone."

I ignored him—he wasn't wrong—and typed in "Valeria Torres bookstore Pomona, California" and got "Bruja & Botanica." For a moment, I thought I had pulled up the wrong listing, but no. It appeared Valeria had left out some key details, like she *was* a bruja and her shop's goal was to "revitalize witchcraft for a new generation."

Alarm bells began ringing. The books in her online store were almost exclusively about witchcraft, spellcraft, and magic with a "c" and a "k." The shop also offered readings and spirit ceremonies.

I remembered Valeria telling me her grandfather had wanted to send her to Mexico to learn brujería, but she had declined, saying she had been determined to follow her dream of owning a bookstore.

Valeria had lied.

I clicked on the "about" section, and all the pieces clicked into place.

There was a picture of Valeria Torres wearing a black dress and heavy brown beads around her neck. Except her name was Valeria Torres Alarcon, and by her side was her husband and business partner, Rafi Alarcon, a retired deputy with the sheriff's department.

Note to self: next time, spend more time researching job applicants *before* I hired them.

I tapped out a message to Ron.

Go to my office. Don't say anything to Rafi. Find out dates and times when Valeria Torres entered CR. She's Hernan's granddaughter. Check all feeds for those time periods.

What am I looking for?

Anything suspicious.

Just how powerful was Valeria? Powerful enough to summon ancient predators from Mexico to terrorize Chavez Ravine? But why would she do that? And what was Rafi's role?

A burst of movement made me look up from my phone. It was Sam, his tail all fluffed up, staring toward the ridgeline separating La Loma from Elysian Park. Then he was off like a shot, darting up the steep side of the gully. Junie called after him, then scrambled up the slope.

"It's just a cat," Ruben said.

"Oh, no, it's not." I stepped over Ruben.

Sam had plopped himself down in the middle of the street. The moon cast an eerie glow on the deserted pavement. Junie had almost caught up to him. That guy was fast.

"Hey, gatito, come back," Junie called.

Sam, being Sam, did the opposite. He darted further down the road, and Junie gave chase, running at superhuman speed. Revenant speed.

Panic bubbled up in my chest, and I cursed myself for not leaving Sam at home. I couldn't trust him around birds of any kind, even killer birds that dwarfed him. My phone rang, but I ignored it. A shadow appeared in my peripheral vision, and I turned. A vampire bird was swooping toward Sam, talons extended.

A scream rose in my throat. Panic seized me while I watched helplessly. And then I remembered I *wasn't* helpless. I had my magic and Little Lencha in my pocket. Before I could act, Junie leapt forward with lightning speed, snatching up Sam. The bird's talons missed their mark, but just barely.

Sam wasn't the least bit appreciative Junie had just saved his ornery little life. He was struggling wildly to free himself from

Junie's grasp. The vampire bird turned around and headed straight for them.

Something flew over my head. For one terrible moment, I thought it was another bird, but there was no familiar rush of air, just a trail of heat. A blur of movement to my right. I spun around. Ripper and the other revenants were pounding toward me.

My phone chimed. Then chimed again.

La Luz Mala broadsided the vampire bird, sending it flying toward a tree. The red orb circled back, but the monster skimmed the tree's top branches, tumbled to the ground, and burst into flames.

By the time we reached it, Ripper was holding La Luz Mala, and the creature was a pile of ash.

"It worked!" Ripper and Pete said at the same time.

To our left, another enormous creature moved quickly over the trees. Then a second and third emerged, forming a solid line of terror.

Ruben whirled around, spotted the approaching monsters, and shouted, "Throw it, Ripper!"

Ripper took a step back and, in a fluid, graceful movement, snapped his wrist and sent La Luz flying. The red orb surged through the air, pulsing brightly, striking the birds like a bowling ball. It knocked them in different directions in a chaotic spiral of feathers and agonized screeches. They plummeted to the ground in a flurry of fire and smoke.

"Take that, you pinche pajaros!" Pete yelled.

The revenants whooped and cheered. Lights flicked on inside several nearby homes.

Great. People would call the security number, and Rafi would answer. Then his next call would have been to his wife. Valeria would probably hop on her broom and be here in no time. To do what, I had no idea.

Sam howled. Junie still had a death grip on my cat, and I could tell he was pissed off at being kept from the action. Not far away, tires screeched.

"Jefa, look out!" Ripper yelled.

I turned just in time. A dark Mercedes was speeding toward me.

I froze. *It's going to hit me. It's going to kill me.*

My right arm flew up as if to ward off the speeding sedan, but my hand was as bright red as La Luz Mala and was alarmingly hot. Red sparks, so bright my eyes closed, flew from my fingers. When I opened my eyes, the Mercedes was hurtling down the gully. A sickening crunch echoed through the night when metal met wood and glass shattered.

I felt lightheaded and dizzy. My magic had worked. It had saved my life but might have killed the driver of the Mercedes. My hand was still raised in the air, but the color had returned to normal. My fingers itched. Ripper and his men rushed toward the smashed car.

Junie finally released Sam, who was headed straight at me, but as I bent to scoop him up, he dodged me and shot past.

"Dammit, Sam!"

The scolding died on my lips when I noticed what was coming for us both—the largest of the vampire birds flying low down the middle of the street, like an airplane coming in for a landing, streetlamps lighting its way. Its face was contorted in rage, jaws opening hideously wide, revealing needle-like teeth that would suck me dry given the chance.

"Ripper!" I shouted.

But the men were already down in the gully with the Mercedes. La Luz Mala was momentarily forgotten down the street, hovering in the air, with no one around to throw it where it needed to go. But if I could summon it, I could direct it too, couldn't I?

I spun around, pointed at the pulsating orb, and imagined a cord tethering me to it. Then I whipped it toward the men in the gully.

"Ripper! Catch it!" I could make out the surprised expression on his face when the deadly orb flew toward him. Then understanding when he registered the giant bird bearing down on me.

"I got you, Jefa!" Ripper caught the light in one hand, then spun around like a discus thrower and hurled it at the monster just yards away from me.

La Luz Mala flew toward its target, connected with a flash of white, and exploded in a burst of orange flames. The heat hit my face, and I closed my eyes before ashes and dust covered me.

When I opened them, I was surrounded by piles of burning feathers. On the pavement at my feet was a ball of red clay.

I took several deep, calming breaths. My muscles were still tensed for action I hoped wouldn't come.

"Buenas pinche noches," I muttered.

"Jefa!" a voice yelled from the gully.

I ran over and peered into the brush. The revenants had pulled the driver out of the wreckage. She was unconscious, but there was no mistaking who it was. Valeria Torres Alarcon. Her face was covered in cuts, and there was blood on her blouse.

The front end of the Mercedes was a tangled, steaming mess.

Ripper stared at me. "You know her?"

"I do now."

Lalo was sitting on the ground, with Valeria's bloodied head in his lap. Her dark hair was splayed across his knees. He looked up and said, "I used to work as an orderly at the French Hospital. This lady needs a doctor."

"She doesn't deserve no doctor," Ripper said. "She tried to kill our Jefa."

Ruben snorted. "How many times have I said women can't drive?"

"I'll call an ambulance," I said. "Just try not to move her too much, please."

"Who is she?" Lalo asked.

"Her name is Valeria. I'm pretty sure she's the witch who summoned the vampire birds."

Lalo edged away from the unconscious woman while the others backed off, giving the bruja a wide berth.

My phone chimed, then chimed again. That time, I checked the screen.

Valeria T entered CR Bishop Gate at 9. Camera feed showed her entering cactus garden. Birds showed up. Fucking Rafi scrubbed the footage, but I recovered it.

Wow. Go, Ron.

I was certain now that Hernan's granddaughter had summoned the ancient predators.

After I called for an ambulance, something bumped against my ankle. Sam, finally looking for some attention from the woman who fed him. I picked him up, and for once, he allowed it, relaxing into my arms.

It had been a long and crazy night.

The adrenaline left my body, and my muscles felt strangely weak. "Buenas pinche noches," I said again to no one in particular.

"Buenas pinche noches, Jefa," a chorus of voices said behind me.

When I turned, the men were standing together, looking more solemn than I had seen them that entire night. For a moment, I thought maybe fatigue had blurred my vision because they appeared faded.

"I think our time is up…or something," Ripper said.

The others nodded. Pete Chavira sniffed. It sounded like he was about to cry.

"I thought I'd have a chance to look around."

Head hanging, Chito shuffled his feet. "I really wanted to say a little prayer at El Santo Niño Church or at least light a candle or something."

"I was hoping we'd have time to see if my old house was still there," Lalo said quietly.

Ruben exhaled loudly. "I thought we'd have a chance to hang out a little bit, where Genaro's used to be. You know, pay our respects to the old place."

A lump rose in my throat. The men continued to fade.

"Thank you. All of you. For helping me. Us. I'll always be incredibly grateful."

Junie stepped forward. "After what happened to me the last time, it felt real good to kill those things. Thank you. For bringing me back." He waved a vaporous hand. "Adiós, Sam."

Ripper let out a low whistle and clapped his hands. The red clay ball responded with the obedience of a dog returning to its master. It flew and stopped beside the man with the pencil mustache. "We'll take care of this for you."

The other revenants placed their ghostly hands on the orb, and almost instantly, it transformed into a swirling mass of ethereal white mist, shimmering and shifting like a living cloud. The men murmured their farewells, their voices thin and reedy, before turning and walking away. With each step, their forms grew increasingly translucent. They hadn't gone far, maybe only a few yards, when they vanished entirely.

A heavy weight settled on my chest. It felt like I was losing a group of old friends who had come for a short visit, then departed just as quickly. Sam nuzzled up against me as if sensing my sorrow.

Tears welled up in my eyes. I whispered their names. "Ripper, Junie, Pete, Ruben, Chito, Lalo, Cowboy, Richard. Vaya con Dios."

In the distance, a siren echoed through the night.

Chapter 33

The next morning, I ended the lockdown.

Of course, I told Cora, Hernan, and Charlie what had happened, but we couldn't very well tell the residents of Chavez Ravine their head of security had raised a small army of dead people and a flaming light ball to defeat an immortal enemy.

I couldn't even tell Eileen Simpson or Dan Berman. Without knowing the history of brujería and supernatural events in Chavez Ravine, it would sound like a crazy, made-up story, and they would probably have tried to get rid of me on the spot.

People had seen La Luz Mala flying, so I said we had used a special kind of Smoke Bomb to sedate the entities, except this one was red. And it had worked.

That whopper went into the carefully worded email I sent to homeowners, announcing the end of the lockdown.

After firing Rafi Alarcon, which I had to admit I enjoyed just a little bit, I picked up boxes of pan dulce from Muertos Café and called my staff in for a meeting.

I knew the truth would be hard for some of them to understand, but I also knew they were sensitive about my holding things back, so I let them have it.

While I spoke, the team attacked the pastries until there was nothing left but brightly colored sugar crumbles and empty coffee cups. When I had finished, everyone but Ron stared at me in disbelief and something more. A little bit of anger, maybe, that they were doing their best to disguise but not entirely pulling it off.

Bailey was the first to break the silence. She had bike patrol duty and was dressed in navy blue Spandex shorts and a top, her long copper hair pulled up in a messy bun. "We missed out on all the good stuff! Why didn't you have us come with you?"

Before I could answer, Liam came to my rescue. "It's a bad idea to have too many people involved in a risky operation like that. Smaller is better. The stakes were too high for all of us to get involved, and you heard what she just said. She needed to focus on the revenants. There's no telling how they might have reacted to a large group. I honestly can't see how us tagging along would have helped."

"And the operation was successful," Justin added. "No matter how bummed we are we didn't get to fight alongside the undead—which would have been totally cool—Maddy's plan worked just fine. *More* than fine."

Bailey tipped her head back and groaned. "But I would have loved to have talked to them. Isn't anyone else curious about what the afterlife is like?"

I couldn't help but laugh. "There wasn't any time for that."

Ron puffed out his chest. "Yeah. It's too bad you didn't get to see them. They were one hundred percent total badasses. Especially Ripper. He was a boss."

Bailey crumpled up a napkin and threw it at Ron. It hit him on the forehead and fell on his lap. Ron picked it up and flung it back.

"Uh. At least we know how to shoot hunting bows now." Bailey rubbed her shoulder. "It's just too bad they didn't work against those things."

Justin snorted. "There's always next time."

"Around here, that's guaranteed." Liam flicked a pink crumb from the front of his shirt. "Are you reporting Rafi to the police?"

I shook my head. "That would be too complicated. But I'm filing a report against Valeria Torres for vandalism. Ron found video Rafi had tried to delete that showed her spray-painting one of the guardhouses."

"But she tried to kill you!" Bailey sounded shocked.

"True," I admitted. "But what would I say? We were having some kind of witch feud, and she was out to get me?"

Bailey grimaced. "I hadn't thought about that." She paused and frowned. "Do you have any idea how she's doing?"

"Valeria has a concussion and some cracked ribs, but she should be all right. Her grandfather, Hernan Frias, is beside himself. He can't understand why she would do such a thing. And he had no idea she was a practicing bruja. We're going to ask her some questions this afternoon."

If Hernan had taken the trouble to visit her shop in Pomona or done a simple internet search, he would have found out. But then again, so would I.

Liam raised his hand. "Do you want some of us to come with you? Just so she doesn't get any ideas?"

I shook my head. "I don't think that'll be necessary, but thank you."

Especially not with what I had in mind. If it worked, Valeria wouldn't ever give me or Chavez Ravine trouble again.

Chapter 34

Back on the dead-end street in La Loma, I punched in the keycode and let myself through the gate.

The place appeared different in the daytime. It was even bigger than it had looked at night—a long and narrow plot of land flanked by two large houses. It was a little like gazing through the wrong end of a telescope. The long rows of flower beds added to the sensation.

I imagined Lencha stepping out of the little clapboard house she had lived in alone, her long dark hair hanging in a single braid down her back, wearing a traditional Mexican apron. She would head to the shed, where she had spent most of her days.

I poked my head into the shed, and a tingling sensation rippled through me. Whether it was anticipation or something more, I didn't know. But if I ended up inheriting the property, I would restore the shed and use it for my own spell work. Ben Tomas was handy. He would probably help if I asked.

Lencha's garden was one of the few bits of land in Chavez Ravine time had forgotten. Ben seemed to have left it as it was. Some fruit trees. Rose bushes and, of course, an expanse of red clay. It wasn't just in a single mound, like I had thought, but a wide area of the stuff extended all the way to the back fence.

In the shed, I found a dusty glass jar, rinsed it out at the spigot, and dried it with a rag I had grabbed from a storage box. Ben was not only a genius landscaper, but he was also a meticulous organizer. I pulled out a small spade and scooped up some clay into the jar. A surge of energy warmed my hands, running up my arms, over my shoulders, and down my back. It felt like a warm embrace—the magic from the clay seeping into my veins—filling me with purpose.

But more than that, I was overcome with confidence in my magical inheritance, a confidence I had lacked since I first learned of my magical lineage. It seemed a bit silly that all it had taken was some clay to make it all real.

But it wasn't just clay. It was a physical connection to the old ways of Chavez Ravine, and I would need to protect it.

At home, I mixed a bit of the clay with some herbs and a few strands of Valeria's long, dark hair, which I had plucked from her scalp while I was waiting for the ambulance to arrive. I carefully put the concoction into a small cloth bag to take with me to the hospital.

Stu and I exchanged a few texts. He was staying one more night with his brother. I told him the birds were taken care of, but I did not confide in him about the revenants. That was way too complicated for the phone, or so I told myself. In reality, I felt guilty for not telling him before, especially after I had vowed to be more open about my brujería. He had been nothing but supportive, and I had been less than honest.

The fact was, I was used to being alone, doing whatever I wanted without worrying about what someone else thought about me or my questionable life choices. But maybe those days were over. Perhaps I would just have to put on my big girl pants and learn to trust him more.

I checked in with the command center, then took a two-hour nap with Sam. When my alarm went off, I hopped in the shower, dressed, and carefully applied my makeup, going heavy on the black eyeliner. Definitely a power move.

In the kitchen, I whipped up a mango smoothie. The Tajin and sweet and sour chamoy made from pickled fruit would act as the perfect cover for the next ingredient: a half teaspoon of red clay from Lencha's yard. Of course, I added a few other things as well to my magical concoction, which I poured into an insulated thermos. The thing had cost a fortune, but it kept things icy cold.

I shoved the hex bag into the pocket of my red trench coat— another power move—and carried the thermos to the Jeep. When I pulled up in front of Hernan's house, the door opened, and my mother stepped out, wearing a black caftan embroidered in gold along the deep V-neck.

Her eyes flicked up and down, and she frowned. "I hate to say it, Madeline, but red is really *not* your color. The teal and lavender suit you much better."

I sighed. "Really, Mom? That's what you have to say? Hernan told you about the night I had, right?"

"Yes, of course." She lowered her voice. "He's having a very hard time processing all of this. He can't believe his own flesh and blood would use dark magic to such ends. The girl must be loca." She tapped her head. "I told him he doesn't have to go and see her right away, but he's insisting. I'm glad you're taking him. Just make sure he doesn't overdo it."

My mother was very thoughtful when it came to everyone but me. I was not in the mood to babysit her geriatric boyfriend, but it was not the time to pick a fight.

"I'll keep an eye on him," I promised. "Is he ready?"

On cue, Hernan appeared at my mother's side, wearing his usual uniform: black pants and a starched white shirt. But he looked washed-out and tired, with purplish circles under his eyes.

"Ready?" I said in my best jaunty voice.

"As ready as I'll ever be." He sounded like the morose donkey from *Winnie the Pooh*.

Valeria had been taken to LA General in Boyle Heights. Back in the day, the old County General had a gritty reputation. Its specialty had been treating the "medically underserved," also known as poor people.

But the hospital had been transformed into a modern behemoth of glass, steel, and concrete with a world-class trauma center.

Hernan wasn't in the mood for talking on the way over, but he seemed to recover by the time we checked in at reception. He stood straighter, and his mouth was set in a grim line. Since we were there to visit his granddaughter, I planned on letting him take the lead.

Valeria had good enough insurance—or luck—to have scored a private room. She was propped up in bed, forehead bandaged, face bruised, watching, of all things, *Buffy the Vampire Slayer*. Valeria had the nerve to roll her eyes when we walked in.

Hernan didn't seem to notice. He dragged a chair over to her bedside and lowered himself into it, radiating disapproval. "Can you lower that thing?" He gestured toward the TV. "I can't hear myself think."

It wasn't that loud, but I got his point. It was hard to think straight with all that screaming in the background. I grabbed the remote from the tray and turned off the TV.

Instead of looking at her grandfather, Valeria fixed her eyes on me. "What do *you* want?" Her voice could have frozen penguins.

I shrugged. "I think we'd both like an explanation."

Valeria pressed a hand against her head, as if to make sure her bandage was still in place. Even with the sides of her mouth curled in a sneer, she was a pretty woman. "Let's see, where should I start?" Her voice had taken a mocking tone.

"You can start from a place of respect," Hernan said.

"And here we go," Valeria snapped. "Where was the respect for your wife, my grandmother? You never, ever listened to what she wanted for Chavez Ravine, did you? No, you were too busy with your own ideas. You wanted status and power, but she didn't. She never wanted that damn homeowners' association. She thought it was elitist bullshit. But you dismissed her, belittled her, marginalized her. You're always talking about leveling the playing field, but look at what you've done, what you've created. Chavez Ravine used to be called a poor man's Shangri-La, and you turned it into a rich man's playground."

Hernan sat back in his chair as if he had been slapped.

Valeria continued. "I've tried talking to you about it too, but you wouldn't give me the time of day. All you ever wanted to talk about was brujería. You don't know the first thing about what that really means."

I placed a hand on Hernan's shoulder. "That's a little harsh, Valeria."

"Is it? Is it really? It's the truth, but it's not something you want to accept because you're the beneficiary, aren't you? All those ridiculous rules about legacy means you got a free house, didn't it? It went vacant for years. Years! Some hard-working family could have bought it when it was still affordable and benefited from their investment. But no. The HOA was so focused on protecting the old families it created an exclusive community with insane fees that guaranteed only the wealthy could live there."

"The legacy families deserved protection after what happened!" Hernan sputtered.

"It went too far!" Valeria's voice was high and shrill. "You're nothing but a bunch of…fascists."

Hernan brought his fist down on the bedside tray. A plastic water bottle toppled over. "You don't even know the meaning of the word."

I couldn't stop myself. "Since we've reached the name-calling stage, I think 'murderous bruja' sounds about right, don't you? We have video of you painting your graffiti, and you were nearby every time the vampire birds attacked. But I do have one question. Where did you get them in the first place?"

The shift seemed to take Valeria by surprise. She opened and closed her mouth, and the outrage drained from her body. I began to wonder whether the meds in her IV were making her a little loopy.

Valeria lowered her eyes. "In Mexico. My husband and I took a trip to see some ruins, and we visited a butterfly sanctuary. The birds must have sensed my magic because they came out of the trees. I found I could talk to them. The forest was shrinking, and they were looking for a new place to live. So, we struck a deal. They could come and help me shake things up in Chavez Ravine, and then, after I dissolved the HOA, I promised them an occasional sacrifice."

What. The. Hell.

Hernan was the first to speak. "People could have been killed!"

Valeria snorted, and the outrage was back. "Yeah, well…guess whose playbook I borrowed *that* from? I knew what you were up to, Abuelo, when they first hired Maddy to get rid of your creations. Marta knew too, just in case you were wondering. There's yet another woman you take for granted. So yeah, I used my brujería for a little social justice. So what?" She

231

winced. All that yelling couldn't have been easy with cracked ribs.

Hernan seemed to collapse in on himself. He looked small and vulnerable in his chair. "I don't understand. You said you had no interest in learning brujería. I offered to send you to Mexico to learn, but you refused."

Valeria sneered. "I lied. I didn't need help from you. I had my own mentor when I was a teenager. My grandmother helped me."

"Your grandmother helped you?" Hernan echoed. "She didn't approve of brujería."

"The type you and your family practiced," Valeria snapped. "Today, you'd call it performative. I think she called it *self-serving*."

She collapsed into her pillows, knocking one onto the floor.

"I'm just so tired. I'm tired of being angry, but it makes me so sad to see what's happened to the old neighborhoods."

I hadn't always been a fan of Hernan's, and there were some pretty large grains of truth in what Valeria said, but people were capable of changing. Hernan seemed to truly regret some of his bad choices.

I pulled the hex bag from my coat pocket, picked up the fallen pillow, and slid it and the hex bag under her head. It would keep her quiet for the rest of her hospital stay.

"Before we leave, I made you a little something. It's one of my specialties—a mango smoothie." I held out the thermos.

Valeria's mood took another turn. Her dark eyes widened. "Are you serious? I mean, after everything? Now I feel kinda bad about trying to run you over. I guess I lost my shit. I must be perimenopausal or something." She extended a hand, wincing again. "The food is horrible here. And I love mangonadas."

I pressed the thermos into her hand. She unscrewed the lid and sniffed, a little suspiciously, her eyes locked on mine.

I smiled. "There's a tamarind candy stick at the bottom."

"My grandma used to make these." She sounded a little high. Valeria turned to Hernan. "I've been mad at you for so long, Abuelo. I'm still angry. Let's be honest. You didn't treat my grandmother with the respect that you demand for yourself." She gave Hernan a sad smile. "But it looks like you get a do-over. Marta says you're going out with Malena B. So please, try not to fuck it up. Because if you do, I think the new bruja in town will kick your ass."

She wasn't wrong. Valeria was also definitely high. Her pupils were nearly nonexistent.

Hernan was obviously not accustomed to such straight talk. He cleared his throat. "I need to think over everything you've said."

Valeria sipped her mangonada and gave a blissful smile. "It's delicious. And for whatever it's worth, Maddy, I'm sorry. I definitely need to get my hormones checked."

Wow. The apple hadn't fallen far from the tree. When confronted, grandfather and granddaughter both went into deflection mode.

We left Valeria with a smoothie, a hex bag, and Buffy back on the TV.

While I was pulling the stiff seatbelt across Hernan's chest and struggling to click it into place, he said, "You put something in that drink, didn't you?"

"Maybe," I admitted. "I couldn't take any chances."

Hernan sighed. "What was it?"

"Some tasty liquid spellcraft. It'll keep her out of Chavez Ravine until we decide it's safe for her to enter."

Hernan shifted in his seat to stare at me. "You can do that?"

"I can now," I said and drove back to Chavez Ravine.

Chapter 35

On Saturday morning, I woke eager to begin my weekend routine: a thorough housecleaning, including mopping and reorganizing my kitchen.

I opened all the windows to allow in the fresh air and mopped the sunroom. Little Lencha was back in her place on the workbench, wearing a smug expression. I was feeling it too. Thanks to her, my magical skills had taken a leap forward. In just a few days, I had learned to wake the dead, conjure La Luz Mala, and take out five immortal vampire things. That felt pretty good, coming on the heels of my disastrous experience in Pasadena.

There was one big looming question: how could I get my magic to work outside Chavez Ravine? I had a theory about that, and I needed a chance to test it.

But my heart was far from light. The mental picture of Ripper and crew fading when death reclaimed them played over and over again while I moved from room to room, wiping down surfaces, stripping the bed, and doing the laundry.

To clear the disturbing imagery from my mind, I listened to a thriller audiobook set on a remote island in the UK and lifted weights for nearly an hour. Then I showered and drove to Palo Verde Market to shop for groceries. That wasn't the best idea because people stopped me in the aisles, asking questions I couldn't or didn't want to answer.

Why had the creatures flown over all of LA and chosen to terrorize our community?

Didn't I think it odd that Chavez Ravine seemed to be having an unfair share of supernatural incursions?

Some of them even implied I might have had something to do with it all because things had started getting weird just when I arrived.

I smiled and did my best to ease their concerns. What I didn't say was the problems we'd had in Chavez Ravine were nowhere near as bad as the entity mess Los Angelenos dealt with on a daily basis.

In other words, their property values were secure, and they could go about their lives without the fear of strange beings crawling out of holes in their manicured yards.

I had an itch to cook, to make something spicy for dinner, but I had already accepted an invitation from my mother and Hernan to eat with them—a weird first I wasn't entirely looking forward to. My mother had said she was cooking up a "feast" to celebrate my victory, but I really think she and Hernan were looking for an excuse to find out exactly how I had done it.

I spent the rest of the day bustling around the kitchen, organizing the pantry, and cooking ahead for the coming week. All the while, I pondered what, exactly, to tell Stu about the revenants.

I had just finished with a batch of soupy Mexican beans when my phone rang. It was Vicki Wells.

I was having such a productive, happy day that my initial reaction was to let it go to voicemail. Why the hell would Vicki Wells be calling me other than to ream me out about some perceived offense?

But curiosity got the best of me, so after the fourth ring, I answered. Warily, like I was afraid a viper might come through the speaker and bite my ear.

"Hello?"

"Oh, thank goodness you answered. I can't believe I'm about to ask this, but I really need your help. With Clare." Vicki sounded panicked.

My hands went all clammy. "What's wrong? Is she all right?"

"For now. She's trapped by some entities, and Occult Affairs says they won't be able to get there for another couple of hours. The problem is, we're supposed to be somewhere important at six o'clock, and I was hoping..."

She couldn't bring herself to say the rest, but I knew what was coming. I also relaxed. It sounded like Clare wasn't in serious danger, just that Vicki wanted her busted out so they could go somewhere. I wasn't super excited about doing Vicki a favor, after the way she had treated me, but I also wasn't about to let Clare get the short end of that stick.

"Okay. Where is she? What can you tell me about the situation?"

Vicki gave a loud exhale. "Oh, thank God. Thank you. Clare's at the disc golf course in Altadena. She's with Iris. There was an eruption, and they locked down the park, and now the girls can't get back to their car. Clare's phone died, but her last text said they are hiding out in a concession stand."

I pressed a finger between my eyes while I thought it over. Like most places with lots of ground and greenery, the disc golf course was a well-known entity hotspot. In fact, players had to sign a waiver acknowledging the risk and accepting that there would be no refunds due to entity emergences. But players had to be eighteen to sign.

"Did you sign the waiver for Clare?" I asked.

Vicki groaned. "I did. I signed an online form. I was an idiot. The guy at the desk told her they hadn't seen any entities in over a year, so I thought it would be okay, and they've been dying to play."

Well, the guy at the desk had lied. If Vicki had taken the trouble to check the public database, she would have known that. But whatever. Clare was stuck, and I knew how to free her and Iris. Plus, it would give me a chance to test my theory about activating my magic outside of Chavez Ravine.

I thought for a moment. "Did she say what kind of entity? Singular or plural?"

"She didn't know what they were, but she said they were small and ugly, with bat wings. It sounded like there were maybe three or four of them."

I sighed. Flyers, for some reason, usually showed up in small groups. No mention of scary teeth. "All right. I'm heading out."

I grabbed a few extra Smoke Bombs from the closet, and my eyes landed on the bow and quiver. The darn thing might come in handy, but I would have to use foam-tipped arrows. If I accidentally killed a non-lethal entity, I would be in trouble.

The workbench was my last stop. I took a small bit of red clay from Lencha's yard and put it in a plastic bag.

After changing into jeans, a long-sleeved shirt, and comfortable work boots, I threw my supplies into the Jeep and headed out. For a moment, I thought about calling Bailey and asking her to go with me, but this was a personal mission, not an official one. And Bailey deserved a day off.

It took less than half an hour to get to the disc golf course in Arroyo Seco Canyon. Someone had set out orange cones to prevent people from driving into the parking lot, and a sign read: "Temporarily Closed."

I blew past the short line of waiting cars, dodging the cones.

A young man in a T-shirt and baseball cap came running out of a low wooden building. "I'm sorry! We're closed. Entity emergence! You'll have to come back another time."

Yeah, that wasn't going to happen. The only thing that sounded worse to me than golf was disc golf. No, thank you.

I parked the Jeep in the driveway, got out, and began gathering my things. The young man came rushing over to scold me.

"Former Occult Affairs officer to the rescue. Can you tell me where the entities are?"

He wasn't very fit for a young guy. His belly hung over the top of his shorts. His bushy eyebrows squished together when he talked. "They didn't say anything about any former officers when I called them."

I held up a Smoke Bomb. "Do you want help or not? With any luck, I can subdue them quickly, and you can open back up for business. And look like a hero to your manager."

He eyed the line of cars and grimaced. "Are you really authorized to do this?"

"Do you know anyone who handles entities for the fun of it?"

The guy twisted his hands like a character in a costume drama. "Ooo, this is really uncomfortable, but okay."

I should have been nicer. After months in Chavez Ravine, I was losing my touch. What had happened to my soothing voice?

I cleared my throat and forced a smile. "Listen, it's going to be fine. Honest. I've done this hundreds of times. There's nothing to worry about. Which way do I go?"

He nodded, walked past the office, and pointed at the top of a green hill. "They're up there. Look for the signs to the tenth tee. There's a snack stand there. We tell people to go there and hide if there's an eruption."

There was a law making its way through the county that would require all outdoor facilities to provide adequate "shelter-in-place" structures in case of entity appearances, so these guys were ahead of the game.

The disc course was a mixture of oak woodland and chaparral, with a clear view of the San Gabriel Mountains. It was a beautiful, wild setting. No wonder people risked entities to enjoy it.

I grabbed my Smoke Bombs and hunting bow and followed the signs to the tenth tee. There they were, and they were hard to miss.

Three imps, each about the size of a French bulldog but with large bat-like wings. Leathery humanoid smashed-in faces. Yuck. They were showing classic signs of recent emergence: they appeared confused and frightened and flew in unsteady circles a few feet in the air.

The roll-up windows of the concession stand were closed. I walked over and tapped lightly on the steel shutter. "Clare? Iris? You girls in there?"

"Maddy? Is that you?" Clare sounded stunned. "What are you doing here?"

Good girl. She was keeping her voice low. I glanced over at the entities. They hadn't seemed to notice me.

"Your mom called. How many of you are in there?"

"Um. Six. Me and Iris and a couple with two kids. I think there are some other people hiding in a tree down the hill."

The window cracked open just enough for Clare to peer out. Her eyes widened when she saw the hunting bow.

"Are you going to shoot them with that thing?"

I pulled an arrow from the quiver and held it up for inspection. "Don't worry. It has a soft tip. Hang in there. Hopefully, this shouldn't take too long."

Two imps, flying badly, had collided with each other and were now rolling around on the ground, their tongues lolling out of their mouths. I unclipped a Smoke Bomb and flung it to the ground. Purple mist exploded into the air. The entities went limp, then still.

The third one—thank goodness, there weren't any more—had finally noticed me and didn't look too happy. Its wings flapped frantically. It was now or never.

I grabbed the plastic bag out of my pocket and shoved the squishy tip of an arrow into the red clay. The tips of my fingers began to tingle slightly. A very good sign.

I loaded the arrow into the bow and said a few quick words, then carefully took aim and let it fly.

The arrow bonked the creature on its broad chest just when it lifted in the air. I couldn't have asked for an easier target.

The reddish-brown clay on the squishy tip shimmered for a brief, glorious moment, and the entity fell with a thud to the ground. I ran over, heart racing. It was knocked out, as if I had thrown a couple of Smoke Bombs at it.

My theory had proven to be correct. The one time my magic had worked outside Chavez Ravine, when I brought Ripper and his crew back to life, I'd had Little Lencha with me. The figurine was made out of clay from her former backyard, and while the spirit of my great-aunt definitely helped, I suspected it was the clay that had really enabled my magic.

The imps had given me a chance to confirm that. Which was a huge relief. Now I just had to make sure my secret sauce stayed secret from anyone who might want to deprive me of it.

I knocked on the concession stand shutters. "It's okay to come out now."

Clare burst through a door and flung her arms around me. "Oh my God, thank you! This is so embarrassing. You have to rescue me all the time, and I can't believe my mother actually called you! She's such a…"

I detached myself and wagged a finger at her. "Don't you dare, Clare."

We both giggled at the unintentional rhyme. Iris was just as huggy as Clare, throwing her thin arms around me and squeezing.

"You're like our own personal superhero!"

A man and woman stepped out of the hut, dressed in nylon shirts and shorts. Both were slim and fit. "Is it safe to come out?" the man asked.

I nodded. "It's fine."

Two kids emerged. They appeared to be twins, a boy and a girl. The woman walked over to the closest entity and stared down at it.

"Oh! I think those are imps. I had a painting of one that looked just like that back in college."

Why anyone would choose to hang something so ugly on their wall was beyond me. "I believe you're right, ma'am. They can be pretty annoying, but we got these three before they were able to do any harm."

It was a good thing they hadn't come into close contact with Clare and Iris. Imps were in the incubus family and, therefore, were sexualized entities. Occult Affairs had learned its lesson about that from a Russian giant with a thing for the ladies.

Within half an hour, I had reported in to the Occult Affairs command center, escorted the group to the clubhouse, and called Vicki Wells to share the news.

Vicki thanked me profusely, then asked to speak to Clare. I handed over my phone, and almost immediately, Clare began to argue. Something about a party. Iris rolled her eyes, flopped into a chair, and stretched out her long, bare legs.

"And here we go," she muttered.

"What's the problem? I asked, careful to keep my tone light.

Iris sighed. "The engagement party. We've told our parents we're not going, no matter what. End of story. But Vicki can't seem to get that into her head. She bought us dresses and everything." She glanced at a clock on the wall and sat up straighter. "We're supposed to be having our makeup done about now because Vicki, of course, hired a professional photographer, and we're like…go ahead, you don't need us for your stupid party. They might be in the mood to celebrate, but we're not."

I had no idea what the girl was talking about. "I'm not following."

Iris frowned. "Clare didn't tell you? Her mom cheated on her dad with my dad, and now they're getting engaged, and we're supposed to be all happy about it." She took a deep, wobbly breath. "They can go screw themselves."

Poor Clare. Poor Iris. And I had thought my mother canoodling with Hernan Frias was bad. Plus, I was an adult. I couldn't imagine navigating that situation as a teenager.

Clare stomped toward me, her eyes red. She sniffed loudly and held out the phone. "My mom wants to talk to you."

My heart sank. Now what? I was not going to let Vicki drag me into their family drama. No, thank you. I took the phone from Clare's hand. "Hello?"

"First off, thank you so much. And I'm sorry. Really sorry. I'm afraid I've been a total bitch to you when you've been nothing but kindness itself to my daughter."

Whatever I had been expecting, it wasn't an apology—and such a sincere one at that.

"Oh" was all I managed to say.

Vicki gave a bitter laugh. "And since I've been paying big bucks to a therapist, I'm going to be honest about something else. Yes, I had an affair and wrecked my marriage. Yes, I fell in love with someone else, who happened to be Iris's father. But I didn't expect Stu to move on so quickly. It came as a bit of a blow. I know that sounds crazy because *I* cheated on *him*, but he acted happier with you than he had in a long time with me. And then suddenly, Clare liked you too. Much better than she did her own mother, it seemed to me. So yes. That's the story, but none of it's your fault, and I'm sorry. Really and truly."

I was dumbfounded. The woman who had treated me with suspicion and hostility since day one was confessing her deepest regrets and insecurities over the phone. My mind raced, trying to come up with an adequate response.

"Well, okay. Yeah. Thank you for that."

Vicki cleared her throat. "My daughter, on the other hand, is not about to let me off the hook so easily. She's refusing to come to the engagement party, which starts in an hour. And now she says she lost her keys somewhere in the park."

I thought for a moment. We could call a locksmith, but that would take forever, especially with the rush hour traffic.

"Don't worry about it," I said. "The girls can hang out with me until Stu gets back. No problem."

"Really?"

"Really." I glanced over at Clare and Iris, who were nodding eagerly.

My plan was a no-brainer for another reason.

It was the perfect excuse to bail on dinner with my mother and Hernan.

Chapter 36

My devious little plan backfired. Immediately.

I made the mistake of cancelling on my mother on the drive back to Chavez Ravine, with Clare in the passenger seat and Iris in the back.

"Don't be ridiculous!" my mother cried. "Bring the girls. I made plenty of food. Tons!"

The girls heard every word.

"Oh, that would be so much fun!" Clare said. "I've been dying to meet Malena B. How amazing is that?"

"Totally amazing!" Iris gushed.

"And, Madeline, I'm going to call that handsome man of yours and invite him too," my mother said. "We'll have our own little party."

She hung up before I could say anything more.

Clare turned to me. "Can you take us to my dad's house? I want to take a shower and change. I feel so gross."

"Ooo, I want to shower too," Iris said. "Can I borrow some clothes?"

I glanced over at Clare, who had gone all stiff and was staring straight ahead. "How will you get into the house? I thought you lost your keys?"

Clare grimaced. "Ooops. I'm sorry. I kind of lied. My mom wouldn't shut up about the party, so I made that up."

I made a sharp left onto the road leading to La Loma. A little too hard and fast. The tires protested with a squeal. "Made that up?"

Clare dropped her head on my shoulder and squeezed my arm. "I'm sorry, Maddy. I was desperate. I know I'm being a pain in the ass, but I'm super excited to hang out with you and meet your mom."

Clare really knew how to lay it on thick, but I had to give her credit for ingenuity.

"I'm just warning you. My mom can be a little much," I said.

Clare threw her head back and laughed. "Don't worry. I've had plenty of experience."

My mother had not exaggerated. She really had spent the day cooking and had made enough food to feed a small army. Chili rellenos, rice and beans. Al pastor with nopales. Potato taquitos with chili verde sauce and ribeye steak for Stu, who was looking around the kitchen with wide and hungry eyes while I helped transfer the food onto colorful Talavera serving plates.

Hernan pressed a cold Modelo beer into Stu's hands, then hurried out of the room. By the squeals of surprise, Clare and Iris had discovered Hernan's collection of swords at the back of the house.

"Be careful with the rellenos," my mother said. "They'll fall apart the way you're manhandling them."

"I am *not* manhandling them." I carefully slid the last chili from the frying pan onto the dish, ladled some red sauce on the top, then stepped back to survey the results. They were perfect. I had no idea how my mother did it. While I had no problem roasting the poblano peppers or stuffing them with cheese, my egg batter never cooperated. It turned into a gummy mess that fell apart in the frying pan. Usually, they ended up in the garbage.

"You're going to love these," I said to Stu.

He got up and wrapped his arms around my waist. "I'm going to love everything," he said into my ear.

My mother giggled. "I never thought I'd see my daughter be so lovey-dovey."

Here it comes. A long story about my loser boyfriends.

I knocked my hip into hers. "Behave yourself."

My mother batted her eyelashes. Fake eyelashes, I was pretty sure.

"Do you see how she treats me, Stu? It's terrible, really." My mother had been flirting with Stu since the moment he walked in, wearing a crisp blue shirt with the sleeves rolled up.

There was no sign of Marta, but she had obviously been there because the house was spotless, the windows sparkled, and the whole place smelled like the lobby of a fancy hotel.

It was a far cry from the stuffy, dark place it had been before Hernan met my mother.

And then, just when Hernan reentered the kitchen, my mother lobbed a bombshell. "Maddy, I should tell you that I've sold the house in Beverly Hills. Now that the gnomes are taking better care of the yards, the property values are coming back up, and I made a pretty penny. Besides, I've been spending so much time here. Hernan and I decided I might as well move in permanently. I'm finally living in Chavez Ravine, after all these years!"

Oh, yay. My mother was going to be my neighbor.

I looked at Hernan, then back at my mother. "I mean, congratulations, of course. But aren't you a little worried about entities following you here? I know the board's been very concerned about that since I started."

My mother sniffed. "Well, it only took you three seconds to find fault with our happy news. I think that might be a new record, Madeline. Excuse me while I put the food I made for you on the table." My mother coldly brushed my shoulder and carried a platter to the dining room table.

Hernan waved a hand. "I'm not worried about entities, Maddy. The spell you created will keep them out."

"But what will you tell the board?" I protested. "That the famous entity whisperer Malena B is moving into the community, but it's okay because her daughter cast a spell? Nobody knows about that but you and Cora!"

"No, Charlie knows too. They'll help me figure out what to say to the rest of the board. And they can't stop her from moving in. This is *my* house. And we plan on getting married. So there."

When I picked my jaw up off the floor, my mother brusquely flashed a marquise diamond.

"You're kidding?" I said.

Stu poked me in the side. "I think you meant to say, 'It's beautiful, Mom.'"

I gave a long, noisy exhale, which sounded like a bull about to charge, but I leaned over and kissed my mother on the cheek. Her perfume almost knocked me over. It was like walking through a jasmine garden at night.

"It's beautiful, Mom," I repeated. "I'm really happy for you."

Hernan grabbed both my hands and squeezed. "I promise to take good care of her."

I wondered if he was thinking about what his granddaughter Valeria had said about his not-so-nice treatment of his wife.

My mother giggled. She was doing a lot of that, and it was annoying as hell. "I can't believe we're beating these two to the altar."

My face felt like it was engulfed in flames. When I glanced over at Stu, he was grinning.

Hernan came to the rescue. "Just think. Nearly dead and about to wed. Hah! Never count us old people out."

My mother's nose wrinkled as if someone had just farted. "I don't know about you, but I do *not* identify with my age. It's just a number. I've never felt more alive, more myself." And with that, she swept from the room.

Hernan patted his chest. "I just can't get over what a lucky man I am."

Um hm. They hadn't known each other for that long. "Let's see what he says after a few months," I muttered to Stu.

From the back of the house, Clare called, "Mr. Frias! We need you!"

Hernan headed for the hall, chest puffed out and smiling. A minute later, he was back, asking if dinner could be delayed a bit because the girls were asking for a sword-fighting lesson.

My mother flapped a dish towel at him. "Of course. Go on and have a good time." She turned to Stu. "You have such a beautiful and charming daughter. I'm just going to put this food on the stove to keep it warm. Maddy, why don't you two take your drinks out to the back?"

I hesitated. It wasn't like her to be so gracious. It had to be a trap, but I couldn't figure it out.

My mother rolled her eyes. "Go on. Go get some fresh air. I'm going to pour myself a glass of wine and watch the sword fighting."

Raucous laughter drifted from the hallway.

Stu grabbed my hand and pulled me through the living room and out the back door. A few minutes later, we were sitting under a tree in the cool evening air. Hernan's shed, where he practiced his iffy magic and once had tried to stab me, was a few yards away.

It reminded me of Lencha's shed. Maybe *my* shed, if Ben was right.

Stu crossed his legs and studied me. "Something's on your mind. What's up?"

"A confession?" I grimaced.

"What kind of confession?" He frowned. "Is it going to make me sad?"

I thought of his ex-wife's engagement party and shook my head. The betrayal had left Stu with some deep scars. "No, but it might make you think I'm nuts. I'd like to tell you how I got rid of those vampire birds, but it's a little out there...I'm just warning you."

Stu scratched his temple. "All right. I've been warned. Hit me."

So, I hit him. Gave him the whole story. When I was finally finished, he had drained his margarita and was pacing in front of the shed.

"If you weren't the one telling me this, I'd have a hard time believing it. It's crazy. I always thought revenants were just from the movies. And that La Luz thing. It's wild. But it's like fate. It all happened for a reason, you know? Because it led you to your great aunt's property and the clay. That's what's been missing all along, and now you've found it. Problem solved." He winked. "There's no stopping you now."

I watched Stu continue his pacing. The depth of his understanding and acceptance sent a shiver down my spine. "I thought you were going to be angry I hadn't told you what I was planning."

He stopped, his blue eyes narrowing and crinkling at the corners. "Why would I be angry?" He sounded mystified.

"Because I promised to be more open with you, and instead, I kept my plan to myself."

"Maddy, I run a security company. I keep people safe from all kinds of threats, but I don't know the first thing about the undead or how to take out immortal beings. That's your turf. You were under the gun and had some decisions to make. You didn't need my permission. Sure, if you'd wanted to talk it through, I would have been there for you. But you worked at Occult Affairs and made critical decisions all the time. You certainly didn't need my help, and I wouldn't presume to think you did."

I had underestimated him. It might have helped to talk things over before I went to the cemetery. I would never know, but I wouldn't make that mistake again. Just as I wouldn't underestimate my skills as a bruja.

My mother called us from the kitchen. Dinner was served.

Stu and I walked back into the house arm in arm. We were the last ones to take our seats at a table that held a truly amazing Mexican feast. Soon, the room was filled with laughter and the sounds of glasses clinking together.

Hernan waved a bottle of red wine in the air. "I broke out the good stuff. Shall I make the toast?"

My mother gave him a playful nudge. "Of course. You're the host."

With another flourish, Hernan produced a bottle of sparkling cider from a silver bucket for the girls and poured out four glasses of cabernet sauvignon for the adults. "To us. And to some well-deserved peace and quiet in Chavez Ravine."

My mother lifted her glass. "Darn tootin'."

Great. My mother was even beginning to sound like Hernan.

If this kept up, they would become known as "Hernanalena."

Clare and Iris giggled.

Stu clinked his glass against mine. "To peace and quiet in Chavez Ravine."

That sounded good. Really, really good. And long overdue. And well deserved. I had assembled a great team, but we had run from one crisis to another, and I'd had little time to do the basics, like setting up training plans and establishing basic security protocols. I was longing for time to do that boring but necessary work.

While I looked around me, I couldn't remember the last time I had felt happier or so optimistic about the future. One by one, I toasted everyone at the table. "To peace and quiet in Chavez Ravine."

The moment I had finished taking the first sip of wine, my hands began to itch, and my heart beat a little faster. I dropped my hands on my lap, waiting for them to start glowing and for my phone to come to life with an emergency call from the command center, but neither happened.

By the time we had finished our delicious meal, I'd had an epiphany: I spoke too soon. Celebrated too early. Counted my chickens before they had hatched. And even though it was perfectly ridiculous, I reached under the table, rapped my knuckles against its underside, and whispered, "Knock on wood," under my breath.

After all, it was best not to invite disaster. Especially in a place like Chavez Ravine.

My hands began to itch, and my veins turned a strange reddish-brown, the color of clay.

Somewhere in Chavez Ravine, something was not right.

Author's Note

If you think Ripper is an unusual name for a character, I agree with you. Ripper was my mother's first husband, except she never told me about him. She accidentally blurted out his name at the end of her life. By then my poor mom was in no condition to answer questions and my dad didn't want to talk about it, but my mother's best friend was more than happy to fill me in. She grew up in Chavez Ravine too and knew Ripper, who lived down the street from the Castanedas.

By all accounts, Ripper was a good guy, but for some reason my grandmother didn't like him. Despite that, my mother married Ripper when she was nineteen. The marriage didn't last long, mostly due to the interference of my grandmother.

Over the years, I was left to imagine what kind of person would earn such a nickname and eventually, he had become so real in my head that he appeared as a character in *The Monsters of Chavez Ravine,* then was resurrected in *Mortal Magic.*

I have no idea what Ripper looked like, but I drew inspiration from a picture of a group of guys hanging out in front of Genaro's store in La Loma. The photo appeared in Don Normark's beautiful book of photographs and interviews, *Chavez Ravine, 1949, A Los Angeles Story.*

Coming Fall 2025

Books by Debra Castaneda

Maddy Madrigal Mysteries
Monsters, mayhem, and Mexican food

Barely Magic
Maddy lands a cushy security job in a gated community but must confront a supernatural threat and come to terms with her magical heritage.

Somewhat Magic
In the heart of Los Angeles, Maddy Madrigal battles legendary creatures and unscrupulous developers as an old protective spell begins to fail.

Desperate Magic
Maddy Madrigal must unravel a web of supernatural clues and confront ancient predators to stop a string of brutal murders.

Mortal Magic
Something ancient and deadly is roosting outside Chavez Ravine, and Maddy's weapons, magic, and extremely agitated cat aren't enough to fight it off.

Dark Earth Rising

Themed novels that can be read in any order

A Dark and Rising Tide

When a massive storm surge hits the central coast of California, the ferocious surf destroys buildings, floods streets, and washes up something sinister from the depths of the Monterey Bay.

The Devil's Shallows

Eight miles of mystery. One night of terror. Residents trapped in a remote neighborhood confront the unimaginable.

The Copper Man

Haunted tunnels. Unexplained deaths. Eerie sightings. Decades after The Copper Man killed her brother, Leah Shaw returns to the remote mining town of Tribulation Gulch where a lethal mystery awaits.

The Root Witch

A beautiful forest. A terrifying legend. It's 1986. Two strangers, hundreds of miles apart, grapple with disturbing incidents in a one-of-a-kind quaking aspen forest.

Circus at Devil's Landing

Creatures that howl in the night, a mysterious circus, and a clash between a ringmaster and a woman determined to rescue her captured lover.

The Spore Queen
A charming reporter, an ailing tech mogul, and two strangers hiding secrets are brought together by a mysterious fungus, one that will either save them or destroy them.

Chavez Ravine Novels
Stand-alone novels set in Chavez Ravine, Los Angeles during turbulent times

The Monsters of Chavez Ravine
A 2021 International Latino Book Awards Gold Medal Winner! Before Dodger Stadium, dark forces terrorized Chavez Ravine.

The Night Lady
A rebel curandera, a plucky seamstress, and a young reporter are pulled into the investigation of a killer terrorizing Chavez Ravine.

The Haunting of Chavez Ravine
La Llorona is terrorizing people in the hills of Chavez Ravine, and a sassy curandera and her clever young niece must stop her.

The Christmas Cucuy
It's Christmas Eve, 1949, and Kiki's dreams are about to come true: she'll be singing at Palladium with her old bandmates. But when she threatens her rambunctious son with El Cucuy, her plans change.